Gates of Paradise

BY MELISSA DE LA CRUZ

Blue Bloods
Masquerade
Revelations
The Van Alen Legacy
Misguided Angel
Lost in Time
Gates of Paradise

Keys to the Repository
Bloody Valentine

Wolf Pact

Gates of Paradise

A

Blue Bloods

NOVEL

Melissa de la Cruz

www.atombooks.net

ATOM

First published in the United States in 2013 by Hyperion
First published in Great Britain in 2013 by Atom
Reprinted 2013 (twice), 2014

Copyright © 2013 by Melissa de la Cruz

A CIP catalogue record for this book
is available from the British Library.

ISBN 978-1-907411-50-2

Printed and bound in Great Britain by
Clays Ltd, St Ives plc

Papers used by Atom are from well-managed forests
and other responsible sources.

MIX
Paper from
responsible sources
FSC
www.fsc.org   FSC® C104740

Atom
An imprint of
Little, Brown Book Group
100 Victoria Embankment
London EC4Y 0DY

An Hachette UK Company
www.hachette.co.uk

www.atombooks.net

For my Blue Bloods family

Your time will come.
You will face the same evil, and you will defeat it.
　– Arwen to Aragorn
　　Peter Jackson's *The Fellowship of the Ring*

Knock, knock, knocking on heaven's door.
　– Bob Dylan

PART THE FIRST

SHOULD OLD ACQUAINTANCE BE FORGOT

*Blood and fire are too much for
these restless arms to hold.*
—Indigo Girls, "Blood and Fire"

ONE

Schuyler

*T*he fireworks burst into a dazzling array of color and sound, shooting a rainbow above the London skyline as the crowd on the Victoria Embankment cheered lustily for the beginning of the New Year. Schuyler Van Alen watched the festivities from the balcony of a town house across the way in Primrose Hill, admiring the spectacular view of the London Eye glowing silver and lavender against the night sky, bordered by a glittering framework of blue lights from the row of trees surrounding the park.

"It's almost midnight," said Oliver Hazard-Perry as he appeared with two champagne glasses and handed Schuyler one with a smile. He was wearing a crisp black tuxedo with shiny silver cuff links, and she was struck by his grown-up manliness—the gravity in the way he carried himself, the newfound confidence in his step. His sandy brown hair was combed back from his forehead, his hazel eyes crinkled with a few fine lines. The London girls couldn't get enough of him—his phone beeped constantly with texts to meet them for drinks at Loulou's or to join them for yet another Pimps and Ho's party at "Harry's." Oliver had told her all about his love affair in New York, with the witch who had healed his heart and cured his blood of the longing he used to carry as Schuyler's familiar. He was back to being just her human Conduit, but he was still the dear boy who had been her best friend since the beginning.

"Cheers," she said, accepting the glass and clinking it against his. She had agreed to the party despite her mood, and was wearing a black velvet dress that suited her. A mourning dress, she couldn't help but think as she had slipped it over her shoulders earlier that evening. It was cut with a deep V-neck, sleeveless. Against the dark fabric, her clavicles were sharp lines, and she knew her arms looked painfully thin. She was wearing her bonding ring on her left hand, and a silver circlet on her forearm that Oliver had given her as a birthday present years ago.

Her friend appraised her thoughtfully. "You look beautiful and tragic, just the way a heroine should on the eve of battle. Like Joan of Arc in her silver armor."

"Nice of you to say, although I don't feel particularly brave," Schuyler said, fiddling with her new short haircut, a pixie with a bit of a "fringe"—what the Brits called bangs. "But maybe the champagne will help." She smiled even as she felt a strange chill, not from the cold breeze, but from an inexplicable, unshakable feeling that she was being watched. Standing on the terrace, she suddenly felt vulnerable and exposed, but she refrained from telling Oliver. She didn't want him to worry any more than he already did. But still— it was there—the feeling that someone was watching her. Watching and waiting.

She shook off her nerves, and they watched in companionable silence as the fireworks popped and the Ferris wheel spun. In the months they had lived in London they'd had yet to visit any of the usual tourist spots. Not that they were there to have fun—although with Kingsley Martin around, fun was never far from the agenda.

"There you two are!" Kingsley boomed, joining them on the terrace with a jolly crew of guests. The party was his idea—rounding up what was left of the London Coven, rallying the troops for one last hurrah before the end. His color was high, and he was handsome and dashingly disheveled in black tie—the bow unknotted and dangling roguishly from his shirt collar. They had Kingsley to thank for the formal costumes and the vintage champagne. "Let's meet the new year with style!" he'd insisted.

Kingsley and his friends were wearing conical hats and tooting brightly colored horns that shot out crepe paper tongues. He handed Schuyler a sparkler, and she waved it off the balcony, sharing a smile with Oliver as the sparks flew in the night air. The countdown began and they joined the

Venators in chanting, "Ten, nine, eight, seven . . . three two one . . ."

The noise was deafening as the orchestra blared Beethoven's Fifth and the fireworks exploded with canon-sized booms.

"Happy New Year," Oliver mouthed.

"HAPPY HAPPY HAPPY!" Kingsley yelled, giving each of his friends a sloppy drunken kiss on the cheek before leading the merry group into a rousing rendition of "Auld Lang Syne" in his rich baritone.

Schuyler exchanged a droll smile with Oliver over Kingsley's antics. For the last few months the two of them had effectively acted as the Venator's jailors, parents, and confidants; and while Schuyler was glad to see him in high spirits, Kingsley could be reckless and she worried about him.

"Happy New Year, Ollie," she said, kissing him lightly on the cheek, remembering past New Year's Eves spent with him, watching the televised Times Square ball drop, perennially uninvited to any of the raucous celebrations that their fellow Duchesne students were famous for throwing. Once upon a time, Schuyler had yearned to experience a really great party—a date for the evening, someone to kiss at midnight, the opportunity to wear a beautiful dress, to look forward to the coming year in the arms of a boy she loved. She gave Oliver's arm an affectionate squeeze even as her heart ached for her true love.

It had been several months since she'd said good-bye to

Jack Force in the deserts of Egypt. Another climate, another life, it felt like. She had promised him she would move forward with her quest, with her mission; to forget about love in favor of duty. She remembered their last night together, the way he had held her close, the way they had burrowed into each other, skin against skin, breath against breath, not wanting to separate, not for a moment. What had happened to Jack? Was he even still alive? Had Mimi killed him? Schuyler didn't know. There was no way to know. There had been no sign of either of the Force twins for months, and with the Covens broken and the vampires in virtual retreat—there was no news anywhere.

"I'm sure Jack's alive," Oliver said, reading her thoughts as always.

She didn't answer, just took another sip from her glass.

"Mimi, too—somehow, I don't think either would be able to destroy the other. I just can't see it," he said.

If Jack was dead, she would know it, Schuyler thought. Somehow she would know, wouldn't she? She would *feel* it. But all she felt was numb. As if a limb had been cut off, as if her heart was so tired of fearing and grieving that it had given up hoping. It was too difficult to think of Jack and what they'd had together. A promise, a bond, a joy, a love for the ages, for the history books. . . . But what was love but pain? It hurt to think of Jack; it distracted her from her work. She had to keep him out of her mind. Had to forget so she could concentrate on the task at hand. Lucifer was moving his pieces across the chessboard. Endgame was upon them. The survival of the vampires was in question. The fight for Heaven and Earth would begin and end with her.

"I know Jack would never lay a hand on her, and I hope you're right about Mimi," she said.

"I know I am," Oliver said staunchly.

He had been defending Mimi for months. Schuyler wasn't as certain as he was of Mimi's change of heart. Mimi had ever been hell-bent on destroying Jack, on seeking revenge, but Oliver was convinced her affections ran elsewhere now. Schuyler wasn't sure how much she believed that Kingsley had supplanted Jack in Mimi Force's heart. Besides, Kingsley never talked about Mimi and whatever happened between them. According to Oliver, Mimi had given up her soul to get him out of the underworld—which was even more troubling, because if Mimi had lost what little soul she'd had—then what did it mean for Jack?

Kingsley was certainly a lot more subdued than Schuyler remembered him—plugging away day after day, buried under Repository books. There had been rumors in the underworld that the demons had discovered a weapon more powerful than the White Fire of Heaven—but if there was such a thing, the Venator had not yet figured it out, and it troubled him that the Blue Bloods remained oblivious to the Dark Prince's malevolent designs. But he certainly wasn't acting as if he were heartbroken—the sly dog was out every night with a different girl on his arm, drinking, carousing, in a whirlwind tour of every nightclub, bar, and pub in the city.

Between Kingsley and Oliver and the skeleton crew of hard-living Venators, their flat—a Venator safe house—was crawling with girls. At first Schuyler had been amused at their bachelor lifestyle—it was such a contrast to her and Jack's quiet domicile as newlyweds in Alexandria. But her patience had been worn thin by the constant parade of lovely "English chippies" or "Chelsea birds" who flocked to their apartment. The bathrooms stunk of perfume, the kitchen counter was always lined with lipstick-stained wineglasses, and once she had even pulled a pair of lacy underthings from beneath the couch pillows.

Schuyler downed her glass and Kingsley appeared at her elbow with a magnum of Bolly. She raised her hand in protest, but it was futile. He filled it to the top until the bubbles overflowed.

"Bingo, Archie, Gig, and the rest of the crew are talking of streaking through the crowd on the Thames—you guys in?" he asked, his blue eyes sparkling with mischief.

"In this weather?" Oliver balked.

"Come on, man, it'll be a hoot!" Kingsley said.

Oliver hesitated. He looked at Schuyler, who shook her head. "You'll be all right?" he asked.

"I'm fine, go ahead. Kingsley's right, it'll be fun." Schuyler smiled at the two of them as they joined the merry crew already shedding clothing at the front door.

* * *

Since the three of them had arrived in town, they had accomplished a lot, including identifying the physical location of the Gate of Promise, a closely guarded secret that only they shared. Kingsley, as the highest-ranking among them (Schuyler had not yet achieved a real place in their society) had sent word out to the remaining Covens to come to London and await orders, and little by little, vampires had made their way back into the city. A number of them were at the party that night, but they were anxious and suspicious, and many were talking about returning underground instead. They had no idea what they were waiting for, and Schuyler wasn't yet ready to tell them. Kingsley had cautioned against sharing what they knew of Lucifer's plan—fearing more traitors within their midst.

The Gate of Promise had been established during the glory days of the Roman Empire, when the Order of the Seven was founded, with the discovery of the Paths of the Dead. Allegra Van Alen, or Gabrielle, as was her true name, determined that the Gate of Promise was bisected, and that while one path led to the underworld, another path, a secret path, led back to the paradise they had lost. Charles Force, the archangel Michael, had suspected such a path existed, and it was why he had ordered the paths to be guarded but not destroyed.

So what had happened in Rome? Why had Gabrielle kept her discovery a secret from Michael? It had been during the Crisis in Rome that the Blue Bloods had discovered that the Silver Bloods were hiding among them. Caligula was unmasked as Lucifer, but the archangel Michael had triumphed, sending him back to the underworld. The Silver Bloods were supposed to have been defeated. But instead, they continued to thrive in the shadows, and to menace the Blue Bloods for centuries after, preying on the young, until the present chaos. The victory Michael had won had been temporary at best.

Gabrielle's daughter will bring us salvation. She will lead the Fallen back into Paradise. Her grandfather Lawrence Van Alen had always believed it, and Schuyler knew in her heart that he was right, that she held the key. There was just one problem: she had no idea what that meant. The gate was immovable, as solid as a vault, and immune to every spell and incantation she threw at it. She had been trying for months and failing. Time was running out—the Dark Prince had set his sights on destroying the gate and was gathering his forces for battle to reclaim the throne he had been denied. The Silver Bloods could attack at any moment and take up the rebellion that had been subdued so long ago.

So where do I fit in? How do I fulfill my legacy?

Schuyler was still mulling over the questions when the boys trooped back in, cheeks blazing red from the cold, in various states of undress—Kingsley stripped to the waist, his strong chest heaving with deep breaths as he sprawled down on the couch in his tuxedo pants; Oliver standing in his boxer shorts, holding a flask of whiskey and grinning.

"You didn't get caught? I thought the bobbies were out in force," Schuyler said, taking a seat across from them and crossing her arms, feeling a bit like a schoolmarm tending to her naughty pupils. "Where's everyone else?"

"After-party in Notting Hill," replied Oliver as he threw the flask to Kingsley, who caught it and took a slug.

"Jolly good show," Kingsley said to Oliver. "Didn't think you'd be able to keep up with us."

Oliver smirked, flexing his broad shoulders. All those workouts in the underworld had paid off. "Your age is showing, old man. . . ."

"Anyway—good news, yeah?" Kingsley said. "Tell her."

"Tell me what?" Schuyler asked, fully expecting to hear of some new conquest one of them had made.

"While we were running across the riverbank, we bumped into someone." Oliver grinned.

"Who?"

"Lucas Mendrion, a retired Venator captain. He—ahem—recognized Kingsley."

"Venator tattoo." Kingsley explained with a smirk. "Invisible to the human eye."

Oliver ignored him. "He said he didn't know any vampires were still around—he'd thought everyone had gone underground—he hadn't heard Kingsley had sent out a bulletin, and we got to talking and it turned out he'd been one of Gabrielle's Protectors during Rome."

"What's that?"

12

"Exactly what it means. Venators assigned to her protection," Oliver said.

"And?" Schuyler leaned forward.

"He said he has something important to tell you." Kingsley grinned. "About your mother's legacy."

"You think it might be about the three remaining gate-keepers?" Schuyler asked. She had thought that if anyone knew anything to help them unlock the secret of the Gate of Promise, it would be one of the surviving members of the original order. Three left of the original Order of the Seven—Onbasius, Pantaleum, and Octilla were still alive, their whereabouts unknown.

"Maybe. He said it wasn't safe to talk, so he's coming to meet with us here. Tomorrow. I mean, tonight," Oliver said, looking at the clock, which showed that it was half past three in the morning. "Caught a break finally." He punched Kingsley on the shoulder, and the two of them looked at Schuyler like eager puppies hoping for a treat.

It was just as Jack used to say—one lead was all they needed—one light against the darkness and all would be illuminated. Jack . . . if only he was here with her now . . . but Schuyler couldn't continue to dwell on his absence. She had vowed to move forward. There was that feeling again—that odd sensation that she was not alone, but she ignored it. She was just paranoid.

So Schuyler returned their smiles, happy to bestow praise. "Happy New Year indeed."

"Whhat are you singing?" Jack asked, whispering.

Mimi started. She hadn't noticed she was humming out loud. She began to sing: "'Leaving on a midnight train to Georgia . . .'" Her voice carried through the empty cabin, low and soft. They were on a train headed from the Ninth Circle of Hell back up to the gatepost at the crossing, back to their world, at their master's bidding. Unlike the dirty subway car that had taken her back to the surface last time, now she was seated in a first-class carriage, complete with reclining seats and troll attendants on call. There was a difference in trying to escape from Hell and willingly leaving with its master's permission.

"'Bought a one-way ticket to a life he once knew,'" Jack sang, his voice a complement to hers. When the song ended, they shared a rueful smile, identical down to the dimples on their chins. Just like looking in a mirror, Mimi thought, glancing at her twin. How could she have ever hated him? Jack was part of her, had always been. She didn't know how she could have survived all these long years in the underworld without him by her side. Time was different down here: she understood it intellectually, but it was still disorienting to live outside of the circadian rhythms. There was no day, no night, just an endless present. She had no idea how long they had been away from their own world.

Once again, they had been yoked to each other for a difficult task—Dark Angels secretly fighting for the Light, hiding their better natures in order to win their freedom from each other.

She removed a jeweled compact from her purse and powdered her nose, admiring her reflection. She was the Mighty Azrael, Angel of the Apocalypse. The most beautiful girl in the underworld. Even the Dark Prince—that old rat bastard—had hinted that if she ever tired of Abbadon, he wouldn't mind getting to know her a little better. How ironic that her legendary beauty had not been enough to keep her twin by her side.

No, she had never been enough for Abbadon, which was why they shared this burden. She had loved him once, more than he had ever loved her, and the rejection still stung, but now it was like the buzzing of a gnat, a flea bite, inconsequential, annoying at best, merely a hairline crack in an otherwise formidable fortress. She had been living with it for so long—his worship of Gabrielle, casting his lot with that . . . Abomina— No, she couldn't call her that anymore. . . . With *Schuyler*. There. Mimi could not bear to *think* her name even if they were adversaries no longer. Schuyler had won, for sure. Not that it mattered.

It was too late to think of what might have been. She had committed to this task, and she would see it through. She looked out the window, the landscape a monotonous gray rock, the red-hot cinders from the Black Fire the only light for miles. It seemed like centuries since she had felt sunshine on her face, even though Jack had assured her they had been in Lucifer's service for only a few months, and that when they reached aboveground it would be right around New Year's.

Do you think we'll find it? she sent to Jack.

I hope not.

Don't, she warned, alarmed at his cavalier attitude. *They might hear.*

They can't hear us, Mimi. I told you. Not when we talk like this. The bond allows us that privacy at least.

He was her twin. The same dark star had birthed them. Bound to each other from the beginning. Sealed in blood and fire.

The bond was the reason they were slaves to the Dark Prince in the first place. Its unbreaking had cost them an internship in Hell. Divorce lawyers had nothing on Lucifer. Mimi was appalled and yet amused at the same time. Was it worth it? They were playing a dangerous game. If Lucifer suspected they were false . . . She shuddered to think of the consequences. He held their very souls captive unless they delivered. They would pay the ultimate price if they did not.

Whose idea was this, anyway? Mimi remembered how close she had been to destroying Jack, holding her sword aloft, ready for revenge. She could have struck him down. It was so *tiring* being good. Sacrifice just wasn't her style.

Oh, well. Too late now.

At least they had each other. Mimi would have gone mad if she hadn't had Jack to lean on. Their former commander had kept himself scarce. Lucifer was always thus, Mimi remembered—aloof, withdrawn, prone to seek his own counsel. And once they had returned to the dark fold, they had been surrounded by old comrades and enemies. Angels with whom they had fought side by side. Angels they had betrayed during that last terrible struggle for dominion of Paradise. Needless to say, they had been given a chilly reception.

That first night back in the underworld they walked in to find a hostile crowd at the local watering hole. She and Oliver had frequented it during their sojourn, but the management had changed, and the place was not what it was.

"Look, everyone—it's the ones who lost the war for us," Danel had said. He had been one of their oldest friends, a warrior, tall and golden and proud, beautiful as ever except for the ugly scar that bisected his face. Now he sneered at them. "If it wasn't for you . . ."

"Traitors. Thieves. Turncoats," came the silky voice of the angel Barachiel. "Welcome to the underworld. You will find you are right at home here." He smiled.

"You are kidding yourselves if you think you can return to his service so easily," hissed Tensi, a formidable avenging angel who had led the charge from the left flank all those millennia ago, when the world was young.

But in the end the angels left them alone. They still feared Abbadon's hammer, still cowered at the flaming sword of Azrael.

"We have no place here," Mimi had said to Jack later in their private quarters. The twins had merited a lavish suite in the palace, a rival to the ducal estate that Kingsley had once called home. "Michael and Gabrielle never trusted us—and neither does this sorry lot."

"They will come around. They have no choice."

Jack had turned out to be right. While the Silver Bloods were strong in number, they were also fearful and scattered. They still remembered the power of the White Fire of Heaven, the wrathful armies of Paradise, how they had been cast out of Elysium and into hellfire. Since Leviathan was tasked with assembling the demon army in the deep bowels of Hell, Jack had stepped into his former position as the head of the Dark Fallen.

Every night Jack drank and feasted with them, singing old war songs, drinking the blood ale, skirmishing in the training courtyards, testing his strength against theirs, gaining their trust, their respect, their admiration, and whatever tenderness was left in their Corrupted souls that passed for love. He impressed them with the depth of the power at his command. Abbadon had truly returned to Hell, they said. Abbadon, Destroyer of Worlds. Hell's true son.

How strange that after their long and twisted history, Mimi and Jack were only just friends now, with a deep and abiding affection between them. They would always share their past, but their future together was unknown. She still loved him, she would always love him, but it was the kind of love that was muted, safely seen through the rearview window, like a place you used to call home but no longer visited. There would always be a wound there, but the healing had begun.

All because of Kingsley Martin, the boy who loved her.

How could she have lost her heart to a Silver Blood?

If she was to have a future with anyone, she would have it with Kingsley. She held on to her love, to the memories of his wicked smile, to the feel of his strong arms around her, his soft tears on her cheek. She had broken him, he had broken her, there was no more posturing, no more lies. They had pledged their love to each other. It made the deception and the fear easier to bear. What a naked fear it was. Azrael, Angel of Death, who was afraid of nothing and no one on earth, was afraid. She was afraid for her life, for her love. If the Dark Prince knew the truth. . . .

Lucifer could unmake her. He could unmake her and

Jack both . . . would do to them what they had failed to do to each other.

Was it worth it?

All this for love?

All this for Kingsley?

Yes. Yes. Yes.

Mimi sighed. The last time she'd seen him she had been soulless, and she had screamed at him to get away from her, had laughed in his face and mocked his love. Did this mean they would have to start all over again? She wondered what he was doing now. Having a great old time, probably. Kingsley Martin was never down for long.

At least she and Jack had done something right. They had arrived in the underworld at just the right time. The demons of Hell had discovered the secret to a weapon that would stand up to the White Fire of Heaven—they aimed to create a godsfire of their own. But there was a catch. None of their tools, which had been wrought in the underworld, could be trusted to hold and direct the blaze.

The Dark Prince needed the Holy Grail to hold his weapon. Only the sacred chalice would contain the righteous flame. And so Mimi and Jack had been dispatched to fetch it. There were many cups, many grails in the history of the world. The task was to find the right one.

Once they crossed into their world, Mimi would make her way to a chapel in Scotland, while Jack would travel to Spain. And if they were successful in finding the Holy Grail, what then? Would they turn it over to the Dark Prince? Mimi wasn't sure what Jack was planning, although he'd assured her he would never let that happen. If they found it, they would lie and say they had not, and Jack was counting on the knights to have hidden the grails well. Mimi was certain Lucifer would not be so understanding of their failure and would suspect treason, but Jack was adamant in his belief that it would all work out, that they would figure out a way to get what they wanted without forfeiting their souls or destroying Heaven and Hell in the process.

The train reached its destination and stopped at the crossing. They disembarked, walking to the same barriers guarded by the same handful of trolls that she had encountered during her journey with Oliver. Once they got past the First Circle of Hell, then they would slip through the gates and find themselves back in mid-world.

A troll slouched over to block their way. "Papers?"

"Papers?" Mimi said, affronted. "Do you know who we work for?"

"Helda hasn't approved your transfer," the troll sneered. "You'll need to go back to get the right papers if you mean to leave the kingdom of the Queen of the Dead."

Without a word, Jack raised his hand and stunned the troll, sending him flying, crashing against the barrier. The other troll guards lifted their spears, but Jack stood his ground. "Let us pass. I shall not be so gentle next time."

Mimi was impressed. She was sure he would have turned back and done the right thing. But that was the old Jack Force. The former Venator, the one who used to follow the rules. There were no rules now.

The trolls backed off, fear in their ugly faces.

The Force twins stepped through the Gates of Hell.

"Admit it, you enjoyed that. You *like* being evil again," Mimi teased.

Jack did not reply, but the sly smile on his face said it all. "Come on. Let's find this thing and end it once and for all."

merging from the Passages of Time was always a disconcerting experience, as if your entire being had been taken apart and then re-formed, the molecules and the memories haphazardly patched together. Bliss Llewellyn felt the familiar dizziness and disorientation, but it was worse now, since they were not just traveling through time but back to the underworld, back to her father's domain, back to Hell, where the wolves were turned into Hellhounds, where Lawson and the pack had been kept in chains.

She had come upon the boys by chance—had been shown a vision of a wolf in the glom, and had tracked it to a butcher shop in a small town in Ohio. There, she had befriended Lawson and his brothers, and together they had traveled to the dawn of Rome, to the beginning of the Empire, to solve a mystery of the wolves' ancestry. Lawson was revealed to be the wolf Fenrir, the greatest wolf of the underworld, and he had bested Romulus, the Beast of Hell, the Hound of Hounds; had killed him with Michael's sword, an archangel's blade. With the help of his pack, he had stopped the Sabine massacre, and in doing so had saved the wolves from extinction. Now they had returned to Hell to fulfill his promise to free his people from the Silver Blood demons.

Lawson turned around, his dark eyes sparkling, and he smiled. The sigul on his cheek, the one that matched Bliss's and marked them as part of the same pack, the blue crescent moon, shone in the dim light. "You okay back there?" he asked.

Bliss nodded, keeping pace with his long step. She was scared but determined to see it through. This was what her mother had tasked her to do—to bring the wolves back into the fold, to help the vampires in their war against their enemies—but she had her own reasons for pursuing this quest. Bliss had a dark history behind her: for centuries upon centuries she had been an unknowing party to evil. As the vehicle for the Dark Prince, she had kept his spirit alive on earth, and in doing so had brought death and grief to the vampires. Bliss wanted not only redemption, but revenge.

She had pinned her hopes on the pack—Lawson, impulsive, reckless, and powerfully strong, and his brothers—Edon, Rafe, and Malcolm—loyal soldiers all—along with Ahramin, the dark one—the wolf who had been turned into a hound and reclaimed her soul. They surrounded her now, and Bliss found solace in their number and strength. They were ready to fight.

Lawson stumbled out of the passage, and everyone else followed after. Bliss looked around—steeling herself for the worst—expecting to breathe the smoke of the underworld—to see gray skies and barren lands—or to be met by a thousand demons with crimson eyes and burning tongues, wielding swords of dark flame.

But what was this? There was grass beneath her feet. Trees forming a canopy over her head. The sweet smell of morning dew. This wasn't the underworld. . . . This looked strangely familiar. . . . This was . . . Ohio?

"Where are we?" she asked Lawson, who was standing next to her. She looked to the rest of the pack. Malcolm wiped his eyeglasses on his sleeve. Rafe appeared confused, and Ahramin and Edon were whispering to each other.

"Guys?" she asked. "Um . . . are we where I think we are?"

Lawson nodded grimly. "Yeah. We're back in Hunting Valley." He kicked a tree stump. "We must have made a wrong turn somewhere."

They'd landed in the middle of rural suburbia, not far from where Bliss had found them in the beginning. This was the clearing in the woods, a few miles away from the center of town, where the boys lived above a butcher shop.

"Well, what are we waiting for? Let's go back in." She

removed the chronolog from her jeans pocket. The time-keeper was rotating, its hands spinning out of control. "Wait—there's something wrong with it. Mac, can you look at it?"

"Sure," Malcolm said. He took it from her hand and studied it. "It looks like it's trying to make a reading, but something's preventing it from doing so."

Bliss looked back from where they came from. The passage had closed behind them. "Maybe because we're out of the passage? Lawson, can you open it back up?"

Lawson nodded; his face took on a look of deep concentration.

They waited, but nothing happened.

"Come on, Lawson, get on with it," Ahramin said, a trace of annoyance in her voice.

"I'm trying," Lawson said. "Something's wrong. I can't open the portal."

"Are you doing something different?" Malcolm asked. "Can we help?"

Of course he'd offer to help, Bliss thought. Malcolm was the youngest in the pack, and by far the sweetest. Bliss had come to adore him in the time they'd spent together. Edon and Rafe had been tougher nuts to crack, though she felt close to them as well. As for Ahramin, the former Hellhound was one of them now, her past transgressions forgiven when she'd proved herself worthy of the pack by fighting against Romulus's will and breaking her collar. They were a team, a unit, and if Bliss had any lingering suspicions concerning Ahramin, she chided herself for them. For if she felt that way about Ahramin, how could she expect anyone to forgive her for her own dark past? Ahramin was merely a former Hellhound, but Bliss was Lucifer's daughter. The Dark Prince had cursed the wolves, had turned them into slaves. In the underworld, the Silver Bloods had been the wolves' masters.

"Tell us what you need us to do," she urged Lawson.

"This has never happened before," he grumbled. "But sure, why not? Guys, everyone focus. We just need to clear our minds, imagine the passage opening. Maybe if we all work together we can do it."

The pack huddled together. Bliss pushed away her fear, pushed away her doubt, and pictured the Passages of Time opening before her. Her head ached, and she put her hands to her temples, feeling them throb and pulse, and for a moment she was convinced it was working. She could feel the passage opening behind her, felt the wind through the tunnels.

Then it stopped.

The feeling went away.

She opened her eyes and looked around. Nothing had changed.

They were still standing in the clearing.

"What's going on?" Rafe asked, frustrated.

"Did you do something?" Ahramin asked Lawson.

"Like accidentally seal the passage behind us when we went through?"

"Why do you always assume it was me who did something wrong?" Lawson protested.

"Because you've screwed up before," she snapped. "Remember how I got left behind the last time?"

They sounded like an old married couple, Bliss thought. Which implied a certain kind of intimacy that she didn't want to think about too much. Besides, it was ridiculous to even consider. Ahramin and Lawson? If they hadn't been in the same pack, it was clear they would have despised each other. Besides, Ahramin had been pledged to Edon from the beginning. No, they weren't like a married couple—more like bickering siblings, which made more sense.

"Don't be so hard on him, Ahri; he's doing his best," Edon said.

"It wasn't Lawson," Malcolm said. "It's like the passages have closed up on their own. Can't you feel it?"

Rafe nodded. "It did feel different, like something was blocking them."

"Or someone," Bliss said.

FOUR

Tomasia (Florence, 1452)

The castle came into view at the edge of a black and winding river, its tall gray walls rising forty feet above the dark waters. Steep cliffs backed the fortress, which meant the stone bridge was the only way in or out. The keep was well fortified, designed to repel a siege. But its defenses would soon prove useless.

"We'll stop here, lest we give away our location," Tomasia Fosari decided, and the team drifted into the shadows of the forest. The air was damp and smelled of the rotting river, its murky waters rippling with the current.

"Are you certain you can do this?" Giovanni Rustici asked. In the moonlight his hair was like a halo around his handsome face. Gio was not only the best Venator among them, he was also a fellow sculptor at Donatello's studio, and Tomasia's closest friend. He knew how hard this was for her. They had spent days on the road tracking the Dark Prince to his hiding place in Verona.

"Yes," Tomasia told him, her face set. She had believed that Andreas del Pollaiuolo was the love of her life. Michael to her Gabrielle. But she had been deceived. Dre carried the spirit of Lucifer within him. Simonetta de Vespucci had named him as the father of her baby. "The Mistress," Simonetta was called, consort to the Dark Prince, his human bride, the mother of Nephilim.

The dark-haired beauty had cowered from Gio's blade.

"We shall not suffer the demon child to live," Gio growled.

But Tomi had stayed his hand. "No. She will be kept under guard, protected and watched by our finest Venators. We would be no better than our Silver Blood brethren if we kill her. We shall not shed devil blood, not in the name of all that is Divine."

Simonetta had revealed Andreas's location, had begged them to show her lover mercy. They had left the weeping, pregnant woman in the care of the Petruvian priests tasked with her safety.

Tomi shivered at the thought of what might have been if they had not discovered the deception. She would have bonded with Dre, with Lucifer. She would have pledged her troth to his. How could she not have known? How was it that she had been able to see her mate in his soul? It did not make sense.

She looked at the castle looming in the distance. Andreas was hiding inside with a Coven of Silver Bloods, and she was going to burn it down with the Black Fire.

"I know you loved him once," Gio said softly. "I know how hard this is."

Gio—Dear, lovely Gio. Tomi put a hand on his. "I cannot love one who has been false." She scanned the castle once more for any sign of life. Torchlight flickered in a distant window. She heard horses neigh, and a shadow of a hawk passed over her head. Otherwise, the night was quiet and nothing moved. The castle towers' red terra-cotta roofs glowed in the dark. Truly, no terrestrial fire could harm this place, but the Black Fire of Hell was another matter.

She pulled a tinderbox from her cloak and motioned the others to gather around. There were five of them in all. Five Venators, five sides of a pentagram.

The small container glowed with an unearthly light, and the air around it hummed with energy. Tomi ran a finger along the box top, and the lid slid open to reveal a small glowing spark, red flames with a black heart. The air smelled of sulfur and smoke.

"The Black Fire is held in check by a containment spell for now. The spell will not abate until I release the enchantment," she said as, one by one, the Venators lit their wooden torches with the dark flame.

"Each of us will take a corner of the castle. Wait for my word. Once released, the flame cannot be extinguished.

31

It can destroy stone as well as flesh, and immortal souls as swiftly as mortal. Toss the torches onto the castle, then run away as fast as you are able." Her voice trembled a little. "Remember, the Black Fire of Hell is treacherous; it will burn you as easily as it will burn our enemies."

The team disbanded, carrying their torches high in the air. The three other Venators disappeared along the river's edge, while Tomi and Gio sprinted across the bridge, toward the keep. Tomi watched as the dark flames flickered on both sides of the wall, the Black Fire sucking all light from the murky night.

They crossed to the far side of the bridge.

When she was certain the team was in position, she gave the signal.

Now, she sent to each Venator as she released her torch, sending the flame to the sky.

Gio sent his flying to the air, toward an open window. "RUN!" he yelled, as they fled the black flames.

Tomi knew the danger, but couldn't stop from looking backward. The sight was magnificent in its horror. The Black Fire erupted over the castle wall, melting the gray stone as if it were made of wax. The two towers and the mighty gate collapsed backward into a black hole of swirling flames. The far side of the bridge toppled behind them, pulling one of the bridge's broad pillars with it into the dark waters in a thunderous crash.

The black flames began to consume the river, making

the water steam as the fire raced across its length. The smell was hideous, sick and rotten; it consumed everything in its path: air, water, and rock.

When they reached the far bank and the edge of the forest, they heard the first screams from inside the castle. They ran along the riverbank, the fire receding behind them. A mile from the castle, they reached high ground and looked down at the valley below. The river rode in a broad circle around the promontory and back to the castle, and the Black Fire would not spread beyond it once it had consumed the soul of the Dark Prince. Two of the three Venators appeared out of the smoke.

"Where's Dantos?" Tomi asked.

"The Black Fire caught his eye. I tried to subdue it, but it was no use," Bellarmine said.

"He burned, I saw him," Valentina said. "He rests with the angels now."

Tomi felt her heart wrench in anger. Like Bellarmine and Valentina, Dantos had been part of her loyal Venator team since the days of Rome. Tomi leaned against Gio, blinking back tears.

She watched the castle implode upon itself, and crumble into a thousand dark pieces. Good-bye, Andreas. Her hatred of her former love was as great as her grief for her fallen comrade.

Burn, devil, burn.

The house on Primrose Hill was larger than the typical London town house, with a curved facade boasting several first-floor balconies, a soaring triple-height ceiling in the entryway, a formal dining room that could seat twenty, an industrial-style kitchen, eight bedrooms, a spacious upper terrace, and a suite of offices in the attic. When the Coven had disbanded, the house was kept in pristine condition by the remaining Venators and their Conduits. Schuyler had to admit she was glad for the home comforts, the French soap and the three-ply towels—such luxuries after the months spent in that tiny, dingy hotel room in Egypt.

Even though the staff was due to arrive at any minute, Schuyler spent the morning cleaning up from the party the night before—picking cigarette butts up off the floor, tossing all the dirty champagne glasses into the dishwasher, fluffing up pillows, vacuuming. At the very least, it gave her something to do with her nervous energy. She hadn't been sleeping very much lately, and the thought that they were now nearer to discovering the truth about the Gate of Promise had kept her up all night.

Oliver rolled into the dining room in time for lunch, still in pajamas, his hair sticking up from his forehead, sleepy-eyed and yawning. The cook had set out a "ploughman's lunch" on the buffet table: plates of cheese-and-pickle sandwiches, a tray of "crisps," and bottled water, in deference to their American tastes. Oliver filled up a plate and took a seat across from Schuyler at the long table.

"I just found out this house used to belong to the Ward family before they bequeathed it to the Venators fifty years ago," Schuyler said. "Maybe that's why it feels so comfortable . . . like Dylan is still with us." Maybe that was why she felt the way she did—maybe the *presence* that was never too far away was her old friend watching over them. But why did it feel so detached, then? As if whatever or whoever it was—was judging her and finding her wanting.

Oliver nodded. "I'm sure he's looking out for us in some way . . . wherever he is."

Schuyler was glad for Oliver's faith. Since they'd arrived in England, she had allowed herself to feel nothing but a grim, dogged determination to carry out her mother's plan. She could not trust herself to hope—but without hope, she realized, she had no reason to go on. She *had* to hope it would work out: that she would succeed not only in protecting the gate but in leading the vampires on the path back to Paradise; that Bliss would come through with the wolves; and that in the end, somehow, although she didn't know how, she and Jack would be together. Otherwise, what was the point of it all? Without hope, she was without life. She might as well chuck her bonding ring into the Thames.

"You're right, we're not alone in this fight," she told Oliver. "We'll give it the best we have," she said, reaching across the table to squeeze his hand.

Kingsley walked in at that exact moment, and upon seeing their clasped hands, gave them a curious look, and Schuyler quickly took her hand away from Oliver's, feeling embarrassed. Sometimes Kingsley had a way of insinuating things that weren't at all true.

"Are there any doughnuts?" he asked, looking at the food offerings. Oliver was right—the Venator seemed to live only on sugar and caffeine.

"Let me check; I think there might be," Schuyler said. "There's definitely coffee. I just made a pot."

Somehow, throughout the course of the day, the casual meeting with the Venator captain had evolved into an elegant dinner party. Schuyler ordered the staff to set the table with the fine embroidered linens she'd found in the hall closet. Maybe it was the house's grandeur that did it, but she had fallen sway to the same impetus that had caused Kingsley to throw the swanky New Year's bash the night before—a desire to live up to their surroundings and to celebrate the grand history of their Coven. Schuyler remembered the Countess's last party at the Hôtel Lambert. Tonight was yet another effort to honor what was left of their glory before it was swept away. What would happen to the house on Primrose Hill, Schuyler wondered. Would it be sold to pay the Coven's debts? Or left to ruin when the vampires were finally gone?

"What is this?" she asked Kingsley, as she looked through the kitchen cupboards for the formal china. She held up a white plate and showed him the barely discernable embossed logo on the back of it.

"The Venator sigil." Kingsley smiled and sipped from his eighth cup of coffee. "I carry the same one on my . . ." He grinned and pulled on the waistband of his jeans, as if he were about to moon her. "Want to see?"

"NO!" Schuyler said, with a hand up. Kingsley, ever the joker, had his Venator mark tattooed near his unmentionables.

"Your loss," Kingsley teased. "Anyway, tradition dictates that the Venator set is only used for when the Regis is in town."

"There is no more Regis," Oliver reminded him, having wandered in to refill his coffee cup. Truly he was getting to be as much of a coffee addict as Kingsley. "Charles has been missing since the Silver Blood attack in Paris."

"Right." Kingsley shrugged.

"No more Regis, no more Coven, no more rules," Schuyler decided, directing the housekeepers to use the set in her hands instead of the Spode Blue Italian.

"What are you serving? It smells lovely," said Kingsley, walking over to the simmering pots on the stove. "The house is full of it. We could smell it all the way up in the attic."

Schuyler smoothed the linen napkins so that the same Venator sigil was showing the right way. "Just something I used to make in Alexandria. A local specialty."

"Kebabs is it?" he asked. "But aren't those grilled?"

"You'll see." She smiled. "Get ready. Our guest will be here soon. I've noticed one thing about Brits: they're never late."

Just as Schuyler had predicted, the doorbell rang promptly at seven o'clock. The housekeeper answered the door, and a few minutes later the Venator captain entered the library, where Schuyler, Kingsley, and Oliver were having cocktails.

Lucas Mendrion had the same ageless visage as Kingsley, the mark of the Enmortal. He could have been anywhere from eighteen to forty, it was hard to tell. He was not handsome—his nose was hawkish and a bit too pointed, his eyes sharp and skeptical—but he projected a reassuring gravity. A man you could trust with your life, and with your secrets, Schuyler thought, understanding why Allegra had chosen him. He was wearing the standard Venator blacks.

"Schuyler Van Alen," she said, extending a hand. "Thank you for meeting with us, Venator Mendrion."

He shook it firmly. "Allegra's daughter," he said, staring at her intensely. "You have your mother's face, but not her eyes. . . ."

"They tell me I inherited my father's." She smiled.

"I didn't know your father. Red Blood, wasn't he?" Mendrion said with a raised eyebrow. "Highly inappropriate, but all in the past now. I saw your mother in this incarnation. She came to visit me once, before she disappeared from us."

"What was she like?" Schuyler asked. She knew so little of Allegra, and was eager for any little bits of insight or memory of her mother.

"Exactly the same as when I knew her in Rome," he said. "Impulsive, tenacious, brilliant. She was . . . our queen."

Schuyler nodded. "I'm sorry—where are my manners— this is Oliver Hazard-Perry, my Conduit, and you know Venator Martin."

Oliver and Kingsley both stood and shook the man's hand. Kingsley poured everyone drinks.

"So—shall we get started? It's good of you to have put together this dinner, but I'm afraid we don't have much time for idle chitchat," Mendrion said. "Martin said you were here to carry out Allegra's legacy."

Schuyler nodded. "They tell me you know about my family's work, and about the Order of the Seven."

"Those of us who were not chosen to serve the order served it in other ways," Mendrion said. "Gabrielle asked me to ensure the safety of this city from its founding." He took a sip from his glass. "As you must be aware, all the Gates of Hell are under siege at the moment; although so far London has been lucky enough to escape the Dark Prince's wrath."

"Do you know where the remaining keepers are—Pentalum? Onbasius? Octilla?" asked Oliver.

The Venator nodded. "Yes. We sent all our remaining Venators to bolster the security of the gates, but the odds are against them. The keepers will stand their ground and give their lives to the battle. But they will fall. The gates will fall. It is only a matter of time. The Nephilim walk the earth now. They will grow in number and influence the Red Bloods. Sow war and disease and despair."

Schuyler saw Oliver and Kingsley looking as uneasy as she felt. The Venator's words were defeatist, as if the battle had already been fought and lost.

"You sent *all* the Venators away?" Schuyler asked, her face falling, realizing why there were so few vampires left in London when they arrived; why it had been so difficult for Kingsley to raise a battalion.

"Yes. That is why I am here." He coughed. "To urge you to make your preparations to go underground, as I am."

"Excuse me?" Schuyler asked, startled.

"War has come to the vampires; the Croatan has risen. You are not safe here. Especially you, Schuyler Van Alen, as Gabrielle's daughter."

"I'm not going anywhere! Kingsley said you could help us!" she said, turning to the other Venator in the room, who looked impassive.

"I *am* helping you," Mendrion said.

"By abandoning the city? Abandoning your post? You were tasked to guard this Coven! To protect the city that houses the Gate of Promise—do you know where that path leads? What is behind that gate and its true nature?" she asked, her blue eyes shining with anger and indignation.

"It is too dangerous to know," Mendrion whispered.

"You took an oath! To my mother! To Gabrielle!"

"I kept this city safe for as long as I was able. I financed the Coven, trained the Venators, supported the Regis for as long as I could. But with Michael missing and Gabrielle gone . . . there is no hope for us. When I recognized Martin as one of our own and he told me you were here, I agreed to meet with you so I could warn you to hide. It's the least I could do."

Schuyler felt wrathful, angry at the cowardly Venator in front of her. His ageless countenance wavered, and for a moment he looked centuries old, crippled, weak, and frightened. A sad creature. Her grandmother Cordelia was right—the blood had thinned in their kind. There was little left of their former courage, their former glory, if even the Venators were cowards.

Kingsley said the words that she was thinking: "So there's nothing you can do to help us—nothing except to tell us to cower and shirk our duty," he said, a smirk on his lips.

"Venator Mendrion, you cannot leave London. The attack on the Gates of Hell is nothing but a distraction, and an effective one," Schuyler said. "Lucifer wants the vampires facing the other way. He cares not for the Nephilim, but only for the Gate of Promise, which leads to—"

Lucas Mendrion put up his hand to silence her. "I told you, I don't want to know."

Schuyler frowned.

"You are very young and very brave. Very much like your mother. She would be proud of you," Mendrion said.

Schuyler ignored him. She had no time for his condescension. "You told Kingsley you knew something about the Gate of the Promise, about its creation."

"No, I never said that." He shook his head. "I merely told him of my relationship with Gabrielle, and he must have assumed the rest. Why? What do you want to know?"

"We have the key to the gate," Schuyler said, choosing her words carefully. "But we don't know how to use it."

Mendrion studied her thoughtfully. "If anyone might know, perhaps Titiana might. She was assigned to Gabrielle's protection from the beginning, as I was. They were like sisters."

"Where can we find her?"

"Truth be told, I haven't seen her in centuries." Mendrion said, holding his glass to Kingsley for another drop of whiskey.

"Why? What happened to her? A Silver Blood attack?" asked Schuyler.

Mendrion shook his head. "No, no, nothing like that. Have you heard of the 'mortalize' movement?"

Schuyler nodded. The mortalize movement was a

growing trend among the Blue Bloods—vampires choosing to live as mortals—forgetting their history and passing as Red Bloods. She had heard that it happened a lot, especially during the long peaceful years when the Silver Bloods were all but forgotten.

"I fear that's what's happened to Titiana. She's chosen to turn back against her vampire roots," Mendrion said.

Schuyler tried not to feel too aghast. While it had been a burden when she'd first learned her true history and ancestry—she remembered the feeling in her stomach when she was first called to join the Committee—how she had refused to believe it was true—and how she wished she had come from a normal family, and not one where her mother was in a coma and her grandmother was her only link to her past. But to chuck it all away? To pretend to be what you were not? When there was so much at stake?

Mendrion gave Schuyler a sympathetic smile. "If it helps, I hear that she might be a student at Central Saint Martins. Some sort of fashion designer. Calls herself Tilly St. James."

The housekeeper entered the room. "Dinner is ready."

Lucas Mendrion turned to the dining room eagerly, but Schuyler cut him off. "I'm afraid I've quite lost my appetite. I do hope you understand," she said coldly. Her meaning was clear.

There was no room for cowards at her table.

SIX

Mimi

From the Underworld Express to the London tube, Mimi thought, holding on to the pole in the middle of the crowded commuter car. She had landed at Heathrow and was headed to Euston Station to transfer to another line that would take her to Edinburgh.

"All right, yeah?" Danel asked from the other side of the pole.

He had met her at the airport when she'd disembarked from her flight. It had been a somewhat unpleasant surprise. She'd thought she was to carry out her mission alone, but it appeared that the Dark Prince had other plans. She had merited a bodyguard, it seemed.

"Jet lag," she told him. She had felt woozy when she'd crossed through Hell's gate, and was shocked to find it had only been a few months since she and Jack had disappeared into the underworld. It was January and freezing. Thank

God she still had access to her credit accounts. The first thing she did was buy a new winter coat.

"Jet lag," Danel repeated with a trace of sarcasm in his voice. Up here, the scar on his face was gone. Was it an illusion, Mimi wondered. Like the disguise she had taken? Or was one's true form only visible in the underworld? For this trip aboveground Mimi had dark hair and eyes. To the rest of the populace, the angel was merely a striking gentleman on the subway.

Mimi ignored him. *Danel here with me*, she sent Jack. *I need to get rid of him.*

Hold on, Jack replied. *I'll think of something. Get him off your tail.*

No one sent to guard you? she asked.

Not yet.

She didn't know whether to feel flattered or insulted at that. It had been Abbadon's idea to turn to the Light at the last minute during the War for Paradise, not hers. Abbadon, who had betrayed the Morningstar and won the battle for Michael in the end. She had only followed blindly, doing as her twin bid her, doing as she had always done. She hadn't had a choice then. She hadn't even questioned her actions or his.

What if she had crossed him back then, where would she be right now? What if she had said no? What if she had remained loyal to the Morningstar? Would they have won Paradise? If Lucifer had bested the Almighty, what then?

In the heat of battle, in the gore and the blood and the passion and the fear, Azrael had done as she was asked by her love: to turn against her general, against the Prince of Heaven. She was the one whose sword had pierced Lucifer's armor. Not Abbadon's. *Hers.* It was Abbadon's will that had won the war for Michael, but it was Azrael's sword that had made it a reality.

"Brooding again?" Danel asked. "You're very quiet these days. Remembering the last battle, are you?"

She didn't lie. "Yes."

He nodded. "No one will ever forget what was done to us. It is time for our revenge. And this time, we shall triumph." His knuckles turned white as he grasped the pole. "Swear it."

"I . . ."

"LONDON EUSTON!" the loudspeaker blared.

"This is our stop—" Mimi said. She pushed her way through the crowd and waited for Danel on the platform. She looked around at the signs, for the one that would direct them to their next train.

Among the rush of commuters, jostled by the crowd, Mimi followed the herd toward the tunnels, and for a long time she didn't notice him. When she did, she felt a shock to her system, as if an electric bolt had shot up her spine. Every nerve tingled at attention, and her whole body was alight with love and desire.

What? Did you call me?

Jack's voice in her head was a distraction. An annoyance.

46

What did he want? Then she realized—it was the bond between them. Even if it hadn't been renewed in this lifetime, it was still there, a pulsing thread that kept them together. It had sparked because *she* had sparked with love, lust, longing. . . .

I'm fine. It's nothing.

She kept staring at the boy across the station, across the platform, on the other side of the tracks. He was turned away from her, but she recognized his handsome profile immediately, and she could hear his roaring laughter above the noise. Every part of her body hungered for him. If only she could leap across the train tracks and land in his arms—she wanted nothing but to be with him—and yet—she couldn't. She had to see this through. He couldn't see her. Danel was with her. It was too dangerous.

What was he doing?

Now that the crowd had parted, she saw that Kingsley wasn't alone at all. There was a girl with him. Correction. There were *girls* with him. Three of them. Passing a little flask around, giggling, and he had his arm slung over two of them so that the girls were pressing their bodies closely against his.

Okay, so it wasn't like he was making out with them or anything, but Mimi felt enraged and hurt nonetheless. She was furious. She had spent so much time working to be good, and this was her reward. So she'd been right as usual: all this sacrificing and suffering was for naught. Kingsley had moved on, and their love meant nothing to him—just like before. But what did she think was going to happen? As far as Kingsley was concerned, they were over. She herself had ended it.

Why was it that they always had to start over? She had lost her soul to rescue him from Hell, and here he was . . . acting just like he always did, just as she had feared. What did she expect, really? For Kingsley to change?

"There you are." Danel suddenly appeared by her side. "Our train leaves from the other side of the station."

Mimi stared at Kingsley in disgust. When the girl next to him slipped a hand into the back pocket of his jeans, Mimi turned to Danel with a crazed look in her eyes.

She grabbed his hand and swung him in her direction. "Kiss me!" she hissed, pulling him to her. She threw herself on him, kissing him passionately, as if he were the one she loved with all of her heart and not the boy across the way.

The angel looked shocked at first, but soon he opened his mouth to hers, and Mimi could tell that he was enjoying it . . . a little *too* much. He put his arm around her waist, pulled her hips closer to his. *Ugh.* There was no question that he was *definitely* enjoying this. She had to make it stop before it went too far.

Repulsed, she opened her eyes.

Across the length of the station, Kingsley was staring straight at her. His dark eyes boring into hers. Did he recognize her under the illusion? Under the disguise? Did he know it was her? He stared at her and Mimi panicked.

She impulsively crafted a spell that caused the train that had just pulled into the station to speed up instead of slowing down, almost crashing into a few commuters waiting for its doors to open. Several people began to scream while others backed away nervously, and the station master ordered everyone to keep calm over the loudspeaker. Just the distraction she needed.

Mimi wrenched away and pushed Danel off of her.

He wiped his lips with his jacket sleeve, his eyes glazed. "Never knew that's how you felt about me. I mean, Abbadon's a friend, but we can work something out. . . ." he said.

"Shut up," Mimi said, straining to see across the busy platform.

But Kingsley was gone.

"So what do we do now?" Ahramin asked, when nothing worked.

The passage wouldn't open, no matter how much they tried. Bliss thought her head was going to spontaneously combust, and she wasn't alone—the boys were massaging their temples too.

"This sucks," Ahramin said. "We need a new plan."

"We need to regroup," Lawson said. "Since we're back in Hunting Valley, then we should go find Arthur at the cave; maybe he can help us." Arthur Beauchamp was their patron and their friend; the warlock was the one who had helped the wolves when they'd escaped from the underworld to live aboveground.

They agreed to the plan, and were about to keep moving when Malcolm stumbled against a tree root. "Can we take a break for a minute? I'm exhausted," the young boy said.

"We're all exhausted," said Bliss. They had just defeated Romulus and the Hellhounds, and had plunged from that battle to prepare for another. "I think we need to rest and get him something to eat."

"The cave's too far, then. Let's just find a place right here," Lawson decided. "You're right, we might need to take some time to lick our wounds."

They made their way through the woods and the suburban maze back to the main center of town. It was cold outside, just like when they'd left. Bliss guessed they had been gone a week since they'd traveled back in time, and she wondered how Jack and Schuyler were faring in Italy, and what Mimi and the rest of them were up to.

They found a diner and ordered plates of breakfast—pancakes, eggs, waffles, and they fell on to the food hungrily. "You feel better now, Mac?" Bliss asked.

"A little. I just have a headache—like it feels odd to be here. Like we're not at the right place, like I woke up from a strange dream that lasted too long."

"This might explain it—" Edon said, showing them the newspaper he'd picked up from the next table and pointing at the date.

"It can't be," Lawson said. "No way."

"What's wrong?" Bliss asked, holding her breath.

"A year," Edon said. "A whole goddamn year has gone by while we were in the passages."

The pack absorbed this information. A whole year of

their lives, gone in a blink. Lawson stared at the date on the newspaper. A whole year they had lost, while their enemies were moving, making plans, preparing for battle. How much ground had they lost? Lawson couldn't speak, and Bliss saw the worry etched clearly on his face—a whole year—what had happened to the wolves who had remained trapped in the underworld?

"It's not your fault. Traveling though the passages is unpredictable," she said.

"Not this unpredictable," he argued. "I promised the wolves I would come back, and that was already almost a year ago *before* this. Who knows what's happened down there in the meantime?"

Bliss felt an urge to put her arms around him and console him somehow, but now wasn't the time, and things had been a little awkward between them since she'd revealed that Lucifer was her father. Sure, she was part of the pack, but it wasn't the same easy friendship they'd shared before. Not yet, anyway.

The wolves weren't their only concern. What had happened to the vampires, Bliss wondered—to her friends? She felt the same urgency Lawson did. She had to know. What if everything was already over? What if the Silver Bloods had already won?

"We have to find Schuyler," she said. "Allegra's other daughter. My . . . sister." She wasn't used to saying it out loud. "I'm supposed to bring the wolves to her. She might know why the passages are closed, or at least help us find a way to open them."

"Where is she?" Lawson asked.

"I'm not sure," she admitted. "Last time I saw her was at her bonding ceremony, in Italy; but if a year has gone by, there's no way she's still there. And without my powers, it's harder—I have to do things the human way. But there are Conduits who can help us." She explained the concept of humans who assisted vampires, noting that the boys looked a bit fearful when she talked about her past. Ahramin didn't seem to care, but that was Ahramin. "The best place to start is New York," Bliss said.

"We shouldn't all go," Edon said. "Arthur might have answers, too. Some of us should stay behind."

"Take Malcolm," Ahramin said.

"No—I'll go with Bliss," Lawson said suddenly.

Ahramin raised an eyebrow.

"You and Edon can take care of things here with Mac and Rafe. I should be the one talking to the vampires," he decided. "I should speak for the wolves."

"Fine," said Ahramin, as if it didn't matter either way.

Malcolm reached out and held Bliss's hand. "I don't want us to be separated now that we're a pack," he said.

"Don't worry," Bliss said. "My friends will be able to help. Lawson, are you sure about this? I can go alone. It's not like I haven't done it before."

"Positive," Lawson said. "I'm coming with you."

So it was decided. Lawson and Bliss would travel to find the vampires, while the rest of the pack would regroup with Arthur.

Bliss rented a car, a subcompact Hyundai, which was a far cry from being chauffeured around in a silver Rolls, but although she still had a working credit card, she had to be careful. After battling hounds and moving through the passages, the ten-hour drive to the city was surprisingly relaxing. Bliss let Lawson take the wheel, even if he drove like a speed demon.

"Hey, lead foot, give it a break will you?" she teased. "Sort of following that car closely, aren't you?"

"Am I? I didn't notice," he said, giving her a sheepish grin.

For a moment Bliss was keenly reminded of the night they'd spent together, when they had almost . . . well. No point in thinking of that now. It was just a mistake anyway. Lawson had been mourning Tala, the mate he had lost, and Bliss had been too drunk to truly understand what was happening. They were friends, and that's all they were going to be. She decided not to press. What was more annoying than a girl who wanted everything spelled out? *What's going on with us? How do you feel about me?* She cringed at the thought that she could be so needy.

So instead she filled the time by telling him about vampire society, about the Committee meetings, the life cycles of rest and reincarnation, the Covens and the Conduits, and Schuyler's quest to protect the Gates of Hell from the threat of the Silver Blood demons.

"I know it's a lot to lay on you right now," she said.

"The better I understand what's going on, the more helpful I can be," he replied. "Don't worry, I like listening to you."

She smiled at him but didn't want to let herself think that everything would go back to normal—what was normal, anyway?—but it was comforting to know that maybe they could resume their friendship.

"So what's our strategy?" he asked, as they drove through Pennsylvania.

"First, we go to Schuyler's house, see if she's there. She probably won't be, but it's worth a shot. Then we go to Oliver's."

"Her Conduit, right?"

He'd been paying attention. "He used to be, anyway. That's a whole other story, and not worth getting into right now. Last I heard, he was serving as Conduit for Mimi Force."

"Jack's twin. I'm starting to catch on, I think."

They drove the rest of the way without speaking, listening to the radio. A year didn't change much, Bliss thought. Most of the songs were the same ones she'd heard before, and the new ones sounded just like the old ones.

When they reached Manhattan, Bliss directed Lawson to the Upper West Side. She noted with some amusement that Lawson's driving seemed to be getting more cautious now that he was around the aggressive New York City taxi drivers.

"Okay, just double-park in front of that building," she said, pointing to an elegant, if slightly shabby mansionette on Riverside Drive. "We can always move the car if Schuyler's here."

"Are you sure? What if we get a ticket?" he asked, but he did as she suggested. Quite a change of pace—she was used to either being in Lawson's world or in a place neither of them was familiar with. Here she was at home, and it felt good to be in charge.

No surprise to find Schuyler not at home. The brownstone was shuttered, the curtains drawn, and the place looked as if it had been abandoned. Bliss directed Lawson to the Upper East Side, and going crosstown took almost an hour in the early evening traffic. "That was hell," he grumbled.

"Welcome to New York," Bliss said with a smile. "They say the subway's faster, but . . . ."

"Don't tell me: you've never taken it. Lifestyles of the rich and famous," he teased.

"Well, I've never been in a Hyundai, that's for sure."

They left the car in front of Oliver's building and went inside. The doorman must have been on a smoke break, because the desk was vacant.

"Should we wait?" Lawson asked.

Bliss just grabbed his arm and went to the elevator, then pressed the button for the penthouse. She'd only been to Oliver's place a couple of times, but it was hard to forget. Lavish even for New York, it took up the top three stories of the building. Oliver had his own floor, complete with the game room that had made going to his house so popular with Schuyler and Dylan.

Dylan.

Bliss didn't want to think about him now.

The elevator opened into the apartment, so they didn't have to worry about knocking. "Oliver?" Bliss called out. "Mr. Hazard-Perry? Mrs. H-P? Anybody home?"

Her voice echoed in the silence of the apartment.

"Looks like we struck out," Lawson said.

"It's a big place," she replied. "Let's make sure."

Bliss walked through the enormous formal dining room, through the kitchen and up the stairs to Oliver's floor. His bedroom door was open, and it was a mess in there. Not like Oliver. The bed was unmade and there were clothes everywhere.

"Ransacked," Lawson said.

Bliss shook her head. "He was packing. Must have wanted to get out of here in a hurry." If she was right, things were worse than she'd thought. Still, he'd left some books on the desk, journals and a few loose papers pressed inside that looked like e-mail printouts. Could be handy. She grabbed them all.

"What do we do now?" Lawson asked, looking uncomfortable.

"There's another place he might go, or where people might be able to help us," she said. "Come on, let's get out of here."

"Lucas said you wanted to see me?" Tilly St. James was a striking girl, with a thick row of severe bangs across her forehead, her long red hair falling in a straight line down her back. She was wearing a black turtleneck and black leather trousers, and was holding pushpins between her teeth. "Sorry—we're doing a fitting for the final show. Come on—why don't you guys take a seat and watch the run-through, then we can talk."

Schuyler and Oliver took seats in the dark auditorium. Central Saint Martins—a design school located in central London—ran one of the most prestigious undergraduate fashion design programs in the world. York Hall was a madhouse of students rushing around getting ready for the winter showcase, a hive of activity as young designers ran backstage with fabric rolls, muslin patterns, and tape measures looped around their necks.

Schuyler took a sip from her cappuccino and smiled to herself, remembering her brief encounter with the fashion industry. Three years had gone by since she was pulled out of the crowd at Duchesne and tapped to be a Farnsworth girl. She had been such a little mouse then. Unable to say "boo" to the intimidating and beautiful Mimi Force. Schuyler felt affection for the scared little girl she had once been. She had weathered the worst—her mother gone, along with Cordelia and Lawrence, and saying good-bye to Jack in Egypt was the most difficult burden to bear yet—but Schuyler felt stronger than she had in years. Jack's love made me stronger, she thought. And letting go of our love has made me stronger still.

The theater was empty save for a few curious first- and second-years eager to see what the seniors had up their designer sleeves. Tomorrow night, the whole world would be watching to see the latest creations hatched from the experimental laboratory, with reporters from the trade and popular press eager to document the birth of a new design star.

The curtain parted and Tilly jumped down from the stage and ran up to Schuyler. "Sorry—we're short a model— you're about the right size and look. . . . Would you mind walking for us?"

Schuyler laughed, feeling flattered. But before she could answer, a glamazon—six feet tall, all cheekbones and thick dark hair; an exotic, wild creature—stomped down the aisle in three-inch clogs. "Tills! Sorry, the tube was blocked—some sort of accident at Euston Station—had to call a minicab."

"Gooch! Thank God!" Tilly shrieked as they exchanged effusive air-kisses.

Oliver nudged Schuyler. "Close call," he said with a grin.

"Ollie? What are you doing here?" the model asked, upon spotting Oliver. "Brilliant party the other night, by the way! I had a colossal hangover the next morning!"

Oliver tried to explain, but he too was given the frantic double air-kiss before the two gorgeous girls disappeared back behind the curtain.

"I guess I shouldn't be surprised?" Schuyler asked with a wry smile. "You do seem to know half the girls in London."

Oliver didn't even blush. "Oh, that's just Gucci Westfield-Smith. A friend of Kingsley's."

"Uh-huh. Right," Schuyler said.

The lights went out and the show began; the overhead speakers blared a song that was all thumping bass line and sultry breathing. The model—Gucci Something-or-other walked out wearing nothing but a feather headdress and a nude bodysuit. She walked with her hands on her hips and gave Oliver a seductive glower at the end of the runway before twisting away.

Tilly came out from behind the stage and took a seat

next to Schuyler and Oliver. "Shhh," the designer said, smiling with anticipation.

There were more variations on the Nude/Native theme. More elaborate headdresses, fringed Navajo ponchos, suede moccasins, and dresses made out of multicolored plumage and rows of beads.

"So, what did you think?" Tilly asked, when the lights came on and the models had returned backstage.

Oliver clapped and stood. "Fantastic. Brilliant."

"I loved it too," Schuyler agreed. "You know what might be great? Have your makeup artist draw masks on the girls," she suggested, recalling the after-party of the Four Hundred Ball, when Mimi had taken "masquerade" to a new level.

Tilly nodded thoughtfully. "That might work. I like it. Let me just tell the girls a few things, then I'll take you for coffee across the street and we can talk."

NINE

Mimi

Where did he go? How could he disappear like that? He knew it was her, didn't he? Knew it was Mimi underneath the brown bob and the brown eyes that were part of her disguise? Underneath the illusion, underneath the *glamour*—he knew her intimately, he knew her soul, he had to have seen her—truly seen her, hadn't he? She would recognize him anywhere. In any guise, under any mask. Why couldn't he?

She followed Danel through the tunnels to the other end of the station, relieved that he seemed to have taken the kiss in stride. It probably wasn't the first time a girl had thrown herself on him for an impromptu make-out session. Maybe he was used to it. They took the escalator up to the next level. And that's when Mimi saw Kingsley on the escalator going down the other way. He was laughing and chatting with the same girls.

Mimi realized her jealousy was irrelevant. This was her chance to let Kingsley and the vampires know what Lucifer was up to. Maybe then he could help somehow.

When she stepped off the escalator, she turned to Danel. "I don't feel well—I need to go back down to the ladies'."

"Okay, I'll wait for you here."

She nodded and hurried down. She pushed her way through the crowd until she was standing right behind him on the platform.

Kingsley Martin.

She wavered. She could smell him—that blend of cigarettes and coffee and whiskey that she knew so well. She could reach over and touch his hair, his neck, slip her hand into his, and they could get away from all this. What did it matter? Let the Dark Prince take Paradise. She and Kingsley could make a heaven here on earth.

Who cared about the coming war? Who cared about the Covens and the survival of the vampires? Was she even a vampire anymore? She had expected the thirst to come back, once she was free of the underworld, but there was nothing. She hadn't had a bite in weeks.

They could forget all this. She could whisper in his ear and tell him to escape with her.

But he would hate her. He would hate her for giving up, for giving in, for being selfish. She was no longer that girl. She had grown up so much. She couldn't do it. Not to him, not to Oliver, and more important, not to herself.

Plus, what hope did any of the vampires have if she and Jack couldn't break the demons from the inside? The Coven was in ruins; Michael and Gabrielle had abandoned their people.

Even if she and Kingsley wanted to run away together, she knew that when it came down to it, they wouldn't do it. Kingsley was a Venator and Mimi was a realist. Duty was more important than love. She understood that in her bones.

Mimi bumped into Kingsley's shoulder.

"Sorry," she said.

"No worries," he said, smiling at her from behind his dark bangs. She was wrong. Kingsley didn't *see* her. He didn't know it was her. He gave her the flirtatious grin he gave every pretty girl on the tube.

But the smile turned into a frown. "Hey——"

"Yes?" she asked, holding her breath.

"You dropped this," he said, holding up a postcard with a picture of a chapel.

"No—that's not mine," she said. "Sorry."

"Oh." He stared at her and blinked, staring hard at her now. "Do I know you from somewhere . . . ?"

She smiled nervously, shook her head, and bolted back up the escalator. If Danel knew what she was up to . . . If Lucifer found out . . . She pushed through the people and jostling elbows. Danel was waiting for her at the top, talking on his phone.

"Sorry, I feel much better now," she said.

"Yeah, jet lag." He nodded. "You told me." He closed his phone. "So that was your boy."

Kingsley? she almost said. Then realized he meant Jack.

"He's run into a bit of trouble with those monks in Spain. I'm going to have to help him sort it out." He sighed. "He doesn't want to make too much of a mess. It would alert the Blue Bloods as to what we're doing. Keep it quiet, you know."

"Oh, okay."

"You think you can handle Rosslyn on your own?"

"Yeah . . . I mean . . . Yeah." She nodded.

"All right, gorgeous. But we've got unfinished business, you and me," Danel said, chucking her chin. Then he was gone.

You're welcome, her twin sent.

Mimi boarded the train to Edinburgh. She only hoped Kingsley would understand the meaning of the postcard.

She wanted nothing more than to fail at this quest.

Bliss

liss remembered the days when the Repository had been housed underneath a pair of nightclubs. The Bank had been one of the hottest spots in Manhattan, but now it attracted more of a bridge-and-tunnel crowd. Block 122, next door, was exclusively for Blue Bloods and their guests. Together, they'd provided perfect cover for the building that housed the documents detailing the history of the Blue Bloods. All of their knowledge, all of their secrets.

But the Repository had been relocated, and now it was housed below Force Tower, in a corescraper miles underground.

"A corescraper?" Lawson asked.

"You know, the opposite of a skyscraper," Bliss said. "The human Conduits watch over it. Maybe some of them will know where everybody is. They might also have some information about how we can get back to the underworld—you never know."

Lawson's face brightened, and Bliss felt a little guilty for bringing it up. It wasn't all that likely that the Conduits would be able to help, at least not with the wolves. Vampire knowledge of wolf lore was relatively limited. Oh, well. They'd find out soon enough.

Bliss led Lawson through the front door of Force Tower, to an elevator at the very back of the elevator bank. It was the only one containing a panel that would allow them to travel down instead of up.

"It smells weird in here," Lawson said.

He was right—it smelled musty and unused. The buttons on the panel were dusty. Bliss worried about what they would find when the doors opened.

She had been right to worry, because when they did open, she could see that the Repository had been all but destroyed.

What once had been a beautiful and welcoming library, with luscious leather chairs and rows of old-fashioned carrels, was now essentially a pile of rubble. Ransacked and left to burn. There were still some small fires burning in parts of the room, and everything smelled like smoke. There weren't as many books piled up as Bliss would have imagined, so maybe some of them had been saved.

"I take it this isn't what it usually looks like," Lawson said.

"Not even a little bit. I don't know what happened," she said, struck by a feeling of a deep sadness and nostalgia. They wandered through the library, looking in at the more formal offices of Committee Headquarters, the private reading areas, the rare book rooms. All trashed.

"Whoever they were, they were pretty thorough," said Lawson. Then he stopped and sniffed at the air. "Someone's here."

Bliss whirled around. "Where?" she asked, ready to fight or flee.

"It's human, don't worry," he said.

"Hello?" Bliss shouted. "Anyone here?"

From the recesses of a dark corner of the stacks, a figure emerged. He looked stooped and broken; his overly formal clothing was tattered and smeared with ash.

"Are those velvet pants?" Lawson whispered. "Who is this guy?"

"He's a Conduit," Bliss whispered back. "Sir?" she said out loud. "I believe we've met before, a long time ago. I'm Bliss Llewellyn."

"I know who you are, Miss Llewellyn," the man said, in a voice that Bliss recalled as being haughty but which now sounded frightened. "Renfield," he said.

"What happened here, Renfield?" she asked. "Where is everybody?"

Renfield shook his head. "We Conduits tried to store away as much as we could before going underground with

68

the Coven, and I went back to grab a few more books and saw this."

"What do you mean underground? Where is everybody?"

"Gone. Everyone's gone. There are no vampires left. It's all chaos. The Regent is missing, the conclave has been disbanded."

"That can't be true," Bliss said, tears welling in her eyes. "I've only been gone a year. Things can't have changed that much. It can't all be over."

"I'm sure it's not over," Lawson said, and took her hand. "We'll figure it out."

"There may still be some hope," Renfield said. "A Venator bulletin went out."

"Show us," Bliss urged.

"It came over the wire the other week," he said. "I was disseminating the information to the remaining members of the Coven when I heard you out here. Come to my office."

Bliss and Lawson followed Renfield through the stacks, to a room tucked away in a back corner, where Bliss had never been. The door was beautiful and intricately carved, as were all the doors in the Repository; the fact that the solid wood remained undamaged made Bliss start to feel safe.

Until Renfield opened the door and a demon ripped out his throat.

few minutes later, Schuyler, Oliver, and Tilly
were settled into a cozy corner of a small tea
shop, which was decorated with traditional, comfortable,
grandmother-like touches—chintz couches and damask flo-
ral pillows. "So, did Lucas tell you why we wanted to see
you?" Schuyler asked, sinking into a plush and decidedly
lumpy armchair that Cordelia would never have allowed in
her elegant Manhattan town house.

Tilly smiled. "Yes he did. Although, for a moment there,
I thought you guys were from *Chic*. They're supposed to
interview me."

Schuyler ignored the comment. "We wanted to talk
about what you might know about the Gate of Promise."

The designer sighed. "Oh yes, yes. The Order of the
Seven and all those *grave* responsibilities . . ."

"Forgive me if this sounds rude, but responsibilities like

guarding the Gates of Hell? I would say that *is* pretty serious," said Schuyler, a bit taken aback by Tilly's irreverence.

Tilly shrugged. "It did seem terribly urgent back then. But you have to understand—you're a new soul, right? Lucas told me about you. The half-blood. Gabrielle's daughter. You don't have the blood memories. You don't know what it's like."

"Tell us, make us understand," Oliver urged.

Tilly fiddled with the rings on her fingers. "In the beginning, the danger was great. Lucifer had been discovered, and the paths had to be guarded or the demons would be unleashed into our world. Lucas and I were assigned to Gabrielle's protection, as was everyone from our old legion. Your mother did what she had to do in London, then we left Lucas behind." She motioned for a second cup of tea. "That's all I remember from that time. Of course, the Crisis in Rome was just the beginning of the trouble. I was with your mother in Florence when . . ." Her voice faltered and she shivered.

"When?" Schuyler prompted.

Tilly closed her eyes. "When Gabrielle discovered that Lucifer had tricked her. That the Gates of Hell she had built during the founding of Rome were no match for his power."

Schuyler and Oliver exchanged an uneasy glace. "What happened in Florence?"

"Lucifer was vanquished, of course. Michael saw to that, as he always did."

71

Schuyler looked at her keenly. "You don't seem so sure."

Tilly stirred her tea. "I don't know. I tried to forget about it, it was all so horrible. Anyway, the years went by . . . centuries upon centuries, and nothing happened. . . ."

"Not nothing . . . There have been deaths. Young ones taken," Schuyler said. "Even here, in the London Coven."

"Yeah, I guess, but it wasn't like . . . it wasn't like it was *everybody*. It was one at a time. . . ." Tilly said, her voice fading a little.

"What are a few souls here and there in the grand scheme of things, right?" Oliver said brusquely.

"I know you think it's terribly awful of us. That we let your mother down somehow, with Lucas going underground and all. But it's not as if evil isn't everywhere. It's all around. We're not the only victims anymore. The Red Bloods . . . are much more violent and vicious than we ever were."

"Lucas mentioned that you had mortalized. . . ."

"Did he? Such an old goat. 'Mortalized.' I guess I did. I got bored, I suppose. . . ."

"Bored?" Schuyler said coldly.

"Yeah. I don't know, sucking blood and all that . . . seemed so . . ." She shuddered. "Well, it's not really *good* for you, is it? All that protein? I mean, I'm a vegan now. . . ." she said weakly.

A vegan-freaking-vampire. Schuyler decided she had certainly heard it all.

"So you don't . . . perform the Sacred Kiss?" asked Oliver.

"No. Haven't needed one in centuries. Thought I'd fade away at first, and I did get brutally sick. I remember it was during the eighteenth century sometime, when I thought I would just fade away. But then I recovered, and I haven't touched a drop since."

Tilly hadn't performed the Sacred Kiss in centuries. And neither had Schuyler for at least year, ever since she'd left Oliver to be with Jack. Come to think of it, when she and Jack had been together, neither of them had taken familiars. She had forgotten the taste of blood and she had survived.

"By the way, we prefer the term 'gone native,'" Tilly said.

"We?" asked Oliver.

"Are there so many of you?" Schuyler asked.

Tilly tapped her finger against her teacup. "Yeah. Tons. It's not something the Repository or the Covens or the Regis ever wanted to accept. But yeah, a lot of us aren't living as vampires anymore. We don't cycle, we don't reincarnate."

"It's just another word for Enmortal isn't it?" Oliver mused, meaning the vampires who chose not to rest but remain awake for their immortal life.

"Yeah. Maybe. I guess. Except . . ."

"We get it, no blood, no human familiars. Do you still have fangs even?" Schuyler asked, wondering what had become of her own. She hadn't felt them in so long.

"Yeah, they're still there. Sometimes they pop up, but you learn to control them." Tilly put her coat on. "Anyway, I'm sorry I can't help. Lucas said things are looking bad for the Covens. Everyone's gone underground again. But maybe that's for the best."

"For the best?" Schuyler asked, an edge in her voice.

"Seems unfair, doesn't it? The whole vampire-elite thing? What gave us the right? Maybe the Silver Bloods have a point. Maybe we're useless, in the end. Who needs us?" She nodded. "Thanks for the tea. And for the suggestion on the masks. I'll use them tomorrow."

*H*is breath was sweet in her ear, his lashes soft on her cheek. "I give myself to you and accept you as my own," Gio whispered, his voice low and trembling with emotion.

Tomi clasped her hands around his back and pulled him closer, and said the same words to him. With that vow they were bonded, just as they had been since time eternal.

She pulled him away from the window and into the bedroom. Gio had seen to everything—that morning Tomi had moved her small things to the new home they were to share. It was a palace in Florence, above the Arno. The room was aglow with a hundred tiny candles flickering in the dark. She smiled at him shyly, even as her breath quickened in excitement. He kissed her again, starting from her lips and toward the base of her neck, and she kissed him back, with an urgent passion that rose as they moved ever closer together.

She felt his warm hands reach for the straps of the simple blue dress she wore, and then his hands were on her skin. Soon they were lying on the bed together, and he was moving against her and she was pressed against him, and when she looked into his eyes, she saw that they were filled with love. He was so beautiful. She moved her body with his, quickening to his rhythm. His hands on her hands, holding them behind her head, his hips sliding against hers, the two of them joined, bound, together now, just as at the beginning of time.

"I've wanted this . . . I've wanted you so much, for so long," he said, and kissed her fiercely now, biting her lip, and he pushed against her with a ferocity that excited and frightened her.

"I've wanted you too, so much," she said, sitting up so that she could see him clearly, and show him just how much she loved him.

He pushed against her, harder and harder, faster and faster, and his strong hands on her waist gripped her so tightly she almost cried out in pain.

"I want to drink in every part of you," he seethed, burying his face in her neck as he shuddered against her, slamming her body with his.

"Michael," she murmured. "Michael, my love and my light."

"Shhhh," he whispered. "Shhhh . . ."

* * *

The next morning they were awoken by a barrage of fists on the door. "Gio? Tomi? Gio! Wake up!" The voice belonged to Bellarmine. He had been on watch the night before.

"What is it?" Gio called. "What is so important that you must disturb us on the morning after our bonding?"

"My deepest apologies for this intrusion, but we do need to consult with you in this matter," the Venator captain explained.

"I suppose we should see what he wants," Gio sighed.

Tomi removed her arms from around his chest, her legs from around his. "I suppose we should. Alas," she said with a smile.

They dressed quickly and walked out to the courtyard, to find Valentina and Bellarmine standing at the door with white faces, looking agitated and upset.

"What happened?" Tomi asked, feeling a dread rise in her stomach. There was something terribly wrong, but she did not know what.

Valentina turned to her, her face ashen. "The Mistress—Simonetta has been killed, and her baby gutted."

Tomi gasped and Gio turned to the Venators angrily. "No harm was to come to her! How did this happen?" he growled, his handsome face flushed an angry red.

"We were bespelled. When we awoke, Simonetta was dead, and we found this by her bed," Bellarmine said, offering up a bloody dagger.

"Andreas's blade," Gio said with a scowl.

"Then he survived the fire," Tomi said, her heart sinking. She had been certain they had triumphed, that the devil had been destroyed. "But why would he kill his own child?"

"So that we would not torture it?" Valentina offered.

"It doesn't make sense," Tomi said, confused.

Gio grasped the dagger. "We will find her killer. We will find Andreas and we will destroy him."

Tomi shuddered at the anger in his voice, at the wildness in his eyes. She had never seen him this way before. Kind, gentle Gio. He was on fire with rage. Tomi shrunk back from him, frightened, and remembered their lovemaking the night before, the wildness of it, the ferocity.

She looked at him and he was a stranger to her. She did not know who he was.

THIRTEEN

Schuyler

The sound of breaking glass woke her from her sleep. Schuyler glanced at the clock on her bedside table. It was four in the morning. She put on her robe and walked out to the living room. "Who's there?" she called. She padded through the dark hallway, looking for the light switch.

She turned on the light and saw Kingsley in the middle of the room, with a broken wineglass in his hand. "Oh, sorry, sorry—we were trying to be quiet and I tripped over the damn rug. . . ." he said.

"I'll get the vacuum." Schuyler frowned and pulled the vacuum cleaner out of the closet.

"Bye, Dani," Kingsley said, as a sleek blonde walked out of his room, dangling her stilettos on one finger. She was a dead ringer for Mimi Force. The same almond-shaped green eyes, the same mane of lustrous platinum hair. The same sexy-pouty expression.

"Bye, darling," she said, kissing him on the cheek.

"Mind the mess," he warned, motioning to the broken glass on the rug.

"Always do," she said, delicately picking her way around it.

Schuyler gave Kingsley the look he had given her when he'd had caught her holding hands with Oliver.

"What?" said Kingsley, with an innocent smile on his face.

"Bye, King-king," another girl said, this one equally stunning and equally blond. She wore only a bra and a miniskirt. But at least she was wearing shoes.

"Bye, Antoinette." Kingsley smiled and kissed her on the forehead. "We were playing strip poker," he explained, just as a third lovely girl stepped out of the room. This one had dark hair cut in a bob, and brown eyes. Not a Mimi clone, then.

"See you, Parker."

The one named Parker winked at Schuyler and pressed her finger to Kingsley's mouth. "Don't be a stranger." She giggled.

Schuyler rolled her eyes. "Is that it? Or are you hiding more in your harem?"

"Schuyler, darling, it's none of your business what I do or who I do it with," Kingsley declared as he went back to his room and shut the door behind him. "Good night," he called from behind the door.

The next evening was the same, but this time there were four blondes and no brunettes, while the next night brought the entire Farnsworth modeling class—the new girls who had arrived in London for the season—to their abode. "Fashion week," Oliver said wisely, as he left to partake of the glamorous festivities himself, holding up a sheath of glossy invitations. "You sure you don't want to go see Stella? I have an extra ticket."

"Since when do you care about fashion?" Schuyler demanded.

"Sky, what's with that face? It's not flattering," he teased. "Don't wait up."

"You've been hanging out with Kingsley too much."

Oliver didn't deny it.

Later that night, Schuyler had been awoken once again by a loud bump, and when she walked out to the living room, Kingsley was playing Twister with two girls, the three of them wrapped around each other in a braided mess of legs and arms and laughter.

She went back to bed, having rejected their invitation to join in, but the next day, as Kingsley was about to go out for another wild night, she stopped him at the doorway. She'd finally had enough of the constant partying, the loud music in the middle of the night, and the condescending looks of pity from the parade of paramours, who seemed to believe that Schuyler was "pining" for Kingsley.

"Do you mind?" he said, reaching for the door.

Schuyler crossed her arms. "What's wrong?"

"There's something wrong?" Kingsley asked.

"Why are you acting this way?"

"What do you mean?"

"The late nights, the girls, the partying . . . I mean, you've always been . . . *social*, Kingsley, but lately you just seem . . . desperate. And I don't know if you've noticed, but they all look a lot like—"

"Don't do it. Don't say her name," Kingsley warned.

"Fine," Schuyler said. "I just . . . I worry about you. What's going on?"

"There's nothing to worry about. I'm just having a bit of fun. You spend time in the underworld, see if you don't act the same."

"Kingsley . . ."

"I told you, nothing's wrong."

"Right."

"You know, Schuyler, she was right, you are a pain in the—"

"Martin!" Oliver warned, having walked out of his room to see what the commotion was all about.

Schuyler stepped aside, and Kingsley went out the door. When he shut it with a bang behind him, she turned to

Oliver. "I'm right, you know. He's not the same. What's gotten into him? What do we do? We can't let him just waste himself this way—he's a Venator! The other teams are—"

"I'll try to talk to him." Oliver said. "Tell him to tone it down. Find out what's bothering him."

Oliver never got the chance to have his tête-à-tête. The next morning, when he and Schuyler walked into the dining room, Kingsley was already at the breakfast table, dressed and ready, reading the morning news on his screen.

"What's with the early-bird act?" Schuyler asked, picking up an apple while Oliver appraised the day's offerings of toad in the hole, kippers, and rashers of bacon.

"I'm, ah—leaving," Kingsley replied, putting down the tablet.

"Where to?" Oliver asked.

"Can't say." He took a drink of orange juice and grimaced, inspecting the glass. "I think this is off. But it could just be that I can't taste it. Oh well, thought I'd try." He picked up a doughnut and began to chew with a moody look on his face.

"Don't change the subject. Why can't you tell us where you're going?" Schuyler demanded.

"Better if you don't know. Safer," he mumbled.

Schuyler exchanged a worried glance with Oliver. "Kingsley, stop playing MI6. Let us help. This isn't a game."

"No!" he yelled, then looked abashed. "Sorry—but I

have to do this alone. I'm not sure it's even something. It could be nothing, and I don't want you to get your hopes up. . . . I don't have much to go on," he murmured, fingering something under the table. It looked like a postcard.

"It's about Mimi, isn't it? She's alive, then? What about Jack . . . ? Kingsley!" Schuyler said, getting up from her seat. "Come back!"

But the Venator had left the room in a flash, and there was nothing left on his plate but a half-eaten doughnut.

"Let him go. He'll come back," Oliver said, spreading butter on his toast. He regarded his breakfast skeptically. "Wonder why it's called a toad in the hole. Are the eggs the toad? Or the sausages?"

Schuyler turned to him. "What if he's working for the Silver Bloods?"

"He's not, Sky. I know he's not. I trust him. Do you?"

"I guess I do. I just wish he would tell us what's going on." She did trust Kingsley—Oliver was right. He was no longer the slippery Venator who had danced with her at the after-party at the Four Hundred Ball and whispered in her ear. Back then, she'd even wondered if he had been the one who'd kissed her at the dance. It was Kingsley who had called forth the Silver Blood that had attacked the Repository, but he explained that he'd done it on the orders of the Regis— it was Charles Force who had commanded him to do it, to test the strength of the Gates of Hell. As a loyal Venator, Kingsley could only obey. She couldn't hold that against him. The gates were supposed to hold, but instead they had proved as permeable as a membrane, and the demon had been allowed to escape from the underworld. Only then did Charles finally accept that the Silver Bloods had returned.

"Kingsley does what he wants, but there's no changing him," Oliver said. "Let him go—he'll work it out."

"Do you think he's gone to see Mimi?" she asked. And if Mimi was alive, what did that mean for Jack? Did it mean then, that—? She felt her heart clench at the thought—but it was too painful and too terrible, so she forcefully pushed it down. Jack—to even think of him brought such a sudden sharp feeling of pain that it made it hard to breathe. She saw his face for a moment—the sheen of his blond hair, his green eyes framed by golden lashes—how peaceful he looked when he was asleep. Would they ever be together again? Or was their last good-bye forever?

"Mimi? I don't know . . . but—" Before Oliver could finish his sentence, the phone rang.

The butler appeared. "A Margaret St. James for Miss Van Alen."

"Margaret? Oh, Tilly. Okay." Schuyler took the call.

Afterward, she went back to the dining room, where Oliver was tucking into a second plate of eggs and toast.

"What did she want? Another fashion show?"

"You wish. No—she said she remembered something that might be useful. There's one more person from the old triumvirate who's still in London. She rang him, and he says he'll meet with us. He knows what happened in Rome, might be able to help us unlock the gate."

"Huh."

"And we thought she was just an airhead who designed clothes," Schuyler said with a wink.

FOURTEEN

Mimi

The tour guide was speaking in hushed tones to a small gathering of tourists, her quiet words punctuated by the snaps and flashes of eager photographers. One man was filming with his handheld video camera, walking in circles around the apse. Behind him, a young couple clearly on their honeymoon posed against the wrought-iron fence, the groom holding his phone at arms' length to take the shot.

Mimi kept her distance from the group. The guide didn't seem to mind that she'd lingered near the entrance, unlike the usual tourist herders, who were strict about keeping everyone together.

She'd arrived in Midlothian earlier that week and had visited the Rosslyn Chapel every day, under a different guise each time, lest the nuns who guarded the place recognize her. So far, she had found nothing, and while she was glad of that, there had been no sign of Kingsley either. Perhaps he had not understood the message. If so, then she was a bit disappointed in him. She wondered how long she could pretend to be "looking" for the grail, and she knew she would not be allowed to return to the underworld empty-handed unless she had a reasonable explanation.

Inside the chapel, every available surface was elaborately decorated in twisted stone carvings. One section depicted the underworld and its inhabitants—an upside-down hanging devil, the mythic "green man" marching a row of skeletons into Hell. The sculptures wound their way around columns and along the arches, across the ceiling and on the floor. There was a term for this, she knew: *horror vacui*—the fear of empty spaces. Every inch of the place was bursting with decoration, as if the chapel's creators had feared blank walls like a literal plague.

What a mess, Mimi sniffed.

"This is called the apprentice column," the tour guide said, coming around to stand next to a nearby pillar. "An apprentice boasted to the master mason that he could carve the design without consulting the original on which it was based. When the master saw that the apprentice had done the work perfectly, he became so enraged with jealousy that he struck the apprentice on the head and killed him. When the master was hauled off to justice, the remaining masons carved an exact replica of his face on the column across from this one," she said, motioning to the other post, which held the visage of a scowling man. "So that forever, the master would be forced to gaze at the perfect work of the apprentice that had caused him so much pain."

Creepy, Mimi thought. But justifiable. She remembered the hot fire of jealousy that she'd once felt over Jack's attraction to Schuyler. If she had never met Kingsley, she probably would have suffered the same doom—forced to endure the reality of the two of them together till the end of time.

The small group chattering in myriad languages shuffled by her on their way to the crypt. Mimi didn't follow. Wherever the grail was held—and it certainly wasn't that jeweled cup displayed at the center of the chapel—it wouldn't be there. The crypt was too obvious. The knights would have made sure it was well hidden.

Look someplace where no one else can look. Find a place no one knew existed.

She walked back outside, circling the chapel in a wide arc. The exterior on each side was composed of a series of flying buttresses that supported the tall center space. In between each one was a stained glass rose window. The stone was sandy in color and worn from erosion.

Mimi looked up and realized she probably should have paid attention to the boring tour. There was something odd about the chapel, but she couldn't figure out what it was. She stepped back, the pebbles crunching beneath her heels.

There was a rough-hewn wall that extended higher than the rest of the building, giving it a lopsided look. The wall was ragged at its edges, as if indicating a temporary construction. Unfinished. Mimi circled the wall, imagining it as a blade that had chopped the chapel in half. When she touched it, the stone was cold and mossy. She walked back to the other side, the lower side, and saw that it had none of the buttresses that lined the other wall.

"The chapel that stands at Rosslyn is only a small fraction of what the original builders intended," a voice said behind her.

Mimi turned to see another tour guide. She was a nun, Mimi realized, from the cross on her lapel. "What was it supposed to look like?"

"The buttressed end was to be the choir, the portion of the building behind the altar. The long cathedral nave where parishioners would have sat was never built. The wall on that side was only supposed to be temporary, like a bandage slapped over the unfinished end," the nun explained. "They dug up the foundations for the remainder of the building in the nineteenth century. It would have been quite spectacular if it had been finished."

Just like St. John the Divine in New York, Mimi thought. The site of her almost-bonding. So much ambition and hubris, so many unfinished churches in the world.

"We'll be closing soon. Feel free to take a walk around, then meet me at the gate. Your group should be leaving the crypt by then." The nun smiled again, but not so warmly this time. The old woman looked a bit tired and maybe eager to finish her day.

When she walked away, Mimi headed to the place where she guessed the buried foundations were located. She knew where the crypt would be, ending just outside of the building's footing.

If I were a Knight Templar, where would I hide the grail?

In a place where no one would ever even think to look, perhaps?

Maybe there was more to this structure—something a nineteenth-century conservator wouldn't even think to look for. She went back and stood at the edge of the rough-hewn wall, the place where the chapel would have continued it if had been completed.

She squinted, and in the dim light she finally saw it. The nave. Hiding in plain sight. One moment she was outside, and the next she was standing within an elegant cathedral.

Impossible, Mimi thought. *I'm not in the glom and not in Rosslyn, so where am I?*

"The wolves call it Limbo. Their historical realm before they were turned into Lucifer's dogs. The nun was wrong—the chapel was built as intended, but not on earth and not by man."

Mimi knew the voice. She turned to the Venator standing behind her. He had come through, just as she had hoped. But she kept her face calm.

"It took me a long time to find the magic needed to unearth the hidden portion of the chapel. Lucky you, to show up and take advantage of my work." He was holding a cup by its lip, letting it dangle from his hands.

"Looking for this?" Kingsley asked with his usual smirk.

FIFTEEN

Bliss

he thing that had gotten hold of Renfield was a crimson-eyed vampire that bared its fangs and drank deeply from the blood gushing from the poor historian's throat. Renfield's legs kicked feebly in the air, and he gurgled as the life was drained out of him.

"Renfield!" Bliss shouted, and ran forward.

But before she could reach him, Lawson darted in front of her and shoved her out of the way. He was strong, even in human form, and she skidded across the floor, safely out of reach from the monster in front of them.

What had she been thinking? She wasn't a vampire anymore; she didn't have the strength to stand up to the demon that had attacked Renfield. A Silver Blood in the Repository—it brought back memories of that other attack not too long ago.

The demon dropped Renfield's body to the ground as

Lawson lunged at the beast from behind. Bliss frantically searched for a weapon, anything that could help Lawson, who was now wrestling with the monster. The Silver Blood had the upper hand, its fangs outstretched, hungry for the kill. It would tear Lawson apart. . . .

Lawson suddenly shifted form, and in a moment he was his true self. Fenrir. The mightiest wolf of the underworld. The change startled the Silver Blood, and the demon roared and jumped back from Lawson, who pawed the ground and growled. They paced around one another, each waiting for the other to attack first.

"Well, well. A dog out of its cage," the Silver Blood sneered. "Heel, boy."

Lawson howled.

The demon raised a whip to strike, and brought it down hard on Lawson's left flank. The wolf whimpered in pain and cowered.

Out of the corner of her eye, Bliss could see a large plank of polished wood, now cracked and broken. A shelf from one of the bookcases that had toppled to the ground. If she could just reach it, maybe she could use it to distract the Silver Blood, slow him down so Lawson would have the advantage.

Quietly, she crawled off to the side and retrieved the plank. The creature was still taunting Lawson, who looked just about ready to pounce. Bliss stood up as quickly as she could, lunged forward, and, swinging the plank low, bashed the vampire below its knees.

Her ploy worked—the demon fell to the ground. It only took a moment for Lawson to attack, taking advantage of the demon's weaker position to rip him to pieces with his fierce teeth and sharp claws.

The Silver Blood was consumed by a bright silver flame, then collapsed into a bag of bones. It was dead.

Lawson panted heavily before shifting back to his human form. Bliss was breathing pretty hard herself—she couldn't believe how close they'd come to being killed. Her clothes were drenched in blood—the historian's and the demon's. They fell into each other's arms in relief.

"You okay?" Lawson asked, letting go as quickly as he had hugged her tightly.

Bliss nodded, blushing a little at the force of his embrace. "You?"

"Nothing that won't heal up quickly," he said. He was covered in scratches and blood.

"Do you need anything? Bandages?"

"Nope. Already on the mend. See?" He held up an arm dotted with small cuts, but as Bliss looked at it, they disappeared. "You saved my life, you know."

"Funny, I thought you saved mine."

"We saved each other," he said. "We make a good team."

"We do, don't we?" she said, and smiled.

"I just wish we'd gotten that thing before it killed Renfield," Lawson said.

"Poor Renfield," Bliss said. "All he wanted was to serve the vampires."

"We'll take him up with us when we leave, so that his body can be found and buried properly."

Bliss nodded. She was exhausted and traumatized, but she knew there was no time to stop and grieve for the poor human Conduit. They had to try to find what they had come for, the Venator bulletin Renfield had spoken of, which had given her hope that the vampires had not been completely wiped out. "He said it was in his office. You think maybe the Silver Blood was after it too?"

"Could be. Why else would it have been here?" Lawson said.

"Let's check it out." Bliss walked over to Renfield's desk and started going through the drawers, but didn't find anything that looked like it came from the Venators' office. Bliss wished she'd paid more attention during Committee meetings. She didn't even know what she was looking for. It had come over the wire, the Conduit had said. The Repository was notorious for relying on out-of-date technology.

"There's a file cabinet over here," Lawson said. "It's locked, but I think I can take care of that." He pulled the handle as hard as he could. Bliss could see his muscles straining through his shirt, and her heart started racing. Was it jealousy over her lost powers, or just a reaction to Lawson's body? Which was a pretty nice body, as she well remembered from their one brief encounter.

Finally the lock broke and the drawers opened. "Files," Lawson said, taking folders out and spreading them on the floor.

Bliss started flipping through them. The first drawer held records of all the vampires who'd originally come to America so long ago. The second contained files on the Venators. It was the third, though, that was the most chilling.

"What is it?" Lawson asked.

"It's the files on the human Conduits," Bliss said. "It says they're dead."

"All of them?"

"Hard to be sure. All the ones whose files are here. See the black marks? That means they're gone. It looks like Renfield was one of the last to survive."

"Didn't you say your friend Oliver was a Conduit?" Lawson asked.

Bliss nodded, trying not to panic. Oliver—dead? There was no way. Mimi would not allow that to happen. Bliss quickly looked through the files to see if his name was there. "His file's missing," she said, somewhat relieved. "He might still be alive. We have to find him."

"Why is he so important?" Lawson asked. "Were you two, like, close?"

Was she imagining things, or did he sound a little jealous? Was it wrong that she hoped he was? "Oliver's just a friend," she said gently. "He was Schuyler's Conduit, and I think more than that, for a while, but there was never anything between *us*," she said firmly. "If we could find him, though, he might be able to tell us what happened. Or help us find Schuyler. He's never that far from her."

She realized she still had the notebooks she'd taken from Oliver's apartment. She took one out and skimmed the pages, but it was all gibberish. It didn't take her long to figure out it was a code—Oliver had just moved every letter over by three. She started making out words, though it was hard to tell how they were significant. *Freya*? *Egypt*? She flipped to the e-mail printout, which she now discovered was addressed to Oliver's parents. "Hand me a pen, would you?" she said.

Lawson waited patiently while Bliss decoded the last paragraph of the e-mail. Finally, she raised her head in triumph. "He's in London. Something about the gates. Schuyler's with him. They're staying at a Venator safe house. They must have received the same bulletin Renfield was talking about."

"Does it mention where the house is?"

"No, but we can find it. We just need to get there." And then she remembered. "Jane! She's in London too. How could I have forgotten?" Jane Murray, the Watcher, had told her that the Venators were gathering in the British capital and for Bliss to meet them there.

Lawson's brow furrowed. "London? We just got to New York."

Bliss realized Lawson had never really been in a city

before, and now she was carting him all over the globe. She knew it made him uncomfortable to have to rely on her, to trust that she knew what she was doing.

"It's going to be fine," she said. "We just have to get plane tickets and passports and some clothes, and we can get out of here."

"You've got a magic wand?" He smirked.

"Something better. A Park Avenue apartment," she said. Her apartment! Penthouse du Rêves. She hadn't been there in what felt like forever. There was no reason to think it wasn't still there: she was the sole beneficiary of her foster parents' largesse, and while the Repository had been destroyed, she had a feeling the Silver Bloods had left the apartment alone. After all, it had belonged to one of their own—Forsyth Llewellyn, when he was alive, had been Lucifer's closest ally.

"I don't have a passport," Lawson said. "And what about my brothers, and Ahramin? I need to check in with them."

"We will. I can arrange for a passport for you, I know I can. We'll make sure everything is okay with the pack before we leave. Don't worry, it's going to be fine." Bliss was back in New York City, back home, and she felt invigorated, glad to be useful instead of helpless.

"If you say so," Lawson said. But he didn't look so sure.

SIXTEEN

Schuyler

*O*nce in a while, Schuyler missed him so much it was hard to put into words. She'd only known him for such a short time before he was taken from her. Nevertheless, he was always on her mind. Lawrence Van Alen. Her grandfather. The vampire who had taught her the four factors of the glom, who taught her about her legacy, who prepared her for her task.

It was amazing how much Peter Pendragon reminded her of Lawrence. Something in the haughty way he greeted her, his aristocratic mien and aloof manner. As Oliver explained, the Knights Templar was a splinter group of Venators, devoted to protecting the holy relics. But as time passed, their importance to the Covens had diminished and their ranks thinned. Peter Pendragon was one of the last remaining members.

They met him in his study at Marlborough Farm, a

sprawling estate a few hours away from the city. The grand old manor had seen better days, most of its windows shuttered, dust motes flying in the air, furniture covered in sheets of fabric. The house was a beautiful ruin, like many historical homes in England that were too expensive for the upkeep, left to linger and decay. Perhaps that was why Schuyler felt at home in the shrouded, dark manor—it reminded her of her own home in New York City. She had been a child among phantoms, surrounded by memories of a better time, living in a dark, secluded place, with only her formidable grandmother as a companion.

She felt that watchful presence again; it came and went, and while it was troubling to feel as if she were being observed, there wasn't much she could do about it. For now, whoever or whatever it was seemed to be benign enough.

"So you are Allegra's daughter," Peter said, looking Schuyler up and down. "And you have come to London to unlock the secret of the Gate of Promise."

"Yes. Tilly St. James sent us. She said you were part of Gabrielle's old team, just like her and Lucas Mendrion."

"I was," he said. "Come, sit down. Will you have tea?"

Schuyler declined politely, feeling as if the world were on a knife's edge, and all she was doing was drinking champagne and sipping tea while her love was lost and Rome burned.

"Nice spread," Oliver said, admiring the furnishings. Schuyler nudged him with her elbow, annoyed.

"What?" he asked. Kingsley's cockiness was wearing off on him.

Pendragon turned to Schuyler. "I know Mendrion and the rest of the Coven are going underground. But I will stay here and make my stand. Besides, I heard through the Venators that something is happening in London soon. Your arrival is fortuitous, I think. Gabrielle's daughter. That I am alive in this cycle to meet you is a wonder.

"I was assigned to Gabrielle when Dantos died in Florence in the fifteenth century, during that ugly mess. I had a shorter run than they did, since I left your mother's service to join the Knights Templar."

"Why did you leave?" Schuyler asked.

"It was Gabrielle's idea, actually. She said I could serve her better as a knight." He smiled. "I tried not to take it too personally. I liked working for your mother."

"Can you help us?"

"Maybe." He nodded. "Tell me what you know."

"Catherine of Sienna told us that the Gate of Promise will only unlock with the key of the twins," Schuyler said. "Do you know what that means?"

"The key of the twins is the *sangreal*. The holy blood," he said, shifting in his chair.

"Holy blood," Schuyler echoed.

"Another name for it is the Blood of the Father."

"The Holy Grail?" Oliver guessed.

"No. The grail is the cup of Christ. There's some

mishmash about it being a person, but that's not true; just some popular rumor, another false concept we released to the Red Bloods to keep the grails safe." He shrugged.

"There is more than one?" asked Schuyler.

"Well, of course; you do not drink from only one cup, do you?" he said. "They are hidden all over the world. Once upon a time, there were enough of us to guard each one, but no more," he sighed, just as his butler entered the room and whispered in his ear.

"Excuse me," he told them, struggling to stand with the help of his cane. "It seems there is a disturbance at one of the grail sites and I must take my leave. Please forgive me. We must continue this charming conversation another time."

"Is it serious?" Schuyler asked, looking worried.

"I'm sure the nuns are just jumpy. Do not worry. The grails are well hidden. A very old and very deep magic keeps them safe from harm."

"Just like the gates," Schuyler said.

Pendragon nodded, appraising her with approval. "The holy blood is about lineage, about ancestry." The old knight looked at Schuyler. "Do you know who your father is?"

Back in the cab on the way to the town house, Schuyler mulled over Pendragon's words and her own history. She was the *Dimidium Cognatus*. The half-blood. The only child of vampire and human lineage. "The Blood of the Father . . .

Do you think?" she asked Oliver. "Are you thinking what I'm thinking?"

"Your father is still alive," Oliver said. "That's what your mother wanted you to know."

"Alive? It can't be."

"What did your grandmother say? What did Cordelia say about him?"

"She always made it clear he was dead, and that's why Allegra was in a coma, because my mother wouldn't take another familiar after he passed. I got the feeling Cordelia hated my father's family. She never spoke of them, especially him. She couldn't stand it that Allegra had married a Red Blood. I never knew much about him." Schuyler fiddled with the latch on her bag. "I mean, I don't even carry his name," she said softly. She remembered all those lonely afternoons by Allegra's bedside, and the time she had come upon a stranger kneeling by her mother's bed, and how her heart had raced at the possibility that her father had returned. But the stranger had turned out to be Charles Force. The vampire Allegra had spurned to bond with her human familiar.

Oliver squeezed her hand in sympathy. "That was your grandmother's fault, not yours."

"Do you really think my dad is still alive?" she asked. "But there's no way that's true. My mom was in a coma out of grief, remember?" But then again, Allegra had so many secrets, it was hard to know what was true and what wasn't, and Schuyler told that to Oliver as well.

"Well, there's only one way to find out. What do you know of your father's family?"

"They owned some big company a long time ago; my father was named after it. Bendix Corporations, I think. But they sold it."

Oliver tapped the information into his phone. "Says here Bendix is now headquartered in Los Angeles, but that the family still retains a percentage of ownership, and sits on the board. I can get us on a flight tonight if you want."

"Let's do it," Schuyler said. Her father was alive? No. It was impossible. She didn't know much about her father, but she knew he was gone. If he was alive, why hadn't he ever tried to come see her? How could someone just let their child grow up without ever once trying to contact them? She had grown up missing both her parents, a mother and father she never knew. She was a product of their great love for each other, and yet their legacy to their only child was a deep and abiding loneliness. She had been alone for so many years.

Not alone: she always had Oliver, she realized. Her human Conduit, her faithful companion. He was with her now.

Mother, where are you sending me? she wondered.

SEVENTEEN

Mimi

*I*t was dim inside the enchanted chapel, the windows black, as if the world extended no further than the space inside it. Mimi was trapped in an insulated world, in Limbo, in the nothingness of the abyss.

"I knew it was you at the station," Kingsley said. "Don't tell me you're with that jerk. What happened to that brother of yours?"

Mimi tossed her hair back haughtily. "We work for Lucifer now."

"Yeah, right." Kingsley laughed.

"He wants the grail to make godsfire, and we mean to give it to him."

"The Mimi I knew—"

"The Mimi you knew is gone," she said. "I told you to forget about me, and it looks like you took my advice to heart."

"Jealous, were you?" he asked. "Now I know you're

lying about your feelings for me."

In reply, she drew out her sword and faced him.

He did the same, brandishing his weapon. "Do you really mean to fight me for it?" He tipped his sword against hers, and a dull ring echoed around the room. He took two steps backward, the grail in one hand, his blade in the other. "All right, then, who am I to stand in your way. You always were a good sparring partner."

Make it look real, she thought. *I've got to make him believe I have gone to the Dark, to keep him safe. Otherwise . . .*

She swung first, and he met her thrust with the edge of his sword, bashing her blade against a stone pillar. The shock reverberated through the steel, rattling her grip. She nearly lost the weapon, but quickly recovered. Kingsley took a step back.

Mimi advanced, crossing her blade against his, then quickly recovering to jab at his chest. Rather than meet her second blow with his sword, he swung with the grail, and she nearly dropped her weapon once more.

"Careful now, you might destroy what you want to take from me."

Mimi smiled. "No chance of that." She held her sword low, scraping it against the hard stone pillar as she brought it up fast toward his left hand. She turned the blade sideways, as he had first done, and struck at the backside of his hand. The blow sent the cup flailing from his grip, and it fell to the ground with a clang.

Kingsley took a leap forward, but rather than striking Mimi, he kicked the grail with the backside of his foot, sending the old cup rolling behind him.

For a moment he was defenseless, and Mimi drew her sword across his chest. Her steel met flesh, drawing a bloody line across his midsection. Kingsley grunted in pain, and she felt the ache in her chest as well, at the thought of hurting him. But her face remained impassive.

She lunged for the grail, but Kingsley kept himself between her and the cup, circling her as they danced around each other.

They were now in the center of the nave. The elaborate stone carvings that were worn flat in the real church appeared newly carved and shining in the otherworldly extension. But Mimi stopped admiring her surroundings when Kingsley's sword nipped her shoulder, cutting through her coat.

"Ouch!" she said, annoyed.

"Tit for tat." Kingsley smiled and motioned to the gash on his chest. "Come on now, let's stop this. I haven't seen you in months and this is how you greet me? I'll say it. I've missed you. What happened to you? Why did you disappear like that? Why did you tell me to leave you alone? Explain what happened—I can help. . . ."

He knows. He knows I don't want to hurt him. She could have cut him deeply on the first strike, but she'd only caused a surface wound. He'd treated her shoulder in similar fashion. He wanted to know how far she would take this charade, how badly she was willing to wound him to recover the grail.

And it was all because she had told him the truth before she'd left. *Remember that I love you, no matter what happens.*

It was her own words that were keeping him from buying her act. If only she could take them back. It was too dangerous for him to know the truth.

"I will take the grail, or I will die trying," she said. "You'll have to kill me for it."

"Fine," Kingsley said. He advanced on her side, swinging his sword in a wide arc, and, knowing his reach would exceed hers, slashed against her torso.

Mimi hissed in pain, but before she could parry, he had cut her again above the knee. She staggered backward, trying to catch her breath. She would heal, but for now the pain was agonizing. He's toying with me, she realized, as he cut her again, and this time the blade grazed her wrist in a thin line. Kingsley was wearing her down, cutting her with a thousand nips and scrapes. He didn't want to kill her, but he would chip away at her defenses until she crumbled. Another cut grazed her ear, and this time she couldn't restrain from letting out a sharp cry of pain.

Kingsley seemed taken aback. "Are you hurt? Truly?"

Mimi saw her opportunity and reached for the chalice, taking it in her hand and raising it in triumph. The moment she touched it, the chapel disappeared around them. The protective spell had dissipated.

They were standing outside the Rosslyn Chapel now, in the early evening.

"You can't hurt me," Mimi said, as she raised her weapon, her eyes blazing. "You were always a weakling. See how easy it was to take this from you? Lucifer would laugh to see you." *Make him believe it, make him hate you.* She advanced toward him and lunged for his heart.

But rather than parry, Kingsley grabbed her blade and wrapped his hand around the steel, letting it cut into his palm. With all his strength, he pulled Mimi's sword away from her so it fell to the ground, and she was forced to drop her hold on the chalice as well. He picked up the grail with his blood-soaked hand, and with the other he raised his sword toward her brow.

"Now tell me the truth," he said. "Why are you doing this?"

She cringed from him. "I told you why."

"I know you still love me." He smiled. "I can see it in your face."

Mimi sneered. "We are with Lucifer now; we have always been false."

"I don't believe it for one second," Kingsley whispered, looking into her eyes tenderly.

"Then you are a fool," she said. She wanted to throw herself upon him, to bring her face to his, to kiss his lips and hold him in her arms, to brush his dark hair out of his eyes.

But instead she disappeared into smoke and air.

Her work was done. The grail was safe in the hands of the Venator she trusted most. She only hoped Jack had been as unsuccessful.

EIGHTEEN

Bliss

er stepmother had named it Penthouse du Rêves. A palace of dreams and an interior decorator's nightmare. Just as Bliss had guessed, the house was still running, and although she didn't recognize any of the staff, they all seemed to know her.

"Welcome back, Miss Llewellyn," the housekeeper said. "Shall we make up some rooms for you and your guest?" she asked, as if Bliss had been away for merely a few weeks and not a few years. She would have received the same welcome, Bliss thought, no matter how long it had been. Forsyth's trust funds would have seen to it—that there was a haven for Lucifer's daughter. Once in a while, her terrible heritage did have its privileges, and Bliss was not shy about using them.

She asked the butler if he could arrange for a passport for Lawson, and tickets to London for the both of them. "Through whatever means necessary," she said, and hoped that this new butler would be as effective as the previous one had been.

The butler gave a nod. "Whatever you request, Miss Llewellyn."

Lawson's mouth had fallen open a bit, though Bliss wasn't sure if it was from the horror of the rococo decor of the apartment or her ease at ordering servants around.

"You're going to catch flies in there," she teased, and Lawson snapped his mouth shut.

"This was how you lived?" he asked, after the servants had gone.

"Oh, it was much worse than this," she said. "Much, much worse. We used to have a chauffeur who drove me half a block down the road to school. In a Rolls-Royce." Lawson was looking at her as if she were a stranger, and she didn't like it. "Yeah, I know, gross. If BobiAnne were here, she'd probably make the driver take me around in a Prius, now that eco-friendly is the new smug."

Lawson looked around and grinned, pointing to a life-size sculpture of a golden-haired princess with heaving bosoms.

Bliss laughed. "Hey, I didn't decorate this place. My stepmother had ambitions for Versailles. The room we're putting you in isn't that bad. We should really get some sleep—we have a lot to do tomorrow."

"I could probably use it," Lawson admitted, and followed her up the stairs.

The guest room was one of the more tastefully appointed, at least in a relative sense. It had a hunting theme—the walls were dark green, and the curtains, lamp shade, and bedspread were all plaid damask, in shades of navy, maroon, and beige. Bliss thought it wouldn't have been so bad were it not for the deer heads dotting the walls. Trust BobiAnne to always find the detail that went too far.

"Sorry about the taxidermy," Bliss said.

"Makes me feel right at home," Lawson deadpanned.

"Oh, and if you're hungry, the cook can make you whatever you want."

"Kind of like that hotel we stayed in." He smiled. "Remember?"

The hotel where they had totally hooked up? Yeah. She remembered. How could she forget? She nodded, trying not to blush.

"Listen, I know we never talked about what happened that night, and I'm sorry that things got a little out of hand," he said. "You were right to stop me when you did."

So that's how he felt about it. That it was all a big mistake. Bliss took a deep breath and avoided looking him in the eye. How could she ever have thought he'd really been interested in her? "Good thing," she agreed. "Would have been a huge mistake, you and me."

Lawson looked a little stung. "I didn't say that. I never said it was a mistake."

"But you think it," she said.

"Is that what you think?" he asked, challenging her.

They stared at each other. Finally Bliss said, "No."

Lawson's face broke into a smile. "Neither do I."

Bliss didn't know what to say to that.

"Keep me company?" he asked suddenly.

Bliss hesitated for a bit and wondered why she was hesitating. She'd been waiting for this exact moment since the first time.

"Okay," she said, not sure what it meant. Maybe it didn't mean anything. Maybe, like her, he just didn't want to be alone.

The lights were off and the house was quiet. She turned toward him at exactly the same time that he turned toward her, and before either of them could say anything, they were already kissing.

Her attraction to him was unlike anything she had felt before. It was instant, powerful, and when they were together she felt as if he knew every inch of her—not just her body but her soul. She fell asleep in his arms.

"Bliss . . . Bliss." He was gently calling her name.

Still half asleep, she reached toward him, thinking it would be fun to do that again . . . but instead of his warm body, her hands only found an empty space where he should have been.

She blinked her eyes open.

Lawson was sitting at the edge of the bed, shirtless in his

boxer shorts. "Mac just called," he said, putting his phone away.

"Something wrong?" she said, pulling up the covers around her chest.

"Yeah. They went back to the cavern to see if Arthur was there, but he wasn't. Hadn't been for a while, apparently. The place was completely trashed, just like the Repository. I don't know if it was hounds or what, but they said it was a disaster. They think he's alive, though—there was no blood anywhere. They don't know what to do next, but we have to find him."

"*We?* But what about my friends?"

"I have to go with them," he said. "They're my pack. My place is with them. With the vampires missing, Arthur's our only chance of getting back into the passages and the underworld for the rest of the wolves. I want you to come with me."

"Lawson . . ." Bliss put a hand on his cheek. "I have to go to London. I can't come with you."

His face turned red. "Why not?"

"My friends . . . they need me. They're counting on me. You saw that Silver Blood in the Repository. They're your former masters; you know how strong they are," Bliss said. "That's what we're fighting. The vampires can't handle them alone."

"But I need you too. Your pack needs you."

"You don't understand," she said, sorrow in her voice.

"You're right, I don't," he said, getting up and putting on his clothes. "You took an oath."

"And you promised you would help me too," she said quietly, reminding him of his pledge to her when she became one of his pack. "Lawson, please."

He laced his boots.

"Lawson—" She struggled to stand up. "Where are you going? Lawson!"

He didn't look back. Not once. Bliss knew before she heard the front door slam and the elevator doors open that he was gone, and she was alone again.

117

NINETEEN

Tomasia (Florence, 1452)

ne day the baptistery doors would grace the most beautiful cathedral in the world. Tomi was satisfied with her work for the day, and took a moment to admire the piece before she returned to her quarters. When she arrived at home, the door was ajar and the room was empty of servants.

"Gio?" she called. "Gio, are you here, my love?"

"In here." That wasn't Gio's voice, Tomi thought, immediately putting a hand on the knife she carried around her waist.

"Who's there?" Tomi walked inside the bedroom and screamed.

Andreas ran to her, and she screamed even louder. "Get away from me! Where is Gio?" she yelled, pushing him away. "WHAT HAVE YOU DONE TO HIM?"

"Tomi, please, Tomi." Andreas shook her. "Gio's gone. He must have known I would return, and escaped before he had to face me. Tomi—it's all right. It's *me*."

"DEMON! Stay away from me!"

"Tomi, listen. I am so sorry—I have been trying to get back to you—but I was detained. I was sure you were safe with Gio . . . until I realized. He's the one we've been looking for all along. He has been turning the Venators against me, spreading lies, alienating my men. He even tried to kill me in Verona."

"The Black Fire," Tomi whispered. "But how?"

"I contained the fire. It responded to my magic," he said.

Tomi looked at him in confusion and fear. Unable to understand. But if it was true, then . . . She held her stomach, feeling sick all of a sudden.

"Lucifer had returned to us. He was alive . . . and his spirit was in Gio," Andreas said. "I trusted him like a brother. I loved him like brother. But he was not who we thought he was."

"No! No! That cannot be."

"He was with Simonetta. He was manipulating her all along. That child was not the first. There are others. He has bred a host of half-human demons, the Nephilim. He has kidnapped brides for the Dark Fallen. The trigylph is a symbol of their union—serpent and sheep."

"No."

"Tomi. I know he was your friend. He was mine as well."

Gio had been more than a friend. Tomi turned away from Andreas, the sick feeling in her stomach only growing.

She was utterly horrified and unable to accept what he was saying. Gio . . . ? Lucifer? But . . .

Andreas walked to her and put a hand on her shoulder. She turned to him slowly. He smiled, and she was stunned as she recognized her love once again.

Just as she had thought: Andreas was Michael. Prince of the Angels, the Valiant, Supreme Commander of the Lord's Armies. Michael, her eternal love. Only an angel with a power like hers could have stopped the Black Fire of Hell. Only Michael, Pure of Heart, the Protector of the Garden, the Champion of the Light.

She had known Andreas was Michael the instant they had met; but as the months passed and he'd kept away from her, doubt had crept in. They had been separated far too long. . . . He had left her, and in his absence, Gio had fed her lies and misinformation.

"It is not too late," Andreas told her. "Thank God you are alive. When I heard he was with you . . . I feared the worst."

"Michael," she breathed. "You are Michael returned to me," she said as she put a hand on his cheek. She remembered what Gio had said to her that night: *I've waited for so long*; remembered the way his love had bruised her, how he had coveted her body with a fierce and territorial pleasure. Something had been off. . . . He was unfamiliar. . . . Her body had known even though her mind had not.

She had been deceived. . . .

She had been betrayed. . . .

"It is all right; you are alive, we are safe. The devil is safe behind the Gates of Hell once more," Andreas murmured, folding her in his arms.

Tomi felt an ache at the deep familiarity of his embrace. She had been right all along. . . . She *had* known. . . . How could she have doubted him? How could she have let Gio manipulate her love? How could this have happened?

Andreas kissed her face, her hair. "I don't know what I would have done if I had lost you again. . . ."

Lost you again. . . .

And there was the knowledge she could not bring herself to accept. Michael had triumphed over the Dark Prince during the Crisis in Rome. Had won the day, won the battle. But it had come with a price.

Tomi returned Andreas's kisses, but she could not bring herself to tell him the truth . . . that the worst had already happened.

That she had bonded with Gio, had said the words, and now . . . Her hand rested on her belly. What had she done? *What have I done?*

She had lain with the devil, and conceived a child in deceit.

PART THE SECOND

THE PAST IS ALWAYS WITH US

I learned to live half alive . . .
—Christina Perri, "Jar of Hearts"

ordelia Van Alen had been a connoisseur of the world's grand hotels, and Schuyler knew she would have approved of the Casa del Mar. The hotel on the edge of the Pacific had a panoramic view of the coastline and the Santa Monica Pier. Oliver had chosen the hotel for its proximity to Los Angeles and its excellent bar. He had booked them separate rooms on the penthouse floor. They were in Schuyler's room, having gotten into the city via a stopover in New York. The remnants of a late room-service banquet were littered around the living area—silver platters of shrimp and salad, along with empty green bottles of sparkling water.

"You only live once." Oliver smiled and admired the view.

"Not if you're a vampire," Schuyler reminded him.

"Point taken," he agreed. "Now, shall we have a dip in the

pool and enjoy the scenery, or should we get right to work?"

"I'm a little too anxious for relaxation right now. If my dad is alive, I want to see him as soon as I can. Let's get started," she said.

"Excellent." Oliver got out his laptop and started searching. "Let's see . . . the Bendix Corp Web site doesn't have much information on its board of directors or officers, so that's not going to do it. Checking for Stephen Chase in LA, but there's only about a million listings. . . . This is going to be tough."

"Look up Bendix, or Ben Chase—I don't think he always went by Stephen, at least not when he was younger."

Oliver checked again. "Nothing for Bendix. Another million for Ben. We need to try something different."

Schuyler peered over his shoulder at the screen. "Are there any news articles about the family? Maybe they're not in LA proper?"

Oliver ran a search for news articles on the Chase family. "Looking to cross-reference the Bendix Corporation," he muttered to himself. "Got something—a charity event sponsored by the Chase family. In Malibu. No names or pictures, though."

"That's okay," Schuyler said. "We can look for phone numbers in Malibu—maybe there won't be as many as in the other places. Stephen, Bendix, Ben, whatever."

Oliver typed furiously. "No Bendix, which is too bad— that would have been the easiest. No Ben or Stephen, either—found an S. Chase, though. What do you think?"

"Worth a shot." Schuyler got out her cell phone and dialed the number.

A deep male voice answered. "Good afternoon, Chase residence. Who may I say is speaking?" Schuyler recognized the voice of the butler, of the help.

"This is Schuyler Van Alen. Is this the number for Stephen Chase?"

A pause. Then, "This is the home of Mrs. Chase, his widow."

"Widow?" Schuyler blurted out.

"May I ask why you're calling?" the butler asked, sounding a little suspicious.

"I'm, uh . . . Stephen Chase's daughter."

The man coughed. "I'm afraid that's quite impossible," he said. "Are you certain you are calling for Stephen *Ronald* Chase?"

Stephen Ronald Chase. Her paternal grandfather. Her heart beat in excitement. This was her *grandmother's* house. "My name is Schuyler Van Alen and I'm looking for his son, Stephen Bendix Chase. Ben is my father," she said quietly.

There was a much longer pause.

"I will relay the message to Mrs. Chase, Miss Van Alen. Where can I say you are calling from?"

Schuyler gave him her room number at Casa del Mar and hung up the phone.

"What happened?" asked Oliver.

She told him. She could barely process the idea before the phone rang. It was the butler calling back, with the Chase home address and instructions. Schuyler thanked him profusely before hanging up.

"So apparently my grandmother wants to meet us tomorrow. She's in Malibu, not too far."

"*Us?* I think he just meant you, babe."

"Ollie! I'd hate to go alone," Schuyler said.

"If all goes well, you won't be alone. You'll be with family," he said firmly. "I'm sure your grandmother won't want an audience. Shall we discuss it over cocktails?"

Schuyler wondered if she should be concerned that Oliver seemed to be a little too carefree, getting to be more like Kingsley than trying to save the vampires. But then she could really use a drink herself.

The lounge at the Casa del Mar looked out over the ocean, and the bartenders were attentive mixologists, who made up special drinks for each of them. Schuyler's was a bittersweet (appropriate, she thought) mix of orange blossoms and something she couldn't quite put her finger on—Pimm's? Oliver's was some kind of martini made with absinthe.

"Warn me if you start hallucinating," Schuyler said.

"A snack will take the edge off, just in case," Oliver replied, and ordered oysters and sushi. "Now, why are you so nervous about meeting these people? Isn't this what you've always wanted?"

"I guess," Schuyler said. "But I know so little about them, and I don't think they know anything at all about me. I mean, that butler didn't really sound surprised that there might be some secret granddaughter roaming around, although maybe that's just how butlers are supposed to sound. What if my grandmother doesn't want to have anything to do with me? Don't you think it's weird that she agreed to meet with a stranger off the street? And what if this trip turns out to be pointless? We could be wasting valuable time here."

"Or what if we find exactly what you've been searching for all your life?" Oliver said.

"What do you mean? We're here to find the *sangreal*, aren't we? That Blood of the Father thing."

"That's what *we* need, or the vampires need," he said. "But it's not the same thing you've been missing."

"What are you talking about?" Schuyler said, annoyed. She pointed her cocktail fork in his direction. "Stop being so cryptic."

"Let's take a step back," he said. "For most of your life you only knew your mother as an unconscious figure in a hospital bed. You were told that your father was dead. The only family member you thought you had in the world was your grandmother, and she's gone now, as is your grand-father, who you met only a few years ago. But your father's family is your family too. Your *human* family. I can imagine why that would be a scary thing to think about. But it could also be awesome."

"Awesome how?"

"Well, why assume that they'd be such skeptics about you? Why not assume they'd welcome you with open arms, thrilled to have found you? Isn't that how you'd feel if it turned out your father were alive? Ecstatic?"

"I used to think so," Schuyler said. "I kept hoping. . . . But what if I'm wrong? What if he's awful? Cordelia always intimated that he'd done something terrible. She always told me to stop thinking about him, that he wasn't worthy of my mother."

Oliver squirmed in his chair. "She probably just meant he wasn't worthy of her because he was human."

Schuyler nodded. "You may have a point there."

"Cordelia wasn't a big fan of the relationship, but do you really think your mother would bond with a guy like that?" Oliver asked gently. "Allegra gave up everything for him. He must be pretty special."

"Maybe," Schuyler grudgingly admitted. She'd always loved her father in that obligatory way that anyone has toward an absent relative—like she was supposed to love him because of who he was. But she'd never known him at all. Cordelia had never talked about him, and for Schuyler's entire childhood, Allegra had been in a coma. When she'd woken up, all she'd cared about was the Van Alen Legacy. There had been no time to tell her daughter anything else, it seemed. Except, when she'd really needed her, Schuyler realized—her mother had appeared to her, right when

Schuyler had been torn between choosing to follow her heart with Jack or to remain with Oliver. *You cannot be with someone just because you don't want to hurt him. You have your own happiness to think about.*

But if Bendix was still alive . . . then where the hell had he been all these years? Why had he never visited Allegra? Never tried to contact Schuyler? Not once, not a card, not a phone call. Cordelia might have been an impediment, but what could that matter to a father who loved his daughter?

"Now, finish your drink, eat some oysters, and fortify for your Oprah reunion." Oliver winked.

Schuyler laughed. "You're a good friend, Ollie."

"Happy to be of service," he said, and bent over the table in a mock bow.

"Watch it, you almost dunked your hair in your drink," Schuyler pointed out. "You just missed because it's pretty much gone."

"My hair?" Oliver asked in mock horror, running his hands through his thick locks.

"No, your drink." Schuyler laughed.

"Must be time for a refill, then," he said.

But before Oliver could summon the bartender, Schuyler heard an unusual beeping noise coming from his cell phone. "Did you get a text?" she asked. "That's not what it usually sounds like."

Oliver looked nervous as he picked up the phone to

check his message. "Give me a second," he said, and stepped away from the bar.

Must be pretty bad, Schuyler thought, because she saw his face turn pale.

He walked back to her chair but didn't sit down.

"What is it?" she asked.

"That wasn't a text message—it was the emergency beacon from the Repository in New York. It's never gone off before, or at least I've never been the one to receive the signal, so it took me a minute to figure out what it was. Something really bad has happened. I have to go back right away."

"Should I come with you?" Schuyler asked, worried.

"No, you have important things to do here. Go find your family tomorrow, and keep me updated on what happens. Stay and finish your drink, and get some food in you. We'll talk soon."

It was just as she'd expected. She was on her own. Except for that lingering feeling that someone was very close—and keeping an eye on her. But she had gotten accustomed to it; and since nothing had happened so far, she chalked it up to nerves and anxiety and decided to forget all about it.

TWENTY-ONE

Lawson

Lawson drove back to Hunting Valley as if the devil was on his tail, his feelings in turmoil. He'd always been impulsive, and he had left Bliss in New York without thinking—he'd been angry and had done the first thing that came to mind. Left. He'd wanted her to come with him, and while he had lied—he *did* understand that her friends were important to her—what he hadn't been able to say was that he wanted to know that *he* was important to her too.

And just as she needed to find Oliver and Schuyler and reunite with Jane, he needed to find Arthur. Arthur had saved them when they were lost, and if he was lost now, it was their job to bring him back.

His wolf pack was waiting for him when he reached the cavern. Malcolm literally jumped for joy when he saw him, and Ahramin unexpectedly threw herself into his arms for a hug. "What was that for?" he asked.

"We missed you," she said, shrugging.

Edon frowned. Ahramin must be trying to make him jealous, Lawson thought. She was always playing games like that. He wanted to tell Edon he had nothing to worry about.

"What do we know so far?" he asked.

"Look around," Rafe said. "The place is a mess. No blood, but no claw marks, either. Doesn't look like hounds from when they attacked the first time. This is new."

"Not hounds, then," Lawson said. Silver Bloods? Maybe they'd drained Arthur, and that was why there wasn't any blood. He hated the thought of it. He'd seen the work of the Silver Blood in the Repository and shuddered to think of his friend as one of their victims.

Malcolm seemed to know what he was thinking. "If it was a vampire, there would be blood," he said.

"We have to assume he got away, then," Lawson said.

"Where would he go? And wouldn't he leave us some sort of sign if he'd had any chance to?" asked Rafe.

Edon nodded grudgingly. "We've been digging around, but we haven't been able to come up with much. Just about everything is ruined."

"Just about?"

"We found a book," Malcolm said. "*Through the Looking-Glass.* Arthur was always getting on me to read it."

Weird thing to leave behind, Lawson thought. "What's it about?"

"A fairy tale about a mirror that takes you to another world," Malcolm explained.

Huh. "Did you go into Arthur's room?" Lawson asked.

"Of course we did," Edon snapped. "We looked everywhere!"

"Remember that gold mirror he somehow lugged down here?" Lawson asked. "How strange we thought it was that he'd carry it around with him? Did that get trashed too, or is it still standing?"

"It's still there," Rafe said. "We tried everything."

"I have an idea," Lawson said. "Follow me."

They worked their way through the rubble until they reached Arthur's room, where the only thing left intact was the enormous old-fashioned mirror. Lawson looked at the ground in front of it.

Footprints.

Lawson grinned as he pushed on the mirror.

Nothing happened.

"See? We tried that too," Rafe said.

Lawson didn't give up. He ran his hands along its length until he felt a button.

"What are you doing?" Malcolm asked.

"Give me a second."

Lawson pushed the button, and the mirror opened outward, nearly hitting him in the face.

"So he did leave us a clue," Edon said. He didn't sound so annoyed anymore, but Lawson didn't have time to be grateful.

"There's a passageway back here," he said. "Let's go."

The five of them entered the passageway single file,

135

with Lawson in front. Rafe closed the door, leaving them in darkness, but Lawson turned on his phone, and the passageway lit up, just enough so they could see their way forward. They only had to walk for a few minutes before they reached a door.

"Is it open?" Rafe whispered.

"No," Lawson whispered back.

"Should we force it?"

"Let me try something else," Lawson said, and knocked.

And waited.

And waited.

And then . . . the door opened.

"Well, it's about time," Arthur said, looking up from his book. "What took you so long?"

The room behind the cavern was enormous. It was really more of an apartment than a room, complete with a kitchen and dining table.

"So this is where you really live," Lawson said.

"An old warlock needs to have his secrets," Arthur said, with a wink. He turned to Ahramin. "Hello, my dear. And you are . . . ?"

"I'm Ahramin," she said, almost shyly. Lawson had never seen Ahramin nervous like this, but it was probably because she'd never met a warlock before. Not that there was anything to be scared about, as Arthur was a true friend of the wolves. He had explained to Lawson that long ago he'd owed a favor to a Fallen angel named Gabrielle, who had turned out to be Bliss's mother. Gabrielle had asked him to help the wolves, and so he had.

"And Bliss?" Arthur asked.

Lawson didn't flinch at her name. He quickly explained what had happened, how they'd fixed the issues with the timeline but got stuck trying to go to the underworld; then how he and Bliss had gone to New York to try to find her friends. "But you still haven't told us what happened here. How did you escape the attack? Who attacked you? And what can we do to reopen the passages?"

Arthur laughed. "One thing at a time, my boy, one thing at a time. The Hellhounds left me alone once you disappeared. That mess up there is merely an illusion. As soon as it became clear you weren't coming back anytime soon, and there was danger afoot, I knew I needed a better hiding place. What better way to escape an attack than to convince potential attackers that one has already occurred? I made the place a glorious mess."

"You did a good job," Edon said.

"Too good," Lawson said. "We almost didn't figure it out."

"Oh, I knew you would. Such a simple clue, really. I almost worried that whoever came to attack me might cotton to it."

"Did anyone come?" Rafe asked.

"Trackers, but they left. No hounds."

"Well, what have you been doing here all year?" Malcolm asked.

"Don't be rude," Ahramin said.

Said the pot to the kettle, Lawson thought, but he was curious to hear Arthur's answer.

"I've been working on your problem," Arthur said.

"But we only just found out about it," Lawson said, puzzled.

"When it took you such a long time to return, I started to worry and thought I would look into it. As it happens, I've discovered why the passages are out of sync. There's been a rift in time."

"What does that mean?" Edon asked.

"I'll show you," Arthur said. He retrieved a map from a drawer, one Lawson had never seen before. "This is a time map I discovered. Do you see this image here?" He pointed.

Lawson looked closer. The map was largely made up of pictures, but where Arthur pointed, there were two identical images, side by side, followed by a series of images that looked similar at first and then started looking different. But after studying the images for a minute, Lawson realized the first two weren't identical. They were mirrored.

"Do you notice the difference?" Arthur asked. "The images on the map should all be unique, because there should only be one true path through time. But something broke, and now there are two paths. They've been there for a while. It's amazing you've been able to move through the passages until now, since that break has caused a ripple effect that slowly created enough of a blockage that the passages are rendered useless. If that blockage is allowed to spread, time as we know it will cease to exist, and the world will crumble into chaos and disorder."

Lawson had a feeling he knew what that meant. The wolves were members of the Praetorian Guard, keepers of the timeline. If something had gone wrong, it was their job to fix it. "What do we do?" he asked.

"You have to find the passage and fix the broken part. You'll have to travel to its location since you can't use the passages themselves anymore."

"How will we know where to look?"

"I know that the break took place during the Roman Empire, during Caligula's reign, so you'll have to go to Rome and try to find the ancient path, the one that led to the creation of the first Gate of Hell. That's the best I can do, for now."

"Did we cause this?" Malcolm asked. "When we went back there? Is this all our fault?"

"No, dear boy," Arthur said. "Do not blame yourself. This is the work of the Fallen. Bliss is part of this. I'm sure she is. She should be here with you."

Lawson did not disagree.

"If she's really one of us now, then we should be her priority," said Ahramin. "Why is she running to the vampires? She's not one of them anymore."

Much as Lawson hated to admit it, Ahramin had a point. Bliss was part of the pack, and the pack needed her. He needed her. He had told her as much before he left, but maybe he should try again.

Bliss picked up right away when he called her cell phone. "You're not on the plane yet?" He didn't apologize for leaving, but then Bliss didn't expect him to. They had let each other down.

"I'm at the airport," she said. "What's up? Did you find Arthur? Is he okay?"

"We did and he is," he said, and briefly explained what they'd learned. His voice dropped so that no one else could hear him. "Listen, I know you're worried about your friends, and I will keep my promise to you. But the thing is, Arthur thinks what's happened to the passages affects your friends as well."

"Really?"

"Yeah." Then his voice dropped even lower still. "I'm sorry I left the way I did. I didn't mean to."

"I'm sorry too," she whispered.

"So let's be sorry together."

Bliss smiled into the phone. "Okay, I was just about to get on a plane to London, but I can go back to Ohio instead."

"No, don't," Lawson said. "Meet us in Rome."

imi completed the long journey back to the underworld well before Jack. She wasn't sure how to read his delay—had he struggled to fail at his quest, or had failure simply been impossible? The difficulty with being Abbadon and Azrael was that it was easier to do things well than to do them poorly. It was all she could do to force Kingsley to succeed in winning the cup, although certainly he'd always been good at stealing things from her. Like her clothes, or her heart.

She tried to forget the look he'd given her—right before she'd disappeared—a combination of shock and displeasure. He had been confident she would fall into his arms— downright *smug*, even. And while Kingsley was right to believe in her love, she couldn't help feeling a little irritated, especially now that she knew how he had been spending his time while she was working so diligently on breaking her bond so they could be together.

The bastard had expected her to kiss him.

And why hadn't she?

Because then all would be lost. Lucifer would know immediately, and everyone would be vulnerable. Not just her and Jack, but Kingsley and Schuyler as well. If their betrayal was discovered, it would bring death to the two of them as well as to the ones they loved the most.

Where are you? she sent to Jack. But there was no reply.

She waited anxiously for his return, pacing the rooms of their apartments. The Dark Prince had been made aware of her failure, but so far had not requested her to come before him to answer for the fiasco at Rosslyn. Days felt like weeks, which felt like months, which felt like years, while she flinched at every knock on the door, fearful that someone had realized she'd thrown the fight with Kingsley. That she was a traitor. This couldn't go on forever; it would make her insane.

She tried to distract herself, remembering her last time in the underworld, when she'd waited anxiously in her room; when she'd gone back for Kingsley. She'd indulged herself then, with massages and facials and hair treatments, and glorious meals with fancy wine, but those didn't help now. She was too fidgety to sit still, and too nervous to eat. Late nights at the clubs helped release some of the tension, but she couldn't dance forever.

Finally, late one night, Jack returned, weary from his

trip. She could tell from the look on his face that he'd failed, which is to say that he'd succeeded in doing Lucifer's bidding. He'd retrieved a cup. "What happened?" she asked. "Are you okay?"

"We were so close," he said. "I found the cup, and I'd set up this fantastic battle with the monks for it. They'd just about succeeded when you called me."

So it was her fault. She'd insisted that Jack help her get rid of Danel, and in doing so she'd sabotaged his efforts. "I'm sorry," she said, one of the rare occasions she was willing to admit it.

Jack shook his head. "That wasn't the problem. It was a little trickier to make sure the monks won with Danel there, but I made it happen. They destroyed their precious chalice rather than letting us have it. No, the problem is that Danel is a little too good at his job. He figured out that the monks didn't seem sufficiently devastated by the loss of their treasure."

"Do monks ever really seem all that emotional?" Mimi asked.

"It's pretty subtle," Jack admitted. "Even I didn't catch it. But Danel was all over it. Before I fully realized what he was doing, he'd tracked the monks to a second cup."

"What? They had two? How did we not know that?"

"We've been tracking the strongest chalices, the ones that we were sure would suffice to carry the godsfire. The one the monks were hiding isn't among them, but Danel thinks it will work—it's still a cup of Christ—so Lucifer is over the moon that we managed to bring it back."

"Wasn't there anything you could do?" Mimi asked. "Couldn't you steal it when he wasn't looking, or something?"

"Believe me, I did everything I could," Jack said. "Danel was too vigilant. I don't think he was actually on to me, but we have to remember that none of the angels really trust us, still. It would take centuries for us to reestablish their loyalty to us, and we don't have that kind of time right now."

"Not to mention the fact that they're right," Mimi pointed out. "We are traitors."

"There is that," Jack agreed.

"What are we going to do now?"

"Well, finding a chalice was one of the last steps in being able to use the godsfire as a weapon, but it's not the final one. Lucifer wants to meet with us tomorrow to discuss our next series of tasks."

The work of the Dark Angels was never done, Mimi thought.

"We've got time to sabotage the process, still," Jack said. "Whatever these last tasks are, we can fail at those as well. And if we have the opportunity, we'll steal and destroy the cup."

"They'll know it was us," Mimi said. "If we do it here, there won't be any hiding it. And we'll never get Lucifer to dissolve our bond."

"We'll find a way," Jack said. "There's got to be a way."

* * *

They were summoned to the Dark Prince's chambers the next morning. His white robes gleamed against his golden throne, and Mimi was awed once again by his otherworldly beauty. This was the face of the Morningstar, Lucifer of the Dawn, the most beautiful angel in history, who had been banished for his vanity, for his greed. This was the Prince of Heaven, consigned to an eternity in Hell. He was smiling, and his joy radiated an intense, almost angry happiness. He was very close to getting what he always wanted, and he knew it.

Danel and Barachiel stood on either side of the throne, dressed in formal golden raiment, wings spread. Danel was giving Mimi the same look that boys from Duchesne used to give her, after she'd given them a taste of the Sacred Kiss. The lascivious anticipation of physical delight that meant he couldn't wait to be alone with her again. *Ew!* She should never have kissed him at the train station, but it was too late now.

"My Dark Angels!" Lucifer said, his voice seductively sweet and melodious, as beautiful as the rest of him. "Welcome back. I'm so pleased Abbadon was successful in retrieving the chalice; though I must admit, Azrael, that I'd anticipated more success coming from you. Perhaps you were distracted by the thought of Araquiel as your foe?" he said, using Kingsley's angel name.

"It wasn't a problem," Mimi said. "He's a formidable opponent, that's all."

The Dark Prince grunted. "Formidable is not a word I would use to describe that weakling. I was surprised to hear he defeated you in battle. A first for the mighty Azrael, is it not? Regardless, we shall not concern ourselves with that, for now. We have more important things to discuss. There is one more final task we need to complete before we wage war upon our enemies. For the first, I will need Abbadon's assistance."

"At your service, my lord," Jack said.

"We have discovered the location of the Gate of Promise, but before we are able to return to Paradise, a sacrifice must be made, as before," he said. "But not just any sacrifice."

Mimi nodded.

"The gatekeeper must be destroyed in order to obliterate the gate."

"Then we shall destroy the keeper, whoever it is," Jack said.

Lucifer looked amused. "I'm so pleased to hear you say that, Abbadon."

Uh-oh. Mimi had a feeling she knew what was coming.

"The gatekeeper is Gabrielle's daughter, the human Abomination," Lucifer said. "Her blood is the key to our salvation."

Schuyler Van Alen.

The Dark Prince folded his hands under his chin and looked straight at Abbadon. "My spies report that you were once *involved* with this person, that you went as far as to bond with her. Is that true?"

He knows. Lucifer fucking knows. Mimi felt her body grow cold with fear. This whole secret agent thing was a charade. He had been laughing behind their backs for believing that they could earn their unbonding. The Dark Prince knew all along what Mimi and Jack were up to. He had taken them back into the fold only to screw with them precisely at this moment. *This* was his revenge. Mimi drew her hand on her hip, where her sword was within reach. *We can fight it out. We will die trying, but we will fight it out.*

Jack remained impassive. There was no change in expression, no sign that the information had dug deep into his heart. *Stay strong,* Mimi sent. *Don't let him see.*

Jack did not reply. His stance was relaxed, and his tone conversational. It was as if he had expected to hear as much. "My lord, forgive me. You are correct in that I once had feelings for this half-human girl. But there is nothing between us. She was merely a passing fancy, a plaything. I realized my mistake and severed our ties. She means nothing to me. Do with her as you will."

"That is good to hear." Lucifer smiled. "Distractions can be very harmful. Her mother, as well, was nothing but a distraction. And an annoyance." He regarded Jack thoughtfully. "You will bring the gatekeeper to me. Her blood is in your veins, and will call to yours when you are aboveground."

"Yes, my lord." Jack bowed.

"I hope you will not be tempted to drain her completely before you bring her to the gate. We will need her alive for the sacrifice."

"Indeed, my lord, I shall resist the temptation."

"Danel will join you in this task and make sure everything proceeds smoothly."

"Yes, my lord. I will be glad for the help. He was instrumental in acquiring the grail. I could not have done it without him."

"Schuyler Van Alen should never have been allowed to live. Her life is a mockery of our glory," Lucifer declared. "She is her mother's greatest mistake, and will prove to be her deepest sorrow. I will enjoy draining her life's blood and subsuming her spirit."

What a hypocrite, Mimi thought. To call Schuyler an Abomination when you yourself unleashed the half-demon Nephilim into our world. Silver Bloods mating with human women to create a half-mad race of demon children. And good luck with that plan to kill Gabrielle's daughter. I'll believe it when I see it. Schuyler Van Alen is nothing if not hard to get rid of.

"I want nothing more than to please you, my lord. Her blood is yours." Jack bowed.

"And me?" Mimi piped up. "I mean, and me, my lord?"

"Yes, Azrael?"

"Am I going with them?" Mimi asked.

"No, I trust they will be able to handle this on their own."

Can you? Mimi asked Jack, using their bond. *Handle this?*

But Jack did not reply. His face was impassive and as

hard to read as ever. It couldn't have been easy, listening to the Dark Prince's plans for him. *What do we do now?* she sent. *Talk to me.*

Jack? Hello? Jack? she sent, standing with a rigid smile in front of Lucifer. *What are you going to do?*

What I have to do, he finally replied.

Mimi wasn't sure what he meant by that. Would he do what he had to to survive? Or what he had to in order to make sure Lucifer failed and Schuyler was kept alive? Mimi couldn't imagine any reality in which Jack would actually kill Schuyler, of course. His great love for her had ruined both of their lives. He had bonded to her. No, of course not. Jack would find a way to make sure it never happened.

Mimi found the thought of being rid of Schuyler once and for all somewhat appealing. But she knew that, after everything, she would never allow the Dark Prince to touch a hair on that girl's head if she could help it. Just as she knew Jack would never allow Lucifer to hurt Kingsley. They would protect the people they loved. They were in this together.

I'll help you in any way I can.

TWENTY-THREE

Tomasia (Florence, 1452)

*N*ow that Andreas had returned, Tomi wondered how she could have doubted him. She should have trusted herself, but she had not, and now she would pay the price. But the reason for her misgivings could not be dismissed: it lay in the memory of what Andreas—Michael—had done so long ago. The last time they had encountered the Dark Prince. Though she had tried in her heart to understand, she had never accepted his choice. She had never forgiven him for what he had done during the Crisis in Rome.

What happened in Rome should never have been allowed. She had tried to accept, had tried to understand, but now Tomi had to admit that after the crisis passed, it was too late. Ever since then, she had mistrusted Michael's capacity to lead them. . . . She had wondered if he still understood the reason for their sacrifice. The reason for their existence was to seek redemption for their people, to bring hope to the banished, to bring light to those who had been cursed into darkness.

They had come so close to victory in Rome. Michael had been so close to ending it.

Now they had both been punished. As the centuries passed, Tomi's doubt had only grown; and in that doubt, Lucifer had found a way between them, to unmake what could not be unmade.

Their great love for each other.

It was only a matter of time before Andreas would find out what she had done. Lucifer's child. This was a new spirit, a new entity. This was no ordinary pregnancy for their kind. This was a new soul. She could sense its fear, its wonder, and uncertainty. Somehow, Lucifer had stolen the gift of procreation from the Red Bloods and used it to create a child with her.

Their child. Born of love. Gio—Lucifer—she had loved him. Whatever she had done, she had loved him, and she loved this child.

She would do everything to protect her—and it was a daughter, she knew that for certain. She would do everything to protect her from Andreas.

What would happen once he discovered the truth?

Tomi thought of Simonetta—gutted, murdered, an innocent babe slaughtered in her belly. Nephilim. Demon children. But they were still *children*. Worthy of forgiveness, worthy of redemption. The babe had done nothing to deserve such a vile and violent end.

Andreas would never do the same to her, she knew.

But the baby . . .

With Andreas back, they returned to their mission, hunting the remaining Silver Bloods in their midst. Tomi tried not to think about the fact that one day she would give birth to the same thing they were killing.

It felt so natural, working with Andreas. Of course he was Michael; of course there was no one else he could have been. But over time she saw him looking at her strangely. He knew that something was wrong, that something had changed between them.

"You are troubled, my love. What is the matter?" he would ask. "We have triumphed over our enemy. There is nothing to fear."

But as kind as Andreas was, Tomi could not bring herself to tell him the truth. That she had been deceived, that she had doubted, and so she was the one who had betrayed him this time. Instead, she wore dresses that fit tightly at her breasts but bloomed and draped, skimming over her torso, so he could not see the growing bulge of her stomach.

Before long, though, she would not be able to hide it.

At night, she dreamed of Gio. She dreamed of their night together, and she felt the shame in her soul from how she'd responded to his touch. In her dreams, she could see Lucifer in him. Some nights she dreamed that she realized it in time; that she was able to get away; that she realized Andreas was her true mate. Then she would wake up, remember the truth, and the guilt and the shame would fill her again. Some nights she dreamed that she could see Lucifer in him and she did not care: she lay with him anyway.

That was more shameful still.

They were hunting a Silver Blood along the byzantine streets of the city center when Tomi realized she had gotten too big to run. The Silver Blood began to move faster and faster, and Andreas rushed to catch up with him. But Tomi could hardly move. The child was kicking in her belly, and the dress she was wearing to hide her growing waistline was heavy and dragged her down.

She could see Andreas ahead of her, trying to decide whether to catch the Silver Blood or slow down to attend to her. "Go!" she shouted. "Do not wait for me!"

She hoped the pause had not slowed him down too much; she would hate for a Silver Blood to escape because of what she had done. But she could no longer run; she could no longer stand. She sat down on the side of the road and waited for Andreas to return, trying to think of what she would say to him.

It was nearly an hour before he returned, bruised and bloodied.

"Are you all right?" she asked. If anything she had done led to his being hurt . . .

"I'm fine," he said. "It is my opponent you should worry about."

Tomasia smiled with relief, but her face fell when she remembered what she had to do.

"I should ask the same of you, though," he said. "I have noticed, of late, that you seem to be a bit unwell. Distracted, perhaps. I did not want to push you to tell me something you did not wish to share, but I must ask now."

"There is something I need to tell you," Tomasia admitted. "Though I am fearful about how you will receive the news."

Andreas knelt next to her in the road and took her hand in his. "There is nothing you can say that I am unwilling to hear. Nothing can change how I feel about you. Our bond is stronger than that."

Their bond . . .

"While you were away," she began, "I became convinced that I had been wrong that you were my mate, that you were my Michael. I should never have doubted; I should never have believed that Lucifer could ever reside in you, but I am ashamed to admit I did. I believed it because everyone else did, and because everything I saw led me to believe it. And Gio . . ."

"No one could have known about Gio," Andreas said grimly.

"It was more than that, though. Gio convinced me that we were meant to be together, that he was my Michael, and not you. And I already doubted myself so much that I felt that he must be right. . . . We became bondmates."

Andreas stood. "You . . . you bonded with Gio?"

"Yes. I bonded with him. And . . ."

"Stand up!" Andreas commanded.

"Please, Andreas—"

"I said, stand up!"

She did as he asked. She stood up straight and tall, and did not stoop forward so the folds of her dress would better hide her burgeoning stomach. It was time for Andreas to know everything.

He saw right away.

"My God," he said. "He has got you with child? How can this be?"

"I do not know," she admitted. "But I do know one thing: I cannot let you destroy it."

155

TWENTY-FOUR

Schuyler

*S*chuyler lingered over her coffee the next morning, not sure how early would be too early to show up at the Chase house. When she couldn't take the waiting anymore, she had the hotel call her a car and gave the driver the address.

He whistled. "Going to Sunny Dunes, are you? Nice spread."

She could only imagine what kind of house would garner that reaction in a place like Malibu. They drove down the Pacific Coast Highway, snaking through the canyons, right against the beachhead. Schuyler saw surfers in wet suits sitting on their boards, waiting for waves. There were families picnicking by the beach, and a row of colorful houses facing the water, the only clue to their immense wealth the Aston Martins and Ferraris parked in the driveway.

The Chase residence was set right on the beach, an

imposing modern structure that appeared to be made almost entirely out of glass. "It's a landmark," the driver said as he dropped her off. "One of the last houses built by a really famous local architect. Don't break anything!" he joked.

"Thanks," Schuyler said. She had expected a more traditional manor, something like the Nantucket ten-bedroom "cottage" that was Cordelia's summer residence. This house reminded her of a museum, with its jagged roofline and aluminum panels. The driveway led to a double-height front door with a heavy iron handle. Through the glass panels for walls, she could see into the house—a serene and immaculate space that looked out over the ocean.

She buzzed the intercom and peered into the camera. "Uh, hi? I'm Schuyler Van Alen. Mrs. Chase is expecting me?"

"One moment," a voice answered. Schuyler heard the sound of footsteps, and the door swung open to reveal a diminutive young woman in a black polo shirt and khaki pants—a uniform, Schuyler noticed, but a discreet one. The emblem "Sunny Dunes" on the pocket was all that gave it away.

"Hi, Schuyler, come on in. Mr. Jackson is ready for you."

Schuyler followed the girl through the grand foyer and into a sun-filled living room. Double-height glass windows looked out over the ocean; the walls were beige and covered with stunning artwork. Schuyler thought some of the work looked familiar—de Kooning? Chagall? A stern-looking man of advanced age was standing in front of a Lichtenstein mural. "Good afternoon, I'm Murray Jackson. I work for Mrs. Chase. You must be Schuyler, the young lady with whom I spoke on the phone," he said. "Do have a seat. Mrs. Chase will be down momentarily." He gave her a long once-over and left the room.

The furniture was upholstered in a rich creamy leather, and surrounded an enormous metallic coffee table that glinted in the sunlight. There was a grand piano in one corner, and Schuyler saw that the top was covered in framed photographs. There was a beautiful couple—her mother and Ben. Schuyler had never even seen any wedding photos. Cordelia had hidden them all away. They were so gorgeous together, Schuyler found it was hard to look at them, hard to feel connected to the two glowing people in the photograph. So that was her father.

He was so very handsome—not merely handsome but *bright*. There was a gentleness in him. He looked like such a happy person, she thought. A golden boy in all respects— born to sunshine and laughter. His smile was so full of joy that Schuyler had an inkling, for the first time, what had made Allegra give up her entire world for him.

He must be pretty special, Oliver had said.

Looking at the photographs, at the way he gazed at Allegra, Schuyler knew Oliver was right.

But most of the pictures on the piano were of a girl roughly her age, smiling at birthday parties, on the ski slopes, or on a horse bedecked with ribbons. There were photographs of the girl with an elderly couple who had to be her grandparents—Mr. and Mrs. Chase? And a few with a stylish woman who had to be the girl's mother. There were no photographs of her with anyone who looked like he could be her father. The girl was very pretty, and had an appealing merriment to her. There was something familiar about the way her blue eyes crinkled with delight. Who was this girl?

Schuyler moved on to look closely at the art and was too busy inspecting the nearest piece to hear the footsteps on the stairs, but a voice from behind told her she was no longer alone. "How do you like the collection?" a woman asked.

Schuyler turned around to see the grandmother from the pictures: a tall, imposing woman dressed in impeccably crisp cream linen.

"This is a Richard Prince, isn't it?" Schuyler asked. "I always thought he was terribly overrated and overpriced, but this truly is amazing," she said, admiring an oversized landscape with a cowboy in the forefront. She'd always thought the Marlboro Man was such a cliché, but the painting was a revelation.

"Thank you. I'm glad to say we bought it when he was still affordable." The woman laughed. "Decca."

"Schuyler," Schuyler said, shaking the woman's hand, which had a nice firm grip.

"Yes. Jackson tells me you think you are my grand-daughter," Decca said, sitting on the couch across from

Schuyler and studying her with a keen frankness. "I assured him that it was quite impossible, but he insisted I meet with you, so I thought I would humor him."

"I appreciate that," Schuyler said. "And I am sorry to impose on you like this—but I'm looking for my father. I'm Ben Chase's daughter."

Decca nodded. "My dear," she said, pointing to the photographs on top of the piano, "that is Ben's daughter. My only grandchild, Finn."

Schuyler swallowed hard. "My father had another daughter?" Then that meant the girl in the photographs—the pretty smiling blonde with the clear blue eyes—was her sister. She couldn't even imagine it.

"As far as we knew, Ben only had one child. I'm sorry to say this happens sometimes—strangers showing up with a claim to the family. My son did have his share of girlfriends, but he was not . . . shall we say . . . an irresponsible person."

"My mother was Allegra Van Alen," Schuyler said, her hands trembling as she reached into her purse to show Decca the wedding announcement from the *Times*, as well as her birth certificate. "Ben is my father. Her husband."

Decca took the paper and frowned as she read it.

"See, I'm telling you the truth. I'm Ben's daughter with Allegra."

Decca shook her head. "But that can't be." She turned away for a moment, toward the view of paddleboarders gliding through the waves. "It doesn't make sense." She stared hard at Schuyler. "Cordelia told you Ben was your father?" she asked. "Cordelia Van Alen?"

"Well, yeah. I mean, my mother was in a coma, so I really couldn't talk to her."

"A coma," Decca echoed.

"Yeah, she's been hospitalized since I could remember."

Decca pursed her lips, then seemed to come to an internal decision. "Please give me a moment," she said, and left the room.

Schuyler had no idea what to do. Somehow, she had allowed herself to hope, to think of herself as something other than the *Dimidium Cognatus*. To imagine what it might have been like, if her dad had been around. She would have been a normal granddaughter to Decca, like that healthy-looking girl in all the photos. Finn.

Her sister.

What was she like? Schuyler wondered. Certainly she hadn't had to deal with all the things Schuyler had faced growing up. Perhaps she was like Schuyler's Duchesne classmates—wealthy and oblivious, obsessed with boys, clothes, and status.

But maybe not—maybe she was just living the life Schuyler had always wished she'd had. She certainly looked like she was loved. Happy. Peaceful.

Schuyler found herself almost as curious about Finn as she was about Ben. Strange, given that she'd had a whole lifetime to wonder about her father, and only a few minutes to think about the prospect of another hidden sibling.

There had to be a way to make things right with Decca, to make her understand that all she wanted was to meet her father, and now her sister. She wandered around until she found the bathroom, where she could splash some water on her face and reapply her lipstick, hoping to look more like a normal person than like someone who'd just received a shock. She ran her fingers through her hair in an attempt to be more presentable, and went back into the living room and waited for her grandmother.

Finally, Decca returned. She was holding a letter. Schuyler recognized Cordelia Van Alen's elegant handwriting on the envelope.

"When were you born?" she asked.

Schuyler told her.

"We received this a few months before your birth. It was from your grandmother. She told us Allegra had passed away."

TWENTY-FIVE

Mimi

With a wave of his hand, Lucifer dismissed Jack and Danel. "You may take your leave tonight," he said. "Move quickly. We don't want to give our enemies time to figure out what we're doing."

Now that Danel had been sent off with Jack, Mimi wondered if she was going to be stuck with Barachiel. It was a shame that her work on Danel had been for nothing. She could have distracted him with a few more of those kisses, as repulsive as she found them. But getting stuck aboveground with Barachiel was even worse. He was the angriest of all the remaining angels in Hell. She wasn't sure he would ever accept that she and Jack had returned to the fold. Smart of him, she supposed.

"And now we turn to you," the Dark Prince said. "My lovely Azrael, my angel of Death. I was very displeased by your failure to retrieve the grail, particularly as you and Abbadon are here to repay your debt to me."

Mimi opened her mouth to protest, but Lucifer stopped her. "I am not interested in explanations. However, I am more concerned with your ability to prove your devotion to me, personally. Barachiel, please leave us."

Barachiel looked as if he were about to protest, but then smirked at Mimi and left the room quickly. What was all this about? It was true Lucifer had hinted that he'd be happy to take Jack's place as her partner, should she desire it; and she did not. She would much rather French-kiss Barachiel if it came down to it.

Once, a long time ago, she had loved the Dark Prince as her king, her idol. Maybe the old Mimi—who had reigned as the queen of New York and thought nothing of loving and leaving—the Azrael who had brought armies of Heaven to their knees—would have sought Lucifer's love. Would have welcomed it—would have relished being his bride for the power and the glory.

But that Azrael and that Mimi were long gone. Mimi had changed. Maybe it was due to centuries upon centuries of being cursed as a vampire—the many years living away from Paradise and the beauty of the eternal kingdom—but she was no longer the Dark Angel she once was. There was no longer any love in her immortal soul for the bright beautiful prince before her. She saw through his beauty, through his lies. He had brought the angels nothing but ruin and sorrow, she saw now. Evil was seductive and easy, and virtue was difficult and unappreciated.

If he desired her, she would fight him. She would never let him take her like a cheap whore to his bed. She would die before she gave up her body to his lust. But perhaps if he allowed her to be close enough to him, she could do what Michael had failed to do—she could destroy him.

"Yes, my lord?" she asked with her sweetest smile. "How can I please my lord and master?"

It appeared she was wrong about his intentions. Lucifer barely acknowledged the hidden invitation in her words. She studied his face more closely and realized his look of triumph was gone; she wondered if it had been a front for Jack and the other angels. Perhaps Schuyler was not the last barrier to their victory, after all.

"Is there a problem, my lord?" she asked. "Something you didn't tell Abbadon and Danel?"

Lucifer frowned. "If they perform their task quickly and efficiently, then all should go as planned. But yes, there have been some . . . developments. Complications. Involving Araquiel, as a matter of fact. He remains a thorn in my side."

Mimi didn't like where this was going.

"His theft of the grail that you were supposed to steal would not present major problems for us were it not for the fact that he took something from me when he left the underworld."

He couldn't mean . . . there was no way . . .

"Araquiel has the godsfire in his possession," Lucifer said. "And now he also has a grail, which means he has a weapon to counter ours. He can defend the Gate of Promise."

Yes! Mimi had succeeded, then, in arming the Blue Bloods. Kingsley would defend the gate. She felt her love for him expand beyond her consciousness. They had hope yet.

"I am sending you aboveground to deal with him."

"Deal with him? Has he expressed a willingness to negotiate?"

The Dark Prince laughed, a hollow, angry sound. "Negotiate? No, I mean you're going to have to take care of him. *Remove him from the equation.* The vampires must not be allowed to use the godsfire. Do you understand me?"

She understood.

She had been given the same orders that Jack had received.

To kill her love.

Mimi wanted to laugh. She'd been so worried that by sending Danel to Jack, she'd made herself responsible for Lucifer's having access to a chalice; now it turned out that by forcing Kingsley to steal the chalice from her, she'd set him up to die. At her hand, nonetheless.

"You will take this with you," he said, gifting her with an emerald stone. Lucifer's Bane. "It will allow me to see what you see, to hear what you hear. You will report to me directly on this mission. I cannot send any of the Dark Angels or

166

demons with you, as Araquiel will recognize them for what they are. But you—as you must be aware—Araquiel always harbored an unrequited affection for you."

Unrequited? Ha.

Lucifer smiled. "Perhaps you can use this infatuation to win his trust."

Mimi returned the smile. Perhaps she could.

"If you fail me, Azrael, this stone you wear will destroy you and Abbadon both, as well as the lives of everyone around you."

She was wearing a ticking time bomb around her neck.

"Azrael? Can I count on you?"

"Of course, my lord. Your will is my oath." What else was there to say?

TWENTY-SIX

Bliss

Lawson and his pack were waiting for Bliss outside the airport in Rome when she arrived. It felt like forever since she'd seen them, but it had only been a couple of days. She supposed her sense of time was all screwed up because of losing a year. It felt strange to see them all here, in this city, where they'd been so recently and yet such a long time ago. The Rome they had left was the city at its first breath, but the Rome they were in now was a sprawling and crowded metropolis, ancient ruins among medieval and Renaissance structures, a hodgepodge of architecture and industry, the Eternal City and a thoroughly modern one.

Bliss noticed that when Lawson saw her, his eyes lit up, but he kept his cool. She kept her feelings in check as well, even though she couldn't help but hold him just a little tighter when they hugged hello.

"So what's the plan?" she asked.

The boys looked at each other, then at the ground. Ahramin smirked. Bliss had the urge to slap her, but then again, she always had the urge to slap her, even after everything that had happened.

"No plan. Right. Okay, then at least tell me what Arthur said."

"He told us there was a rupture in the timeline, that something had happened that wasn't supposed to, and now there were two versions of the timeline. That's what closed the passages," Lawson said. "We have to figure out what it was and then find a way to open the passages up. Then we can go back to the underworld for the wolves."

"Did he give you any sense of how we should go about doing that?" she asked.

"Apparently we need your help," Ahramin said. "Even though we were doing just fine on our own."

"We know the break in the timeline happened here," Lawson said. "But we don't know when or how. Just that it was sometime after when we were here, during the height of the Roman Empire, during Caligula's reign, when they first discovered the Paths of the Dead and established the first Gate of Hell. Arthur thought you might be able to help us with your memories. That maybe we can find the path that way."

"My mother's memories? Or my father's?"

"Either one," Lawson said, looking uncomfortable. Her father was still a touchy subject.

"Okay, so maybe we'll start digging into what we know about Caligula—if there are certain monuments in the city that he built, or that are associated with him. Maybe we can start there and see where it leads. The Paths of the Dead are hidden in the glom, but they begin with a physical location here in mid-world." Bliss looked at the pack. They were all still exhausted from having traveled back in time and fought a great battle; and she was feeling just as fatigued. "But first, let's all get some sleep. I bet none of you slept on the plane."

"I did." Malcolm smiled.

"All right, where are we staying?"

The boys looked at each other again.

"You haven't figured out anything, have you?" Bliss said, but she tried to say it gently. Lawson looked uncomfortable; she knew he felt embarrassed at how unprepared they were. "We could stay at the St. Regis," she said. "I stayed there last time I was here."

"No. Nothing fancy," Lawson said. "That's not our style."

"Okay. There are lots of youth hostels around here—I'm sure we can find someplace where we can all stay together."

They took the train from the airport and found a cheap place downtown that looked clean. Since it was winter, and past the season for winter break travel, they managed to get a dorm room all to themselves.

"We all have to stay in one room?" Ahramin said, curling her lip.

"At least there's no one else here," Rafe said. "Come on, it will be fun. Like being back in the den."

The hostel was sparsely furnished but cozy. Downstairs, where they'd checked in, was a small common area with scratchy wool sofas and a shelf full of magazines and books that other travelers had left behind. They definitely weren't catering just to Americans, Bliss noted, seeing just about every language she recognized and a whole bunch she didn't. That was probably a good thing, and why the place was so inexpensive. There was also a kitchen where they could make sandwiches—nothing hot, but there was bread and condiments and some cheese in the refrigerator, along with bottles of juice. So depressing to be eating a peanut-butter-and-jelly sandwich in Italy, but Bliss was sure there would be time for a good meal once they'd figured out what they were doing.

Upstairs were several dormitory-style rooms, with eight beds in each. Bliss quickly staked out one of the beds closest to the door. If she'd learned anything these past few years, it was the importance of being able to make a quick exit. Apparently, Lawson was on the same page, because he did the same thing.

Malcolm took the bed closest to the window, so he could leave it open in case he started to feel sick. It was always possible that the break in time had something to do with the Hellhounds, and there was a slim chance that Malcolm would be able to catch the scent.

Bliss watched Ahramin walk up and down the row of beds, trying to decide where she wanted to stake her claim. Sure enough, she took the bed right next to Lawson. Edon looked irritated, but he didn't say anything.

What was going on here? Bliss was confused. Ahramin had been instrumental in their victory over Romulus. The former Hellhound had fought against her collar and lived. Ahramin and Edon had seemed happy enough to be back together again. Had something happened since then? How could it, since Bliss had been present nearly the whole time? Was it something else? Something that had happened back when they were still in the underworld, maybe?

"Guess I'm back here with Mac," Rafe said, throwing his bag on the cot closest to the window.

Edon looked as if he were going to protest, but then put his things down between Rafe and Ahri. "Are we sure they aren't going to put more people in here?"

"They promised," Bliss said. "No guarantees on the bathrooms, though. They're unisex and only one person can go in at a time. And I hate to say it, but they're totally gross."

It was true. She'd been fooled by the cleanliness of the rest of the hostel; the bathrooms were tiny and infested with mold and mildew. She was barely going to be able to make herself shower, and she'd only go in if she had to.

The problem was, where was she supposed to change?

As if to answer her question, Ahramin started stripping off her clothes. "Guess we won't be keeping any secrets from each other," she said lazily, standing in the middle of the room in only her bra and underwear. Bliss was annoyed until she noticed the scars that remained on the girl's neck, and reminded herself that Ahri hadn't had it easy.

Bliss put on her pajamas as discreetly as possible. No need to make a spectacle of herself, as Ahramin had. Pajama top over regular top, regular top removed through the neck hole of the pajama top, bra removed through the sleeves of the pajama top. Piece of cake. Just the pants left, and who cared if she showed her legs?

She looked up to see Lawson stifling, and then failing to stifle, a laugh. "What?" she asked.

"You," he said. "That. I thought you were going to sprain something in there."

"Shush," she said, laughing as well. She smacked him on his bare chest with her balled-up top.

He grabbed it from her and pulled her close. "Hey," he said. "I missed you."

She snuggled into his arms, forgetting where they were for a moment.

"Get a room!" Malcolm yelled.

"We did!" Lawson yelled back, but he let Bliss go and she sighed.

"Good night," he whispered when they were tucked into their respective beds. He stretched his hand so that their fingertips were touching.

"Good night," she said, knowing it would be difficult to sleep so close and yet so far from him.

TWENTY-SEVEN

Schuyler

"Excuse me?" Schuyler asked. "Cordelia told you what?"

Decca shook her head. "I'm sorry—we didn't know. If we had known you existed, we would never have kept away. What you must think of us!"

How could Cordelia have done this to me? Schuyler wondered. How could she have cut me off from my father's family so completely? What was she thinking? But then again, given what Allegra had done, wasn't Cordelia merely acting in the Coven's best interests? From her point of view, she was cleaning up her daughter's mess by severing all ties to Allegra's human mistake.

Decca reached over to the tray on the coffee table and poured two glasses of iced tea. Then, to Schuyler's surprise, she burst into tears. "I knew something was strange. She'd told us not to bother with Allegra's funeral. We didn't even

know where to send flowers, and there was no announcement or anything. I should have tried harder to get to the
truth. I always thought she was hiding something from me.
So your mother was Allegra—of course, I saw it the moment
you walked in the room, and you look so much like your
father. . . . You—"

"Have his eyes." Schuyler smiled.

"Yes." Her grandmother nodded. "I'm so happy!" Decca
suddenly cried out, and clasped Schuyler's hand.

That did it—Schuyler started crying too. And she'd
been so adamant that she wouldn't. "Me too," she sniffled.

They spent a quiet moment holding hands and crying,
and then Decca straightened her back, shook her head, and
composed herself. "Your mother made him so happy. They
loved each other so much."

Schuyler nodded. She hadn't quite managed to stop crying yet, but she took a sip of iced tea and tried to hold it
together.

"After the wedding, they lived in Napa for a while, but
Allegra missed New York. They moved to the city and disappeared shortly afterward, and we didn't hear from them for
a long time. I tried getting in touch—I called your mother,
your grandmother, I wrote letters, but nothing. It wasn't like
Ben, but we respected his privacy. Your mother had always
been . . . *different*, but perhaps I was too cautious, too willing
to step aside, and then it was too late."

Schuyler wondered if Decca could tell that she was

"different" too. Most likely. She had the sense that not much got by this new grandmother of hers. The vampires must have had to work overtime to keep her from figuring out what was going on. "It doesn't matter anymore," she said. "I'm here now, and we're finally meeting each other."

"Yes, it's wonderful, isn't it?" Decca beamed. "I want you to tell me all about yourself. We have so much catching up to do! Are you in school now? Is there a young man in your life? Tell me everything!"

Tell her everything? That was impossible. But she could edit, she supposed. She told Decca about growing up with Cordelia, living on the Upper West Side, and going to Duchesne. She told her about her brief stint modeling, how she hadn't figured out what she wanted to do with her life yet (not exactly true, but at least it explained why she wasn't going to college). And then she took a deep breath and told her about Jack.

How to explain Jack?

"There was someone in my life," she said. "I was in love. It was hard—there were challenges for us, being together— but it was wonderful."

"You're using the past tense," Decca said. "What happened?"

"I'm still not entirely sure," Schuyler said. "All I know is that he's gone, and I don't think he's ever coming back."

"I lost my husband too," Decca said, reaching out to again clasp Schuyler's hand. "I understand that feeling of

177

loss, that sense that a part of you has been physically taken away. That you're diminished, less than you once were."

"That's exactly it," Schuyler said. "There's something missing in me now, and I don't know if I'll ever get it back."

"You're young," Decca said. "I know that's what people say, and it seems impossible now, but your heart will mend, and perhaps in the future . . ."

But Schuyler wasn't ready to think about what her life could be like after Jack. And she had far more important concerns than herself; although the thought of Jack really and truly being gone forever was too much, and she found herself starting to cry again. Get it together, she thought.

"I can see that it's too soon for you to think about it," Decca said. "I understand—even at my age I have friends who try to arrange dates for me. I don't have the heart to tell them I'm not ready and I may never be, though it's been years."

"But you have other family," Schuyler said. "Your granddaughter . . ."

"Yes, Finn!" Decca brightened. "You really must meet her. She'll be so thrilled to hear that she has a sister."

Schuyler hoped that would turn out to be true, but she could easily imagine a reality in which it wasn't.

"Do you have other children?" Schuyler asked.

"No, I'm afraid Bendix was our only child," Decca said. "Of course we tried, for years and years, but we didn't have all the marvelous technological advances you young people have these days. If you couldn't manage it naturally, there was only so much the doctors could do.

"It's a blessing that we've found each other, isn't it?" Decca said. "Where are you staying? I insist that you move your things here and stay with me for a while, if you're not otherwise occupied."

"I wish that I could," Schuyler said, and she really meant it. "But . . ." She had no idea how to explain why she couldn't stay. She'd have to come up with something. "Some friends of mine are in trouble. I'm in the middle of helping them out—I came down here to help—and I need to get back to them."

"I see," Decca said, clearly disappointed. "Well, I won't keep you, then."

"No, it's not like that!" Schuyler said. "I want to stay, really I do. And I hope that if you'll have me, I can come back someday."

Decca smiled. "Of course you can. You do what you need to do. I'll be here when you return."

"There's just one more thing I have to ask before I go," Schuyler said.

"About your father?"

Schuyler nodded.

"I figured you would," Decca said.

"He did come back to you, eventually, didn't he?" Schuyler said.

"Yes, he did." She smiled sadly.

"I need to find him. Do you know where he is?"

"I do," Decca said, giving her a concerned look.

"Where is he?"

"He's here."

The journey aboveground was lonelier this time. The train ride through the bleak landscape of rock and cinder seemed endless without Jack to keep her company; all Mimi could think about was how she was going to get out of this one. The emerald stone hung heavy around her neck. Lucifer's Bane. The burden she carried, Lucifer's wrath, unleashed upon everyone she loved. She and Jack had not fooled him for one moment. Truly, they were the fools.

How had it come to this, she wondered. It was so much easier before, when she and Jack would go through the motions of bonding. Sure, this cycle wasn't the court of Versailles or Florence during the Renaissance, but up until now they had lived pretty fabulous lives in New York. How had everything gotten so complicated?

It was the birth of Schuyler Van Alen, Mimi realized.

Gabrielle's half-human child had triggered everything—she was the catalyst for change—but was this what Gabrielle had wanted? The Coven in ruins, the vampires in retreat, the Gate of Promise on the brink of destruction, and the key to Heaven in the enemy's grasp?

What was Mimi going to do? She had to warn them— had to warn Kingsley and Schuyler and Oliver what was about to happen—but how? She supposed there was a Venator safe house somewhere; that was the only reason Kingsley was in London, she was sure of it. But where? Maybe Jack had found it. It was a pity they hadn't been able to talk before he'd left—hadn't been able to coordinate their actions, their deceptions.

Jack, where's the safe house?

You're here? Why are you aboveground?

Looking for Kingsley. Lucifer gave me a job, too.

What is it?

Can't get into it right now. Do you know where the safe house is?

Still looking.

Let me know if you find it. I can help distract Danel, give our friends time to get away.

There was a time when Mimi could have gone to just about any fabulous restaurant or club in London and found a vampire to point her in the right direction. She hadn't noticed it the last time she was in town, but she did now. It was eerie. London had been drained of vampires—pun definitely intended. There was no one left. Not in the usual hot spots, not in the boys' clubs, not anywhere. She felt a piercing sadness at the reality of the current situation.

She called the old families in New York, spoke to a few remaining brave souls, but no one knew where the Venators were hiding in London. "We're all just lying low until we hear from someone in charge," they told her.

She wanted to scream that *she* was in charge, but it wouldn't help matters. Finally, she went with the most mundane approach she could imagine: she called Oliver's parents. The Conduits had scattered too—but Oliver's family was so predictable. They were like ostriches hiding their heads in the sand while everything else was on display. They were "hiding" in Southampton. Water Mill, to be exact.

"Please, you need to tell me where he is," she said. "It's important."

"We haven't heard from him in a while," Mrs. Hazard-Perry said. "He was in London, but then something happened in the Repository—he could be back in the States. We're worried about him. If you do find him, will you tell him to get in touch?"

"Where was he in London? I'll make sure he calls you when I find him."

"We really aren't supposed to tell anyone," she said. "We're under strictest orders."

"From who?" Mimi said. Who was calling the shots in the Coven?

"Venator Martin, of course."

Of course. Kingsley was leading them.

"It's really important; you know I wouldn't be calling otherwise."

Mrs. Hazard-Perry sighed.

Mimi could tell she was almost there. "He's in great danger. I can only help if I know where the safe house is. I promise I'll do everything I can to make sure he's okay."

Apparently that was enough; Mrs. Hazard-Perry gave her the address.

Mimi barely remembered to say thank you before getting off the phone and into a minicab. She gave the driver the address and tried to mentally prepare for what she was supposed to do. There had to be a way out of this, even if she had a virtual ball and chain to the Dark Prince around her neck. She had to find a way to clue Kingsley in, stage some sort of fight where he could fake his death and she could help him escape.

Traffic was heavy as the minicab approached the address Oliver's mother had given her. That was weird—it wasn't a particularly populated neighborhood, and it was far away from any of the busy parts of London. Then she saw the police cars, and the tape that cordoned off the street. Blue and white for London, unlike the blue and yellow of New York.

"What's going on?" she asked the cab driver.

"Dunno, miss. I'll get as close as I can, but you might have to walk the rest of the way."

He drove down the street, right up to the tape. "I'm afraid this is the address you were looking for," he said. He parked in front of the safe house. Or what used to be the safe house.

It had burned to the ground.

Mimi jumped out of the cab and moved through the crowd congregated on the sidewalk. There was a woman off to the side, crying softly. Mimi approached her carefully. "Are you all right?"

The woman sniffed and blew her nose into a handkerchief. "I'm fine," she said. "Just out of a job." She looked at the smoking wreckage of the house and then started crying again.

"Did you work here?" Mimi asked.

The woman nodded. "I was a maid. It was a good job, it was. Lots to clean with all of those parties, but it was honest work."

Sounded like Kingsley, all right.

"I knew the people who were staying here," Mimi said. "They weren't in there, were they, when this happened?"

The woman shook her head. "The young lady and her friend left days ago. Everyone else left last night. Like they knew something bad was going to happen."

"Did they know?"

"Not so's they told the staff. Though I heard they gave everyone the night off, so perhaps there was something afoot. Didn't tell those of us on the schedule for today,

185

though. We all showed up this morning to find this."

"And you're sure all of them left," Mimi said. "Do you have any idea where they went?"

"None at all," the maid said. "But if you find them, tell them they owe us a week's pay."

Mimi wanted to hug her. They were alive! Her friends were alive! Thank God. Kingsley was alive. She gave the woman a few bills from her purse. "Here. They'd want you to have this."

Who had done this? Had Lucifer sent another convoy without Jack's and Mimi's knowledge? She walked around the perimeter, slipping through the Red Blood barriers easily. In the back of the house, behind the rubble, she found the answer.

Jack was holding the torch.

"You did this?" she asked, shocked.

"It was too late. They were gone."

Thank God. Thank God. You knew they were gone, didn't you? Thank God.

But Jack did not reply.

"Jack? Are you okay?"

"What is the point of this?" he said, kicking a rock on the ground.

"What do you mean?"

"I mean, what are we doing here?"

"Jack, again, I don't know what you're saying," she said.

"All this that we've done—for centuries, Mimi. We

fought on the wrong side during the War, and even when we turned to the Light we were punished for it. Centuries we lived on earth, cycling through our lives. Rome. France. Plymouth. Hoping for salvation. Seeking redemption for our sins. For what? For *this*?"

"What are you saying?" Mimi asked, horrified. She had never heard him speak like this, or look so murderous and frustrated at the same time. She put a hand on the stone around her neck to warn him, but he didn't notice.

"Maybe we're trying too hard. Maybe we should just . . ."

"Give up?"

"Exactly. Why fight it? Why are we here? So that we can leave each other? Why?" He pulled her to him. "Why did I ever want to do that?" he whispered, putting his nose in her hair and breathing in her scent.

She found she was responding to him, to his touch, that familiar way he held her—had always held her. It had been so long since he'd held her that way. But why now? Why did he have to say these things now? Then she realized, even if he meant it, she didn't want to hear it. Even if he wanted her back, she didn't want him back.

She pushed him away from her. "You don't mean it— you don't mean what you're saying." She could feel the tears in her eyes. She loved him, she realized now, because he was always fighting the dark that was in him, that was part of him. He wanted so hard to be good, even though he was made for this. He was made for evil. He was the reason Lucifer had almost triumphed. If Jack had not turned at the last moment, Heaven would have been theirs so long ago.

"I am tired of pretending I am what I am not. That I do not want what I want."

"Jack, stop it, you're scaring me."

"My name isn't Jack Force. My name is ABBADON. I am made of dark and shadow. I am made of the underworld." Then the darkness left him as quickly as it had come. Jack smiled at her, his brilliant, handsome, heartbreaking smile. "Why wait for salvation, Azrael, when we can take it for ourselves?"

TWENTY-NINE

Bliss

The next morning, Bliss woke up early and put her things in her hostel locker. She found Edon and Ahramin whispering fiercely. Edon looked tired and annoyed; his eyes were red-rimmed, and Ahramin had her usual smirk.

"Everything all right?" Bliss asked.

Ahramin gazed at her coolly and didn't answer.

The rest of the boys woke up, and the group headed outside to figure out where to begin the search. "I did a little digging and discovered a few of the projects that were under construction when Caligula was emperor," Malcolm said, holding up his mobile phone. "There's a few bridges and aqueducts, but the most important one is the Circus Maximus—the racetrack he built in the middle of the city, with the Egyptian obelisk in the middle."

"Should we start there?" Lawson asked.

Bliss shrugged. "Sounds like as good a place as any. Where is it?"

"Of course the racetrack doesn't exist anymore. They built St. Peter's on top of it."

"Of course." Ahramin smirked, but everyone ignored her.

"The most famous tomb in the world," Malcolm noted.

"So the path to Hell lies right under Vatican City?" Ahramin asked. "Does that sound right to you guys?"

"Stranger things have happened in the history of the vampires," said Bliss. "Besides, when Caligula ordered its construction, it was an arena—a sports stadium, not the Holy See."

St. Peter's Square was stunning. The weather was unseasonably warm, and the sun brightened the pillars surrounding the square and made them almost glow.

"Did you know St. Peter was the first Pope? That's why he's buried here," Malcolm told them.

"Thanks for the history lesson," Ahramin said. "If we'd wanted to play tourist, we could have hired a guide. Let's just get on with it."

Why did she have to be so awful all the time? "I'm interested in learning about it," Bliss said, more to torture Ahri than out of real interest.

Malcolm gave her a grateful look. "Michelangelo designed part of the dome. But I'm more excited about seeing the Sistine Chapel; not that I'll be able to." He sighed.

Oh, right. Denizens of the underworld were not allowed in places touched by the Divine, and St. Peter's Basilica was hallowed ground, one of the most sacred places in all of Christendom.

"What I don't understand is how *you* can go in, considering who your father is," Ahramin said to Bliss.

"It doesn't matter. Bliss and I will go in and check it out. You guys try to keep your eyes open out here. See if you can see anything in the glom that could be a portal," Lawson instructed. "Come on," he said to Bliss, and they followed the line of tourists entering the basilica.

They walked around the magnificent cathedral, marveling at the grandeur of the soaring ceilings and the breathtaking, dazzling interior. They were pilgrims before the altar of God, dwarfed by His glory.

"Anything?" Lawson asked.

Bliss shook her head.

"All right, next room," Lawson said.

They spent the rest of the day wandering through the various highlights in the Holy See. Bliss wished they could be there under other circumstances; the ceiling of the Sistine Chapel was marvelous, but she couldn't really appreciate it—she was too focused on trying to figure out where a path underground might lead; if there were telltale signs in the glom that could give away the presence of the ancient portal.

But all they saw was beautiful art, throngs of tourists, and gorgeous murals. There was nothing to indicate that the place was anything other than a holy and sacred space.

They found the boys and Ahramin waiting for them outside, with no news either. It was the end of the day and the pack was exhausted. After stopping for *pizza al taglio*, they went back to the hostel.

Ahramin changed for bed in what was becoming her usual striptease, but both Lawson and Edon seemed to be making a special effort not to pay attention, which clearly annoyed her. Bliss was determined not to give Lawson another chance to laugh at her, so she pretended she was alone in the room and changed as quickly as she could. But not before she glanced at Lawson, who quickly looked away.

So he'd been watching her, then. Not Ahramin, but her. She suppressed a smile.

The thought of it made her skin tingle, but it wasn't quite enough to keep her awake, given how tired she was. She fell asleep almost as soon as her head hit the pillow.

It wasn't long before she wished she hadn't, though. The nightmare started right away. She was in a dark place, underground somewhere, as best as she could tell, but it was strange—she could also see herself as if from outside her own body.

Wait—not her own body. Somebody else's. Someone familiar but not known to her.

Allegra? Was it her mother running through the maze?

Whoever it was, she was scared out of her mind. Bliss felt her fear, the sweat on her forehead, the pumping of her heart. Terror. Utter terror. Bliss felt the menacing presence draw closer, and she knew something awful was about to happen. Both of her perspectives seemed to be closing in on one another; it wouldn't be long before they would connect somehow, and maybe then she could figure out what was going on. . . .

But before it could happen, she woke up.

She must have gasped, or made some sort of noise, because she'd barely sat up in bed before Lawson rushed over to her. "What is it?" he whispered. "Are you okay?"

"Just a nightmare," she whispered back. "I'm fine."

"You're not—you're shaking," he said.

It was true—she was cold all of a sudden, and she couldn't stop shivering.

"Lift the blanket," Lawson said, and crawled in beside her. "Here, lie down."

His body was warm and comforting against hers. She buried her head in his chest. "I was so scared," she said. "It was like I was in two places at once, and something disastrous was going to happen. And I couldn't stop it, and part of me might have even been responsible. I was so confused," she said, and then tears came to her eyes. She could still feel the horror in her body. She had never felt so frightened. Who was that girl? What was happening to her? Was it Allegra? If so, what was she running from?

"It's okay," Lawson said. "It's all going to be okay." He kissed the top of her head and put his arms around her. They were lying together so that his chin rested on her forehead, and he began to kiss her gently at first, and then more passionately, as if not only to comfort her but to let her know, finally, how sorry he was about the way he'd left her back in New York.

Lawson moved his body against hers. His hands were entangled in her hair, and her legs were wrapped around his torso, and it was wonderful, he was so wonderful, and she lost herself in the sensation of their being together again, until the blanket slipped and she remembered they were in a room with four other people.

"Not here," she whispered. "We can't."

Lawson said nothing, but he was already moving away. He must have known she was right, though she would have liked him to protest a little harder.

"Our timing is bad," she told him.

He kissed her one more time before going back to his own bed. "Sleep well."

As if.

chuyler texted Oliver when she left Decca's house. *Need you. Come back? I can't do this alone.*

Oliver returned to Los Angeles on the next available flight. Whatever duties he had to the Repository, his duties as her Conduit and friend always came first. Schuyler met him outside the airport and jumped into his arms as soon as he came out the door.

"Oh, hey," he said. "I missed you too." But she noticed he returned her hug rather awkwardly.

"I'm sorry . . ." She felt a little embarrassed at being so enthusiastic to see him, especially after everything that had happened between them.

"It's okay." He patted her back and stepped away from her, just the tiniest bit, and Schuyler understood that, while they were still friends, things had changed, and she couldn't take him for granted anymore. Whatever had happened with that witch in the East Village had really worked. He was his own man now.

"I have so much to tell you, I hardly know where to start," she said. "But first—tell me what happened in New York."

Oliver shook his head. "It wasn't good. The Repository's been destroyed, and Renfield was murdered. The Silver Bloods can break the wards now, so the Coven is basically unprotected."

Schuyler accepted this information; it was nothing new. The vampires' strength had weakened considerably since the Covens had disbanded.

"And it looks like someone else was there too. They rifled through the notes. The files were left open."

"Who?"

"I don't know." Oliver sighed. "Whoever it was used Bliss's code."

Bliss! Schuyler felt a glimmer of hope. "Do you think it was her?"

"Maybe. If luck is on our side. Remember Jane Murray? Our old history teacher? She has the spirit of the Watcher now, and she's back too. She made contact with the Coven. She's helping them to locate Bliss, see if she has the wolves."

So many pieces to this puzzle of theirs; so many things that had to happen before they had any chance of succeeding. And so many complications.

They walked toward the parking lot for the car. Oliver said, "There's more. The Silver Bloods burned down our safe house in London. Don't worry, no one was hurt—it was empty when they torched it. And the good news is that Kingsley's back."

"Where'd he go?"

"He wouldn't say, but wherever he went, he said he knows now what the demons are planning, and he thinks he might have an idea on how to subvert it. He's called for a Venator conclave to plan the attack."

"Attack?"

"He thinks it's better to draw them out, especially now that we know they're on to us and they found the safe house so easily. Since we know where the Gate of Promise is, he'd rather have them bring the battle to us than wait for them to sneak up on us. Show all our cards, as they say. Make it happen."

"Is that wise?"

"Who am I to judge? I'm just a lowly Conduit, not a Venator. But strategically, I think it's wise. We don't know when the Silver Bloods plan to ambush the gate, but this way, we can have the upper hand. We can prepare." He wiped his forehead with the back of his hand. "So tell me what's been happening here? Did you have a happy little reunion with your grandmother? Was she round and soft? Did she bake you cookies?"

Schuyler punched him in the arm. "Don't make fun! No, there weren't any cookies." She rolled her eyes. As far as she knew, neither of Oliver's grandmothers were the cookie-baking type either. Doro Samuels had worked to preserve Grand Central Terminal and Central Park, while Eleanor Hazard-Perry was a children's programming pioneer who taught kids how to read using tactics gleaned from vampire skills of instant memorization.

"She was cool, a grande dame, sort of like Cordelia but, you know . . . warmer," Schuyler said.

"Warm-blooded." Oliver smiled. "And did you find your dad?"

"Yeah," she said. "Come on."

The grass at the graveyard was lush and green, almost too alive, Schuyler thought. It was like a constant reminder of everything that was gone, everything lost. She'd brought a small bouquet of calla lilies, and when they found the headstone, she set them down.

"Sky, I'm so sorry," Oliver said. "I know this wasn't how you hoped it would turn out." He put an arm around her shoulder, and she leaned against him as she read the headstone.

STEPHEN BENDIX CHASE

BELOVED SON AND HUSBAND

The headstone didn't tell the whole story of his life, Schuyler thought, thinking not only of herself but of the sister she had yet to meet. Beloved son, husband, and *father*.

He had returned to his family in a box.

"Cancer," Schuyler told Oliver. "Stupid old cancer. He wasn't killed by a vampire. He wasn't killed by Charles out of revenge, as I'd feared for a while. He was just another young person taken too early."

Decca had told her the whole story: how Ben and Allegra had gone back to New York and how in the end, Allegra had called them so they could say good-bye to their son. The disease had been swift and brutal. When they returned from the funeral, they discovered that they had a grandchild, as his ex-girlfriend had showed up at their doorstep with a baby. Renny had told Ben she was pregnant to get him to marry her, but when she admitted it was a fake pregnancy, he'd left to be with Allegra. Only it wasn't fake: Renny had figured out that he would never love her like he loved Allegra, and she'd freed him to be with her.

"Noble of her, I suppose," Decca had said, though Schuyler could tell that until she'd learned about Schuyler, she'd have preferred that Ben had stayed with the ex, Renny.

"Allegra was so distraught. She kept saying it was all her fault, that she had tried to get him to see a doctor for months, that he'd been coughing up blood but had insisted nothing was wrong. Then Cordelia wrote us this letter not long after, and we always assumed Allegra had died of a broken heart."

It was true in a way, Schuyler thought, remembering her mother lying motionless in a hospital bed.

"What was he like?" Schuyler asked.

"Ben?" Decca sighed. "I know mothers are biased, but Ben was one of the good ones, you know? He had *it*—whatever it was. He was so handsome, and everyone loved him, and he was always so kind—I think that's what mattered more— not his good looks—but that he was a *good soul*. I don't mean nice or polite, but someone who had a strong moral compass, someone with character. He was privileged, of course, but he wasn't spoiled. He was such a generous person. Like I said, he loved your mother so much. She was everything to him. It was a shame that he never knew his daughters. He would have been such a good father. He adored children."

Schuyler knelt down at the grave and ran her hand over the headstone. The granite was cool under her fingers and sparkled in the sunlight, glinting gray and pink. *I wish I'd had a chance to know you. I wish that so much.*

You'd have loved him, said a voice in her head. Allegra, inside her, grieving as well. She had not felt her mother's spirit in a while; it was different from the watchful presence that came and went. Schuyler could feel the warm love she always felt when Allegra was with her. *Your grandmother spoke true. He was a wonderful man. He was the most unselfish, generous person I knew. He was such a happy person, he made me so happy. We were happy together until the end. I thought he would get a chance to know you. When I first met him, I saw a vision of the three of us together, of him at my bedside at your birth. But it was not to be. He was taken away too early. A few weeks after he passed, I discovered I was pregnant with you. Cordelia did what she did to protect you. I hope you find it in your heart to forgive her one day.*

That's why she changed my name, Schuyler realized. To hide me from my father's family. Because I was not supposed to exist. I am half human and half vampire. An Abomination. My father never even knew me, and my mother only cared for the survival of the vampires.

Schuyler realized she had been holding on to a dream— that her father might still be alive and her mother would return.

It would never happen, not now, not ever.

Not in this lifetime, maybe, Allegra said. *But the best that is in you is from him. He was the most unselfish person I ever knew. When he learned who and what I was, he told me to forgive Charles, that it was important I return to him. He wanted that for me, for us. Sometimes love means letting go, he said. Remember that when you arrive at the crossroads. When time stands still. When the path is open to you. Remember who your father was.*

Oliver knelt down beside her. "You okay?"

Schuyler wiped a few errant tears off her cheeks and nodded, then stood up.

"This means we were wrong about the whole Blood of the Father thing," she said. "But there's still one more thing I'd like to do before we go back. Will you help me?"

"Of course I will. What is it?"

"I know this isn't really related to what we're doing, and I understand that we don't have a lot of time, but it turns out that before my father got back together with my mother, he had another girlfriend. And she had a baby. That means . . ."

"That you have a sister," Oliver said. "How many secret sisters can one girl have?" he joked.

"Funny," Schuyler said. "But I don't know if you can imagine what it means to me to know that I have more family out there. I need to find her."

They went back to the hotel and got on Oliver's computer. "Tell me her name," he said.

"Finn Chase, I think. Actually, I don't know—I'm not sure if she was using her mother's name, and I don't know what that is."

But Oliver was typing away. "Just Googled her. Got a Seraphina Chase on Facebook, goes by Finn." He pulled up her profile page. "Could this be her?"

Schuyler peered at the picture and recognized the girl from the photographs. "That's her."

"Let's see what she's like. Binge-drinking photos? Embarrassing status updates?"

Finn must have been a trusting soul, because she didn't have any privacy settings that would prevent them from looking at everything. There were lots of pictures—with her mom, her grandmother, her friends. In all of them she was smiling, happy. Unlike Oliver's predictions, there weren't any incriminating photographs, although there were a few obligatory shots of Finn holding a red Solo cup at parties.

"Hmm. Hopelessly wholesome, but that's U of Chicago for you. Supposedly everyone studies too much there," Oliver said. "A bunch of grinds."

"You'd fit right in," Schuyler teased.

"She looks a little bit like you," he said.

Schuyler couldn't see it at first—Finn was blond, to start. But then she looked closer and saw that they both shared the same blue eyes.

"She's pretty," Oliver said.

There was a time, Schuyler knew, when that statement would have elicited a pang of jealousy. She waited for it, but it never came.

"I want to meet her," she said, staring at the photo stream. It was like looking at what her life might have been, a gallery of everything that she had lost. Finn had a mom who loved her, grandparents who doted on her, and friends who clearly adored her, from the numerous "likes" on her page to the messages they scrawled on her wall. It was hard not to feel a little envious of the sister she never knew.

Allegra's legacy had been one of grief, pain, suffering, and war.

But Finn Chase was Ben's daughter. A normal human girl, with a normal life, a normal heart.

"Will you come with me to Chicago?" she asked Oliver.

A week had passed since Mimi and Jack had parted ways at the burning house. She had no idea what had gotten into him—he had to be lying, he had to be up to something—there was no way—no way he meant what he said. Or did he? They had spent a long time in the underworld, after all. She had to admit everything he had said was something she had wrestled with herself. Why be good? Why do the right thing when being bad was their true nature, when it was so much easier to give in?

What's happened to you? she sent him. *What are you doing? Tell me. I can help.* But once again, there was no answer.

Well then, she would have to figure out how to get out of her predicament on her own, as usual. If she was going to warn Kingsley, she would have to find him first. Where was he now that the safe house was no more? Where would he have gone, she wondered. What resources were left to him, with the Coven bankrupt and the vampires underground. It was too distressing to think that Lucifer might actually win this fight. There was only one thing left to do.

Have a cup of tea.

She was in London, after all.

The Ritz was a little too flashy, and all those shops at Harrods had too much tourist riffraff. Only Fortnum & Mason would do. The St. James restaurant, tucked away on the fourth floor, was sufficiently removed from the bustle of London to give her the feeling she was getting away from it all for a bit.

No sooner had she settled in with a pot of Assam tea and spooned a heap of clotted cream on her scone than a girl sat down in the empty chair across from her. "Excuse me," Mimi said shortly. "Can't you see this table is taken?"

"You really don't recognize me, do you?" the girl asked. She had an American accent—curious. "It's only been a few years. Forgotten the little people from high school already, Mimi?"

High school . . . It seemed like centuries ago. But she'd know the sound of that gossipy voice anywhere. "Piper Crandall?" she asked, incredulous.

"The one and only." Piper smiled. "How the hell are you?"

"What are you doing here?"

"The same thing you are, duh. To answer the call?"

"What call?"

"You know, when the Venators summoned everyone here. Or hadn't you heard?"

She hadn't, at least not officially. But Mimi suspected it wouldn't be in her best interest to admit that. "Right, I thought you meant something else," she said. She realized that if Piper was acting so friendly, it meant, at a minimum, Kingsley hadn't told the Coven that she'd cast her lot with the Dark Angels. Good to know.

"I know," Piper said. "We're a bit late to the party, but I had to convince Max it was the right thing to do. Besides, going underground was cramping our style. I'm so glad we came. Everyone's here! It's like a big reunion."

Mimi nodded. Piper always did like to be in the center of the action.

Piper leaned in. "So—what's going on? No one will tell us, but we know something big is happening." For a moment, Mimi felt like she was back in high school again, with Piper waiting for the good dirt so she could go tell everyone. "Come on, spill. I know you know."

Boy, did she ever, Mimi thought.

"I don't know anything. I'm waiting—just like you," she said.

"But you're our Regent," Piper pointed out. "Someone spotted you on the tube the other day, and sent me to check it out."

"So this isn't just a random encounter," Mimi said. She wasn't sure if that was a good thing or a bad thing.

"Not in the slightest. I volunteered for the job—thought we could catch up. Besides, I didn't believe what everyone is saying."

"What are they saying?" Mimi asked with a raised eyebrow.

"Rumor has it you'd gone back to the underworld, back to the Dark Prince." She sounded a little smug about it.

"Oh?"

"Yes, it's all anyone can talk about." Piper leaned in breathlessly. "So—tell me, is it true?"

Mimi didn't answer.

"So are you . . . ?" Piper asked.

"Of course not! That's ridiculous!" Mimi scoffed. "We pledged our swords to Michael during the battle!"

Piper laughed. "Oh I know, I was just having a bit of fun."

"Right," Mimi said.

"So what's up?" Piper asked again. "Everyone's pretty anxious to feel useful. Hiding is terribly boring. Although, I think the Venators are up to something big. They're supposed to have some sort of conclave in a few days, but they won't tell the rest of the Coven what's going on. Ever since their safe house burned down they're being extra careful."

"They've called for a conclave? Only a Regent or a Regis can do that."

"You want to tell them that?" Piper smirked.

"When is this conclave? And where?"

"I told you, they're not telling anyone anything. You have to be a Venator to know. They're keeping us all in the dark." Piper sighed.

"Is Kingsley Martin part of this?" Mimi asked.

"The Venator who worked the Duchesne case when Aggie died?"

"The very same."

"Yeah. Of course. Kingsley is head spook now."

"Do you know where I can find him?"

Piper shrugged. "Not right now. He's supposedly back in town for the conclave." She lowered her voice conspiratorially. "But he hasn't been out much, which is too bad. Kingsley was a lot of fun before."

"You don't say."

"Yeah, although to be honest, he seemed like kind of a mess. Drinking all the time, lots of girls. But then he was always that way. I heard you guys—?"

Mimi shook her head. "People make up so much stuff these days. Anyway, you were saying . . . ?"

"I heard he woke up one morning with some sense of purpose that he refused to explain, and then he disappeared. Some of us were worried he'd turned, but so far there's no evidence of it."

"So far," Mimi said. "That's why I need to find him."

"He always was a traitor. You can't trust the Silver Bloods," Piper said, loving the gossip. "Like I keep telling Deming Lennox . . ."

"Deming *Lennox*?"

"Where have you been? Deming and Ted got bonded. It was a twin elopement: her sister married his brother. Cute, right? But sort of icky too, if you know what I mean. Think they ever swap?" she asked naughtily.

Sam and Ted Lennox. Kingsley's old team. Of course. They had to know where he was. "Where are they?"

"Who knows? Like I told you, the Venators keep their own counsel these days. They don't tell us anything."

he next morning, Bliss told the pack about her nightmare, about the sense she'd had of being underground but still in Rome. "Is there anything under any of these ancient places? Like tunnels or a part of the city? Maybe under the Colosseum or the Forum or the Pantheon, even? The place we're looking for doesn't necessarily have to have been built during Caligula's time; maybe it just had to exist when he was emperor."

"So full of ideas this morning! So energetic," Ahramin said. "And I thought you surely had to be tired from not getting any sleep last night."

"Who said I didn't get any sleep?" Bliss asked. Had they woken Ahramin up? Had she heard them hooking up? And if so, what was it to her?

"Please," Ahramin said, looking annoyed.

"What's with you?" Edon asked.

Ahramin shrugged and ignored him.

"Don't act like you didn't hear me," Edon said, finally sounding truly angry.

"Stop bickering," Lawson said, ignoring Ahramin's glare. "Bliss, tell us more."

"This dream I had last night, I'm pretty sure it's connected to what we're looking for. I felt like it happened underground."

"Well, there are the catacombs, of course," Malcolm said.

"Breakfast first," Edon said. "We have a long day ahead of us." He went downstairs to the kitchen, pointedly ignoring Ahramin, and the boys followed.

Ahramin lingered behind. "The whole place could hear you," she sneered.

"So what?" Bliss shot back. "What do you care?"

"Ask Lawson."

"I'm asking you," Bliss said, but Ahri had already stormed out of the room.

Great. As if things weren't hard enough.

Bliss pulled Lawson aside as they walked toward the Colosseum, Malcolm's choice for their outing. "What's going on between you and Ahri?" she asked. "She's making me nuts, and I can tell Edon's starting to freak out too."

"There's nothing going on," Lawson said.

"Yeah, right," Bliss said. "Clearly you guys have some

sort of history, and one that Edon doesn't know about. Or didn't, anyway. I think he's on to you, and he's getting pretty pissed off."

"It's not important," Lawson said, but he didn't deny it, and Bliss felt her stomach sink at that. Her suspicions were right, then . . . maybe?

"I'm not sure you're in the best position to decide that right now," said Bliss.

"Well, that's all I have to say about it," Lawson said. "Let it go."

"Not so fast," Bliss yelled as he walked away.

The rest of the pack turned around to look at her.

"Give us a minute," she said, catching up to Lawson and pulling him aside.

"We don't have time for this." He brushed her arm away.

"You're going to have to make time. I don't understand why Ahramin is behaving this way, and I can tell Edon doesn't either. If we're going to work together, we're all going to have to find a way to get along, and I can't have Ahri making nasty comments every time you and I . . . ." Her voice trailed off and she blushed.

She'd felt so close to him last night, and now he was as distant as ever. Would it always be like this between them?

Lawson didn't seem to catch it, though. "What do you mean?" he asked.

"Do you not see it? She's acting so weird lately, like she's jealous . . . of us. I don't understand why she'd care. But there must be a reason for it. If I'm wrong about that, I want to know, and I bet Edon does too."

Lawson sighed. "Is there somewhere we can sit down?"

"There's a bench over there."

He sat with his head in his hands for a moment before speaking. "I'd really hoped this wasn't going to be an issue."

So something did happen between them. Bliss inhaled sharply and tried not to let what he was about to tell her hurt so much.

Lawson shook his head, then in a soft, almost inaudible voice, he confessed.

"It only happened once, the night before the trials. I was so keyed up, so afraid of what was about to happen. I'd trained for weeks. If I lost, I would die." He couldn't look her in the eye. His voice was flat. "She came into my bed, just as I was about to sleep. I didn't know what was happening until it was too late. She seduced me. She was my brother's mate. She knew I was scared and she used it against me. Then the next day, I found out why she had done it.

"I entered the arena. They hadn't told me who my opponent was, but somehow she knew. It was her. I would have had to kill her to win, to make alpha. It was either her or me.

"I couldn't. Not only because of what we'd done the night before, but because of who she was. I loved her too, as a sister. She must have worried that that wouldn't have stopped me, so that's why she seduced me, just to make sure

I lost. I thought the masters would kill me. I wanted them to, after everything that happened. I couldn't face Edon. I don't love Ahri, and I don't think she loves me. I think she's just angry and confused. I don't know. I think she wanted to win. She wanted to be alpha."

"That's terrible," Bliss said, though she wasn't sure whether she was referring to what Ahri had done, or Lawson.

"I figured losing at the trials was my punishment. I meant nothing to her, so I knew she'd never tell Edon, and no one would ever know."

"Did you—" Bliss almost couldn't bring herself to ask. "You didn't leave her behind on purpose, did you? When you guys escaped from Hell?"

Lawson looked as if she'd hit him. "You have to know I would never do that. I'd rather have faced Edon than leave her in the underworld by herself. I would never wish that on her. I wouldn't wish it on anyone. I thought at first that maybe she believed I had, though, and that I was partly to blame for what happened to her down there. But then I realized that if that were true, she'd have said something. To hurt me, or to hurt Edon."

"If she was content to keep it a secret, I don't understand why she's acting like this now," Bliss said.

Lawson raised an eyebrow at her. "You really don't?"

"Why would I?"

"She's jealous."

"Of what?"

"Of you. Of you and me, I guess, but probably mostly of you. There's something special about you, and she knows it. We all do."

"That's ridiculous," Bliss said. "She just saw you with someone else, and now she wants you back. I think maybe she always wanted you and settled for Edon."

"Maybe." Lawson considered the possibility. "But she didn't get quite this bent out of shape when she found out about me and Tala. She was pissed, but she never seemed jealous. No, it's you." Tala had been his mate until she was killed by Romulus, before he and Bliss even met.

"Well, you need to do something about it. We have to figure out what caused the break in the timeline, and we need everyone to be able to work together."

"It will be fine," Lawson said. "Just let it go."

Bliss thought Lawson was such a boy sometimes, hoping that something would go away if he ignored it long enough.

"Let what go?" Edon said.

Bliss hadn't noticed the rest of the pack in front of them. So much for a private conversation. "It's nothing," she said.

"Yeah, forget about it," Lawson said.

"Because it meant nothing to you?" Ahramin asked.

"What are you talking about?" Edon asked. "Ahri, what are you talking about?" But then Bliss saw the look of comprehension cross his face. "No. No, you didn't. You couldn't have."

He could have been talking to either one of them.

"Edon, it's not what you think," Lawson said.

"It's exactly what I think," Edon said. "It couldn't be clearer." He turned to Ahramin. "I love you. Why would you do that to me?"

"Because I wanted to be alpha. I did what I had to do. We needed a leader. A real leader and not one who rolled over and sat up for the masters. I'm sorry, Edon, but it had to be done."

Edon turned away.

"Edon!" Lawson yelled. "Edon!"

Edon shifted into a wolf and growled. For a moment it looked as if he would rear up and lunge at Lawson. But he stumbled back against the wall and then stormed away.

Lawson's face was full of anguish. "Edon!"

"Let him go," Ahramin said. "He'll come back. He has nowhere else to go."

Schuyler

Once upon a time, before Schuyler had discovered she was different, that she was a vampire, that she would have to continue what her mother had started, she had been a regular girl at a competitive and elite private school in Manhattan. And as a student of the Duchesne School, she was expected to attend a prestigious college. Her mother had attended Harvard, and her father Stanford, but Schuyler had been drawn to the smaller schools—the urban schools—the "flowerpot" Ivies—Brown, Columbia, as well as the "brainiac" schools like the University of Chicago.

In another life, she and Oliver could have been these students, she thought, looking around at the young people. Their only anxieties were over exams and dating.

Getting to Chicago had been easy enough, but Schuyler had no idea what to do once they arrived. She supposed she could have sent Finn Chase a friend request on Facebook and asked to meet up, but it seemed so awkward. What was she supposed to say? "I'm the long-lost daughter of the father who died when you were a baby and before I was born. Sorry to spring it on you like this. Let's hang out!"

"Are we just going to show up on her doorstep?" Oliver asked.

"I would if I knew where her doorstep was," Schuyler said. "This place is enormous, though."

The campus was spread out over several city blocks, and it seemed impossible that they would be able to find her. "Did you check to see if there was an address on Facebook? Any references to what dorm she lives in?" Oliver asked.

"I read every post I could find, but there was nothing about where she lived. On campus, that's all I know. She's probably careful not to reveal where; too many stalkers these days."

"What about finding her after class? What's she studying?"

Trust Oliver to always come up with something useful. "She's an art major," Schuyler told him. "There was something about how Finn had gotten all of her requirements out of the way and could now spend her time doing what she loved."

"That means most of her classes are probably in the same building," Oliver pointed out. "If we go there, someone might be able to help us find her. We might even run into her, like the crazy stalkers we are."

"Such a good idea!" Schuyler checked her phone to see where visual art classes were held. "Looks like most of them are in the Arts Center, on South Greenwood. That's just a few blocks from here."

It didn't take them long to arrive at the squat, rectangular concrete building. "Not very attractive for a building devoted to art," Oliver sniffed.

"It's what's inside that counts," Schuyler said.

They looked at each other, took deep breaths, and entered the building. Schuyler had been hoping there would be some sort of secretary they could ask right away, but the lobby was empty. They must have come during class time.

"The administrative offices are this way." Oliver pointed.

The office was buzzing with activity, in contrast to the lobby. Student interns wandered around the suite, making copies and filing paperwork. The receptionist was filing her very long nails when Schuyler approached the desk. "You're looking for who? Is she expecting you?"

"Not exactly," Schuyler said.

"And you are . . . ?"

"Her sister."

"Is there some sort of family emergency?"

Schuyler debated whether to lie, then opted against it. "No, I was just hoping to find her. Is there any chance you could tell me where she is? What classroom she's in? I'm not looking for her home address or anything like that." Though I'd take it if you gave it to me, she thought.

"Can't do that," the receptionist said. "FERPA violation."

"FERPA?"

"Privacy. I know your generation doesn't have much use for it anymore, but it's still the law."

"Well, thank you for your help." Schuyler couldn't help but let the sarcasm creep into her voice.

The woman gave her a look and then returned to filing her nails.

Schuyler walked out of the office, dejected.

"What about the glom?" Oliver asked. "Just *make* her tell you."

"I thought about it, but it seemed wrong somehow," she said. "We'll figure something out."

"Excuse me?" a voice said.

They turned around to see a petite girl with dark curly hair standing behind them. "Sorry to be nosy, but I couldn't help overhearing you in there. You're looking for Finn Chase?"

"We are," Schuyler said eagerly.

"You're her sister? She's a pretty good friend of mine, and I don't remember her having any siblings."

"She doesn't know about me," Schuyler admitted. "Actually, I only just found out about her."

The girl's dark eyes sparkled. "How exciting and mysterious!" She held out her hand. "I'm Ivy. I totally know her schedule. Can I introduce you guys? Please?"

Is she kidding? Of course she can! "I'm Schuyler, and this is my friend Oliver. We'd love it if you'd help us out."

"Awesome," Ivy said. "Are you two, like, a thing? Are

you a potential brother-in-law or something?"

Was she asking out of curiosity, or because she thought Oliver was cute? It didn't matter, Schuyler figured, as long as she'd help them. And if Oliver needed to flirt to get what they needed, then he'd better get cracking.

"I'm quite single," he said. "Schuyler's like a sister to me."

Schuyler breathed a sigh of relief. Perhaps not quite accurate, but it would do the job.

"Class is almost over," Ivy said. "She's taking a grad class on Kandinsky. Such an overachiever." She rolled her eyes.

Well, they had Kandinsky in common, Schuyler thought. Finn's taste must have been influenced by Decca. And Ben, of course. She remembered that he'd been some sort of artist.

"We'll catch her on the way out. Come on."

Oliver and Schuyler followed Ivy down a long corridor to a seminar room. Through a window in the door, Schuyler could see a group of students sitting around a table. They were arguing animatedly, and she felt a pang of jealousy at the thought of Finn as a normal college student, passionate about art, oblivious to the fact that the world might be a horrible and dangerous place, where your love could be ripped away from you.

"Sky? You with us?" Oliver asked.

"Just watching," she said.

The students began packing up their books and heading toward the door. Schuyler jumped back and wondered why she felt as if she needed to hide. Nervous about meeting her sister, she supposed.

A tall blond girl with her hair in a ponytail, her face framed by a pair of severe black eyeglasses, left the room. Schuyler had expected Finn to look sporty, somehow, from the photos of her on the ski slopes and the tennis courts; and while the girl certainly had an athletic gracefulness about her, she carried herself with a serious mien. Finn Chase, Schuyler realized, was a bit of a nerd. A cool nerd, of course—a hipster with her vintage glasses and the polyester blouse and the bell-bottom jeans—but a nerd nonetheless.

Ivy stood by the door and grabbed Finn's arm as soon as she exited the room. "I have the craziest thing to tell you," she said.

Finn rolled her eyes. "Crazier than the time you said your calculus tutor was hitting on you, except he just had a spastic eyelid? Crazier than the time you thought we all had bedbugs because you actually had poison oak from rolling around in the bushes with that random freshman? Crazier than—"

"Okay, I get it, enough already," Ivy said. "Yes, crazier than all of that. Legit crazy." She dragged Finn over to where Schuyler and Oliver were waiting. "Finn, meet Schuyler. Schuyler, this is Finn. Also, this is Oliver. And they're totally not dating."

Finn gave Ivy the kind of look Schuyler suspected she'd given her many, many times before, then turned and smiled at Schuyler and Oliver. "Nice to meet you," she said politely. "What's this all about?"

"GUESS!" Ivy was bursting with excitement. She practically bounced up and down, trying to drag out the moment. "You'll never guess!"

Enough already, Schuyler thought, ready to interrupt. Finally, Ivy squealed, "She's your sister!"

Finn frowned. *Uh-oh.* "Don't be ridiculous," she said. "I don't have a sister. Or a brother. Or any siblings. Who are you guys, really?"

"She's not kidding," Schuyler said. "I know it sounds crazy, but I actually am your sister. I just found out a few days ago. Ben was my dad too. He was married to my mother but he died before I was born."

"You're kidding," said Finn, shocked.

"She isn't," Oliver said. "Not even a little bit."

"But I thought—and he and my mom never even—are we the same age? I'm so confused."

"I think you're maybe two years older than I am," Schuyler said. "It's kind of a long story. If you want to hear it." She still couldn't tell. Finn was looking at her with such skepticism, and Schuyler was struck by how much she looked exactly like Decca—wary, guarded, reserved—that she was prepared to be dismissed as an opportunistic crackpot.

"Um, hello?" Finn asked. "Of course I want to hear it!" She broke out into a broad smile. The one Schuyler recognized from the photographs of her father on the mantel. Ben Chase's dazzling, generous, light-filled smile. "Come to my dorm and tell me everything!"

THIRTY-FOUR

Mimi

*N*ow it was just a question of which city the Lennox brothers and their new brides had moved to. Mimi didn't think it would be that difficult to find them: if she'd fallen into a completely improbably romance and run off to Europe, there's only one place she would go.

Paris.

They'd be in hiding, of course, but no one could hide from Mimi for very long. She had better contacts in Paris than in London, even among the Red Bloods, and a married pair of twins couldn't be completely inconspicuous.

It only took her a few days to find them. They were living in the 3rd arrondissement, in Le Marais.

It felt great to be back in Paris—and with a pang, Mimi realized it was a life she and Kingsley had never had the luxury to experience. *Come away with me*, he had asked her, right before her bonding to Jack. She had said yes—but by then it was too late.

In Paris she felt like her old self again, checking into the Ritz in her usual suite, sinking into those heavenly sheets and lush pink towels. She'd even found a little time to steal away and do some shopping; there was nothing that made her feel more confident than a fabulous new outfit from Lanvin, with Louboutins to match. Suitably attired, she went back to business.

The two couples had managed to find twin apartments as well—they lived side by side in a building that had once been a house, carved into beautiful apartments. And they must have felt safe there, since they'd done nothing supernatural to protect themselves—no spells, no enchantments. Just locks that were easy for someone like Mimi to pick.

She spent a couple of days quietly following them around, breaking into their apartments when she knew they weren't home. No sign of Kingsley, but they'd obviously gotten comfortable. The apartments were structurally identical, like Deming and Dehua, but they were furnished completely differently. Deming and Ted's apartment was decorated in soft pastels, with gauzy curtains and a feeling of openness and warmth. Fitting for the Angel of Mercy, Mimi thought. Sam and Dehua's apartment was sleek and modern, with furniture made of steel. Indestructible, for the Angel of Immortality.

Ted and Sam both had their own offices, as well. Ted's,

in keeping with his detective instincts, was covered in maps and corkboards that detailed his investigation of Lucifer's plan to destroy the gates. Sam's was filled with the most expensive computer equipment.

The one thing the apartments shared was that they were both covered in photographs. Pictures of the couples at their bonding, on their honeymoon, wandering around the streets of Paris together. They all seemed so happy.

And the whole time, Mimi was growing furious.

Why was this happening to her? Why was she embroiled in this crazy plot to double-cross Lucifer when all she wanted was what she'd been willing to go to Hell for: the chance to be with Kingsley? She'd lost her bondmate and found a way to move on, but she still wasn't permitted any happiness. The stone around her neck felt heavier and heavier every moment. No matter what she did, the Dark Prince would know.

She decided to wait in Ted and Deming's apartment and surprise them when they returned. She'd always gotten along a little better with Ted, and she knew Deming better than Dehua, from the time Deming had helped them catch the hidden Nephilim at Duchesne.

There was a pale blue wingback chair that faced the front door of the apartment, so she could sit and wait for them and be sure she was the first thing they saw. Mimi touched her chest, confirming that the small needle of her sword was safely tucked into her bra. She never knew when she might need it. Hopefully they'd cooperate, but Venators could be tricky. Even the friendly ones.

To their credit, Ted and Deming didn't look all that surprised when they came home to find Mimi there. It was as if they'd been expecting her. Now it was just a question of figuring out how much they knew, and how to get them to do what she wanted.

"Congratulations," Mimi said. "It must be nice to settle down and not worry that our world is ending."

Deming appraised her coolly. She didn't seem the least bit afraid. "After Egypt we hunted the Nephilim for months, to stanch the demon invasion. The Gates of Hell remain standing, no thanks to you. I don't recall seeing you at the battles at the Gate of Sorrow, and the Gate of Justice when we lost Octilla and Onbasius."

So the Nephilim continued their relentless assault. It was as Jack had worried—back when he'd still worried about this sort of thing. The Dark Prince would keep the vampires and Venators on the edge, on the brink of exhaustion, and when their forces were weak and unprepared, Lucifer would reveal his true plan: to reclaim the throne of Heaven.

"Sorry we didn't invite you to the bonding. We'd only just moved to Paris and we seem to have lost your address," Deming said with a shrug.

"Now, darling, I think we have Mimi to thank for bringing us together. Let's not be rude to our uninvited guest," Ted said with a guarded smile.

"I would have thought you'd be wondering what I'm doing here," Mimi said.

"We're definitely curious," Deming said. "There are some pretty amazing stories going around about you right now. Care to tell us which ones are true?"

Oh, for the days when it was fun to think about the things people said about her. "What have you heard? Let me guess. That I've gone back to the Dark Prince, that Jack and I have revealed our faithless natures—just as everyone always said we would. Am I right?"

Neither one answered.

"They've been saying that about us for centuries. No matter what we do, no matter what we did—and it was Abbadon, after all, who turned the battle—and you forget that it was my sword that pierced Lucifer's armor," Mimi said. "And yet, what do we get for our efforts—nothing but suspicion and lies. . . ."

"So if you're not working with the Morningstar, then have you returned to the Coven to assume your Regency?" asked Ted.

"I might be. I'm looking for Kingsley."

"Then why did you come here?" Deming wanted to know.

"Isn't it obvious? I find it hard to believe that he could just disappear completely and not tell you where he was going. You're his closest friends. And maybe he's the one who told you some of the crazy stories about me, but I have to say, I'm really worried about him."

"Worried?" Ted asked.

Deming gave him a look. *Good.* Mimi was getting to him.

"You must be aware that the Knights Templar have alerted us to the loss of their most sacred treasures. The holy grails. One in Spain and another in Scotland. I have confirmed reports that it was Kingsley who stole the chalice from its hiding place. Rumor has it he stole the seed of the godsfire as well."

The Venators were shocked. "The godsfire and the holy grails—but that would mean . . ."

"That he would be able to create a weapon to defeat the White Fire of Heaven. And whom do we know who would desire such a thing?" Mimi asked in a silky tone. There was only one angel who would need such a magnificent armament. Lucifer, of the Fallen. The Dark Prince of the underworld.

"Kingsley Martin is not a traitor!" Ted shouted. "You have no proof!"

"I have to agree: that's quite a story you're telling us. Where did you get this information? How do you know?" Deming asked.

"I have my sources."

"He's not here," Ted said. Deming looked at him with disgust. Hope that marriage lasts, Mimi thought. "I mean, he's not here anymore," Ted added.

"But he was," Mimi said.

Ted nodded. He turned to Deming. "We have to tell her—I don't believe that Kingsley has betrayed us, but we have to tell her what we know."

Mimi smiled like a cat. "Please do."

"He first came here for a visit after you freed him from Hell. He seemed really upset—wouldn't talk about it much. Just kept saying that he was worried about you, that something was wrong. Then he went back to London and went on a bender, from what we heard. It was only recently that he came back here, and that was to tell us he was getting an army together, to prepare to defeat Lucifer."

So there was a plan, then. "And you believed him?"

"There didn't seem to be any reason not to," Ted said.

"Where is he now?"

"Enough, Ted," Deming said sharply.

"She said she's worried about him," Ted said. "We don't know where he is right now."

"Really? And you don't know anything about the Venator conclave in London in a few days?" asked Mimi.

"You know about that?" Ted blurted out, and then quickly regretted it.

"Seriously, that's enough, Ted," Deming said. "Mimi, I appreciate that you're trying to help, but the best way to do it is to let us do what we do best. If you want to help, leave Kingsley alone."

"I'm afraid I can't do that," Mimi said. "I'm really sorry."

Before Deming or Ted had a chance to react, Mimi pulled the needle out of her blouse, restored it to its full size, and trained it at Deming's throat. "Take me to that conclave," she said. "Or your blood will be on my sword."

She turned to the Venator's husband. "And you're right, Ted: Kingsley Martin is no traitor. I am."

THIRTY-FIVE

Bliss

don did not return. Bliss had taken Malcolm and Rafe with her to the catacombs as well as the ancient sites of the city, to see if they could find the portal, but returned to the hostel at the end of the day as frustrated as ever. She hoped that leaving Lawson and Ahramin to themselves would allow them to sort out whatever was between them, but she was still struggling to understand it herself. Lawson and Ahri? Now it was her turn to feel jealous, but mostly what she felt was angry. They had bigger problems than the consequences of a random hookup right now.

Bliss knew they were close to solving the mystery of the passages and that Arthur had pointed them in the right direction by sending them to Rome, but this thing that had happened between Lawson and Ahramin was distracting them from their real task. She found Ahramin in the lounge, flirting with some backpackers who were trying to decide whether to stay.

"Where's Lawson?" Bliss asked.

"Can't you see I'm busy?" Ahramin rolled her eyes and pointed to the hostel's back door.

The door led out into a small garden, with a patio and a couple of wire chairs surrounding a table. The surface of the table was littered with old newspapers and overflowing ashtrays. The days when Bliss would step outside of a New York club to smoke a cigarette with Dylan seemed so very far away, and now the smell of the ash made her feel a little nauseous.

Lawson was sitting in one of the chairs. His head was buried in his arms, crossed on the table, but he looked up when he heard her coming. "How did the rest of the day go?" he asked quietly.

"Not well. We're not looking in the right place. I can see it so clearly in my head, and I feel like I know it in my bones—but when I look around—I don't see it. Maybe it's not here?"

"It has to be," Lawson said. "We can't give up."

"What about you? Did you and Ahri talk?"

He shook his head. "She doesn't want to talk to me. I'm not sure I have much to say to her either. I just want to forget any of it ever happened, and I have no idea what she wants. Until the last couple of days, I thought we'd both just put it behind us."

"Clearly not," Bliss said. "And Edon?"

"He hasn't come back. But his stuff's still here. He'll show up eventually. When he does, I need you to tell him how sorry I am."

"Tell him yourself." Bliss felt the hairs on her arms stand up. She had a feeling she knew what was coming.

Lawson shook his head. "I need you to take charge of the pack. I've become too much of a distraction, and I need to leave."

Bliss bit her lip. She had come to the same conclusion. She had hoped for a different outcome—for Ahramin to excuse herself—but she knew as well as Lawson that that wasn't about to happen.

"Are you sure? She should go, not you."

"If I stay, Edon won't come back, and he'll still be angry. And I know you won't admit it, but you're angry too. And Malcolm and Rafe won't know what to think. We'll be fractured and ineffective, and the wolves will be lost. We'll never repair the breach in the timeline. But if I go, Edon and Ahri will reconcile, and you can lead them. You'll heal the rift."

Bliss wanted to tell him that she could forgive him, that she could help him mend fences with Ahramin and Edon, but she wasn't sure she could. She was still too confused about her own feelings. Still, she didn't want him to go. "You're taking the easy way out," she said. "You could stay here and work to earn everyone's forgiveness. You could help us, but instead you're running away."

"I'll still be helping you. I just have to do it in my own way." He stood up, and that's when Bliss saw that he'd already packed up his bags. He'd only been waiting to say good-bye to her.

"There was never any chance of my changing your mind, was there?"

He shook his head, gave her one last, long look, and then he was gone.

Bliss was left to explain Lawson's absence to the rest of the pack, and that he'd left her in charge.

"I have to answer to you now?" Ahri sneered.

"No one's answering to anybody," Bliss said. "We're just going to keep doing what we're doing until we learn something useful. I have no interest in bossing you around. We just need to stop fighting and make some progress here. Edon, Ahri, are you two going to be able to get along?"

Edon, who had returned unexpectedly that morning, looked at Ahri and shrugged. "I have nothing to say to you. I'm here for the wolves," he said. "If my brother is enough of a coward that he won't work with us, then let him be. I will stay."

"Edon," Ahramin said. "Edon—I want to explain."

"There is nothing you can say that I would like to hear," Edon said, and his handsome face sagged with sorrow and disappointment. "Let's just get this done."

"I'm going to turn in early. Boys, you coming with me?"

Rafe and Malcolm followed her eagerly, like cubs. They both wanted Edon and Ahri to make up, and they were confused about Lawson's disappearance. But they trusted her; they'd do whatever she suggested. Lawson had been right about that.

She had a lot more trouble falling asleep that night, even though the dorm room was quiet with just the boys in it. She couldn't stop thinking about Lawson. She alternated between being furious with him and missing him desperately. What if she had another nightmare and he wasn't there to comfort her?

It turned out she was right to worry. No sooner had she fallen asleep than she was plunged back into her dream from the night before. This time, though, she was prepared—the feeling of confusion and dual-vision was familiar, as was her own knowledge that she was dreaming and therefore somehow safe. At least for the moment.

Something was different, though. Her two perspectives were moving through a series of dark tunnels. Candles lit the path, though they only allowed her to see a few feet in front of here.

Where am I? she wondered. It felt almost like she was in a basement—she had the definite sense of being underground—but basements don't have corridors.

She had been here once before. She remembered performances, beautiful music. Then she recognized the columns, the courtyard, and realized this was once the Theatre of

Pompey, expanded and re-constructed by Caligula himself.

The theater was the entrance to the underground city, a network of paths that connected all of the empire, from Rome to Lutetia. The hidden city of the vampires, the hidden life of the Coven.

Now all she had to find was the door.

THIRTY-SIX

Schuyler

inn's dorm was actually a college house called Blackstone. It was much more lavish than Schuyler was expecting; she'd pictured bunk beds in an anonymous cinder block room, especially after seeing the art building. But Blackstone was a beautiful brick building that looked almost like a cathedral.

They entered into a student lounge, which had a fireplace and a grand piano. "This is college?" Schuyler asked. "Or Downton Abbey?"

Finn laughed. "It is here. This place is great! You should see my room."

She led them to an apartment with two bedrooms, a kitchenette, and a bathroom. "I share the kitchen and the bathroom, but the bedroom is all mine," she said. "We can decorate them however we want."

Schuyler let out a gasp when Finn turned on the lights.

It wasn't because the room was a mess, even though it was. No, her surprise was because the walls were covered with paintings of someone who looked so much like her that it had to be Allegra. "Did your—our—dad do these?" she asked.

"Every last one," Finn said. "They're pretty much all I have left of him. Go ahead, take a look if you want. They're pretty great, right? Did you ever see the reviews of his show in *Artforum* or *Art in America*? He could have been something if he'd lived."

"I haven't. I'd love to see them one day," Schuyler said as she stood close enough to the paintings to see the fine brushstrokes, the swirl of the paint, to smell the . . . Wait a minute. That smell . . . it couldn't be. . . .

"Oliver, come here," she whispered, while Finn was puttering around the little kitchen to rustle up some drinks. "I smell blood."

"Where?" he asked. "You're not telling me your sister is some kind of serial killer, are you?" he said jokingly.

"No, in the paintings!" Schuyler said. "I think Ben might have mixed his own blood in with the paint."

"Gross," Oliver said. "What is that, like a Victor Acconci fur, felt, and seed sort of thing?"

"It's not exactly common, but people have done it. You know what this means, don't you?"

Oliver gave her a curious look, but then Finn came back in the room. "Cool, right?" she said. "I always used to wonder who he was painting, but I guess that mystery's been solved. That's your mother, isn't it? You look just like her except for the dark hair."

"I think so," Schuyler said.

"What was she like?" Finn asked eagerly. "My mom always told me it was some sort of tragic love story."

"Well, I guess you could say it was tragic because he died, and after I was born, my mom was in a coma for almost all of my life," Schuyler said. "Your mom wasn't—angry? I sort of figured—"

"Mom's a true romantic," Finn said. "She was pretty crazy about my dad, but she knew the whole time that he was in love with someone else. That's why she lied and told him she wasn't pregnant anymore, so he could go and be with her and not feel guilty."

"And she told you all of this?" Schuyler was amazed. She'd spent her whole life in the dark, and here was this girl whose mother apparently kept no secrets. What a different life she must have led.

"I guess it was really important to her that I grew up with good feelings about my dad since I didn't get to know him at all. You're so lucky," Finn said suddenly.

"Lucky? How?"

"He loved your mom," Finn said simply. "Oh, he was fond of mine, sure, but it wasn't the same."

Schuyler shook her head. "No, you were the lucky one. Your mother loved him so much that she let him go because she wanted him to be happy. I bet she was always there for you, wasn't she?"

"Every moment." Finn didn't deny it.

"Decca showed me all the photos—the birthday parties . . ."

"Yeah, they were pretty epic."

"If your mom hadn't lied, our dad would never have left her. He would have done the right thing. He was a good guy."

"Even if he was, he's still dead," Finn said suddenly.

"Yeah." Schuyler had to agree. Then she realized—she wasn't alone in her grief—in her missing him. Finn was in the same boat. Here was someone who loved and missed him too, and who'd never known him. Her sister.

"Besides"—Finn shrugged—"Mom turned out to be right about the whole romance thing. She met this fabulous guy when I was twelve, and I'm really close to my stepdad. It's almost enough to make me believe in true love."

"Even if you haven't found it yourself?" Oliver asked with a smile.

Wait a minute—was Schuyler seeing what she thought she was seeing? Oliver Hazard-Perry, blushing? She supposed it made sense. Finn did look a little bit like her, and more important, she was awesome—confident, funny, smart. Normal. Oliver deserved someone like her.

"Not yet," Finn said, returning the smile with one of her own.

Schuyler could see where this was going, and it made her happy. But it also made her miss Jack desperately. Could it really be this easy for two people to find each other? Why couldn't it have been that easy for her and Jack? Would she ever see him again? Would they ever be together?

"Earth to Sky," Oliver said, snapping his fingers in front of her face.

"Sorry. It's all just so overwhelming."

"Tell me about it!" Finn agreed. "But I'm just so glad you found me!"

"I am too!" Schuyler said. "Tell me more about our dad, and you. Everything. I want to know everything."

They spent the rest of the afternoon talking, catching up on the things they'd missed out on, not growing up together. Schuyler edited her version heavily, just as she had with Decca. She didn't want to freak out her Red Blood relatives.

"You were a model?" Finn asked, impressed. "Was it fun?"

"Not really," Schuyler admitted. "But I did love the free clothes."

"I guess I was a bit of jock," Finn said. "Field hockey, softball, track. I don't think I took my hair out of a pony-tail until college. But like dad, I was always drawing. And I prepped at Endicott like him. I was a Peithologian too. When I was there, I found he'd carved his name and Allegra's in the woods. It was very romantic."

"I'll carve your name anytime," Oliver murmured.

Schuyler elbowed him. "Subtlety is key," she whispered.

"What's that?" Finn asked.

"Oh, nothing," Oliver said.

"So neither of you is in school right now?" Finn asked.

"We decided to put it off for a while," Schuyler said.

"Didn't want to waste the opportunity," Oliver said. "We're traveling instead."

"Anyplace exciting?"

They looked at each other and tried not to laugh. Exciting was one way of putting it. "In the past year, I've been to London, Egypt, and Italy," Schuyler said.

"And I've been to—" Oliver paused. "I guess Europe, mostly."

Schuyler imagined he'd been tempted to explain that he'd spent quality time in the underworld, but it didn't really seem appropriate for the situation. It must have killed him that her travel sounded more exciting than his. She could barely hide her smirk.

"So you guys have no idea what you're missing, then," Finn said.

"We don't miss going to class," Oliver said.

"Oh, but the real fun starts when classes end. There's a big party tonight. Will you come? Or do you have to leave soon?"

Oliver looked at Schuyler. She'd rarely seen a pleading look in his eyes, so it took her a minute to recognize it for what it was. He'd been partying with socialites and aristocrats in London, and yet here he was, angling to go to a regular college party.

She wasn't sure what to do—they probably should get back to London and meet up with the rest of the Blue Bloods; but that would basically be admitting that the trip was, from that perspective, a wash. And then there was the whole blood painting possibility . . . the Blood of the Father. . . . If she stayed, maybe she'd have a chance to check it out.

"Sure, why not?" she said.

L ove never failed to get people in trouble, Mimi thought. Look at Ted and Deming: either one of them on their own could have stopped her, but together they were so worried about each other's safety that all Mimi had to do was grasp the opportunity when it came to her. She kept her sword pointed at Deming's neck as Deming tied Ted up, using the silver Venator rope. That would keep him until Sam and Dehua found him, anyway, and in the meantime, she and Deming would have a head start getting to the Venator conclave.

"It didn't have to be this way," Mimi said. "And if you cooperate, it will all be over soon. The Dark Prince will reward you handsomely if you cast your lot with ours and join our ranks."

"You disgust me," Deming said. "How could you do this to the Coven? You were our Regent."

Ted wouldn't even look her in the eye, and Mimi realized that while there were those in the Coven who'd always suspected her and Jack of being traitors, Ted Lennox had not been one of them. He had believed in her, and she had let him down. His shoulders sagged beneath the rope.

I have to do what I have to do, Mimi thought. If Jack wouldn't do it, then she would. This was the only way to keep all of them alive.

The conclave was held at a stately old manor on the outskirts of London. It was well hidden and well protected; Mimi would never have found it without Deming. It was blocked from sight by numerous different types of enchantments, and heavily guarded by the Venators themselves.

Mimi had used the *mutatio* to disguise herself as Deming's twin sister, Dehua. The other half of the Chen-Lennox foursome had been called away for some secret mission, so there was little chance the real Dehua would attend the meeting.

The entryway to the manor emptied into a large living room, furnished with antique velvet-upholstered sofas and mahogany tables, but also crammed with folding chairs to accommodate the crowd the organizers had anticipated.

Except there wasn't a crowd. The room wasn't even half full.

Mimi recognized several members of the New York Coven, along with other vampires she'd met over the years in various parts of the world. Several Venators were also in attendance, some of whom she'd never seen before.

"I don't understand," Mimi whispered to Deming. "Where is everybody?"

"This is everybody," Deming whispered back. "Most of the vampires are in hiding, and a lot of them just didn't respond to the call. Some of them have decided to assimilate; others are too scared to fight. People thought you and Jack gave up, and with Michael and Gabrielle gone . . ." Her voice trailed off.

Mimi thought back to other gatherings of the vampires, like her favorite, the Four Hundred Ball, held every year so new vampires could be introduced to the community. There were barely thirty people in this room, if you counted both vampires and Venators.

"How exactly are you guys going to mount a defense?" she asked. "I mean, look around. How is this motley crew going to stop the Dark Prince from taking Paradise? They don't look like they could take down a nightclub."

"I guess you'd know, being so *close* to Lucifer and all," Deming said pointedly. "You are an embarrassment to our kind. You should have stayed in the underworld. It's where you belong."

Mimi was about to retaliate with a sharp nudge of her knife, but before she could say anything, the room started buzzing. It could only mean one thing.

Kingsley was here.

The next morning, Bliss told the rest of the pack about her dream and her realization. "We need to discover a way into that underground city. The Theatre of Pompey was part of it, I remember now."

"But almost nothing of the theater remains," Malcolm said. "It was all destroyed."

"It can't be. I saw it. I saw it standing," Bliss said. "Where are those maps of Rome? Of the old city? And the new one?"

She placed the maps over each other. "There," she said, pointing to a semicircular location in the center of the ancient city. "In that neighborhood. That's where the theater used to be." The foundation of the theater still remained, she was sure, but it was hidden underneath, in the surrounding basements and cellars of the buildings that had been built upon its ruins.

"What's there now?" Rafe asked, leaning closer.

"A hotel," Malcolm said. "The Albergo Sole al Biscione near the Campo de Fiori."

The sky was overcast and gray, and the weather had cooled, so there weren't many tourists around when they arrived at the open-air market. Which meant they were less likely to be observed, but also less likely to blend in. They would just have to be careful.

The Biscione was a grand old hotel, and as soon as they entered the lobby, Bliss felt everyone's eyes on them. The boys were wearing their usual mismatched thrift-store cast-offs, and Bliss felt grubby in her day-old jeans and flannel shirt. Ahramin looked perfectly striking as usual, like an old-fashioned femme fatale in her black clothes, so perhaps the pack would pass as her entourage.

Bliss wasn't the daughter of a senator for nothing. "Most rich American kids look like bums, so just act like you belong and no one will question you," she told them.

"Right," Malcolm said.

But after an hour of surveying every inch of the lobby and visiting the basement restaurant, they were stymied. Bliss looked around helplessly. Nothing looked familiar. The group split up: Edon went with Rafe, Malcolm with Bliss, and Ahramin went alone.

A half hour later, it was Ahramin who gathered the pack together at a corner sofa, hidden from the guests. "I found it!" she whispered, triumphant.

"Where?" Malcolm asked.

"I'll show you," she said, and they followed her down the steps to the underground restaurant.

"We were already here; there was nothing," Edon complained.

But Ahramin kept leading them down. Past the wine cellar. To a stone wall.

"Does that look familiar?" she asked Bliss.

Bliss blinked. It was the wall. The wall of the theater from her dream. This was it.

"Here." Ahramin pointed at a grate in the stone floor that seemed to be useless—it just covered another stone.

"What are we looking at?" Bliss asked.

Ahri looked around to make sure no one was watching, then lifted the grate.

"It's just another rock," Edon said.

"Look closer."

Bliss peered at the stone. Just like all the other ones. But wait—there was a gap between that stone and the one next to it.

"Watch this," Ahri said, then inserted her fingertips into the space between the stones. She pushed, and the stone easily slid back, revealing a narrow stone staircase.

"You really did it," Bliss said, trying not to sound too surprised.

"Let's go!" Malcolm said.

"No, you guys need to stay back," said Bliss.

"You can't go alone," he argued.

Bliss looked at Edon and Rafe. She didn't want to be responsible for something bad happening to Malcolm.

"Take Mac; he's small but he's still a wolf. A fighter. We'll stand guard here," Rafe said. "We'll make sure no one else goes down there; and if you're not back in an hour we'll come and check on you."

"Me first," Malcolm said.

"I don't think so," Bliss said, and made her way down the stairs.

Malcolm followed closely behind her. "I can't see anything."

Bliss turned on her phone. The screen made a dim light, but it was enough. The stairs were narrow and seemed to go on for a long time, but finally they reached the bottom. They'd only walked a few steps before Bliss could see that they were standing in the same courtyard with the columns from her dreams.

"This is it," she said. "The Theatre of Pompey. The entrance to the passages."

chuyler wasn't sure why she was so nervous. She'd been to tons of fancy parties in New York, and even more beyond that. Masquerade balls, elaborately themed galas . . . She should be completely jaded by now. But for some reason, the thought of going to a basic college kegger was freaking her out. She tried to explain it to Oliver as they walked the few blocks to the house where the party was being held. Finn was up ahead of them, with Ivy and a bunch of her other friends.

"Oh, it's not surprising at all," Oliver said. "It's to be expected, really. You're off to a classic Red Blood social function with your newly discovered human half-sister. Have you ever been more out of your element? It's not like we got invited to parties at Duchesne all the time."

"I guess that's it. I feel like it'll be high school all over again, and what a success we were at that," Schuyler agreed.

"Don't worry, this won't be like high school; and besides, haven't you forgotten? You married the BMOC. You're like the prom queen," Oliver teased. Seeing her reaction, he turned grave. "I'm sorry—it was a tacky joke."

"No, you're right, and I'd rather not pretend like Jack's not here, like that whole thing didn't happen."

"He's alive, Sky, I know he is. And he's thinking of you too, wherever he is."

She nodded. "I just wish . . ." *I just wish I knew where he was.* If he was okay. If he and Mimi hadn't destroyed each other, then what had happened to them? Where were they? Was Jack all right? She felt unmoored without him. There was so much she wanted to tell him and to share—about her father, her human family, Finn. It was as if things had not truly happened to her until she told him about it. She was glad for Oliver's company, but it wasn't the same. The watchful presence was still around, she noticed, but subdued somehow. She wondered if she would ever find out who or what was watching her.

"Listen, at some point we have to find a way back into Finn's room when she isn't there. I have to see if there's any way to extract the blood from those paintings. If there's any chance it's Ben's, this might be what we're looking for."

The party was in a house that was, for a lack of a better way to describe it, disgusting. It was a run-down Victorian that was shared by a group of eight boys, none of whom seemed to have any interest in maintaining a hygienic residence. Schuyler's shoes stuck to the hardwood floor when she walked in the front hallway, and it was even worse in the kitchen, where the boys had stored the keg. There were so many people, they had to push their way through the crowd to make their way in.

"Is there anything else to drink?" Oliver asked. "Whiskey maybe? I'd settle for a blend if you don't have single malt."

Finn laughed. "You're so funny! If you go through the cabinets you might be able to find some Soco."

"Soco?" Oliver sniffed.

"Southern Comfort?" Finn laughed. "Ever heard of it? It tastes okay with Seven Up."

Oliver scrunched his face.

"You're such a snob, Ollie," Schuyler chided. "Come on, let's have a beer." She didn't really want one, but if they were going to try to fit in, they had to do what the natives did.

Reaching the keg seemed impossible, though—there were so many people swarming it: preppy boys in their gingham button-downs over T-shirts and jeans, girls in ironic grandma dresses, everyone jostling for red plastic cups. "You have to be aggressive at parties like this," Finn said, and used her elbows to muscle her way up to the keg.

"Impressive," Oliver noted.

A tall boy in a lacrosse hoodie nudged Oliver out of the

way and handed Schuyler a beer. "Here. Pretty girl like you shouldn't have to wait for a drink."

"Oh, thanks," she said, a bit unsure whether it was a good idea to accept.

"At your service, m'lady. May the gentleman inquire as to your name?"

"Oh, leave her alone, Trevor," Finn said, with three beers balanced in her hands. She gave one to Oliver and nodded to Schuyler. "Looks like you're all set, and you've met our resident lothario. Trevor, go find some naive freshman to hit on. Schuyler's with me."

"It was worth a shot." Trevor shrugged and made his way back into the crowd.

"Oh, he was harmless," Schuyler said.

"Sure, if you're looking for a one-nighter with no phone call afterward," Finn said.

"Speaking from personal experience?" Oliver asked.

Already jealous, Schuyler noted. Interesting.

"No, that's Ivy's territory. More beer for us, though." Finn took a long drink from her cup and motioned for Oliver to do the same, then nearly spit it out when she saw the look on Oliver's face as he downed his drink.

"Come on, it tastes like New York tap water," Schuyler said to him. "Don't be so uptight." It wouldn't hurt him to have a few drinks to loosen up in front of Finn, she figured.

After two beers Schuyler felt a little looser herself, so

she decided to go exploring. Unfortunately, the rest of the house was even grimier than the parts she'd seen. The bathroom had apparently never been cleaned; there were rings of mildew around both the tub and the toilet, and the bedrooms were carpeted with what had once been beige shag and was now trampled brown. The undergrads were boisterously drunk, and after watching one of them vomit into the pot of a long-dead plant, Schuyler decided it was time to go.

Oliver and Finn were in the living room, dancing to some horrible pop song. She hadn't seen Oliver dance since the old days at the Bank. She'd forgotten what a good dancer he was. He was pretty smooth, she noticed. He blended in so well with the college crowd that she hated to drag him away. "I think I need to get out of here," she whispered.

"Would you totally hate me if I stayed here with Finn? I'm actually having a really good time."

It was just as she'd expected. "No problem. Our flight leaves first thing in the morning, though, so if you don't come home, text me and I'll meet you there, with your luggage. Finn, would you mind if I went back to your dorm? I think I left something there."

"Oh, sure," Finn said. "Someone can let you in the front door, and my apartment's unlocked. I know it's totally unsafe, but my roommate's always forgetting her keys, and we don't have much to steal."

"Thanks a lot," she said. Easier than she'd expected. She

didn't like lying to Finn, but it was better than breaking in and risking getting caught.

"I'll walk you out," Oliver said.

"You don't have to," she said.

"I want to."

Oliver helped her elbow her way through the crowd until they made it outside. "Are you sure you're okay with this? You know I'd normally go with you, but . . ."

"I understand," she said.

"The thing is, I don't know if this is weird, but . . ."

"You're really into Finn."

He brightened. "Do you think she's into me?"

"It's pretty obvious, and yes. I think you two would be perfect for each other."

Oliver wrapped his arms around her. "Thank you," he whispered.

Schuyler felt a momentary pang of loss. It had been a long time since they'd been together, and they'd never talked about it, but she knew they'd both been wondering what might happen if Jack never came back. She hadn't wanted to fully contemplate the possibility, and Oliver had gone to great lengths to get Schuyler out of his system, literally, but the prospect was always there, an unanswered question between two old friends.

But now it was clear. Even if Jack never came back, Schuyler and Oliver weren't meant to be. Maybe it was too soon to say that he'd found someone he was meant to be with, but Schuyler couldn't imagine anyone better. Her best friend and her newfound sister—what could be more perfect?

"Don't screw this up," she said, and reached up to give him a brief kiss on the lips.

One last kiss.

*K*ingsley stood in the entrance to the living room and waited for the buzzing to stop. He was as handsome as ever, Mimi couldn't help but notice, with his thick, dark, almost black hair and clear blue eyes. He scanned the crowd, and she saw him stop and stare right at her.

He knows, she realized. He can see through the disguise, through the illusion. He knows it's me behind this mask.

She was elated and terrified at the same time.

What would he do?

They locked eyes for a long time. Then his gaze continued to sweep the room.

Would he buy it? she wondered. Would he believe her? He had to, for this to work. He had to believe she was false, that she was a traitor, that she was doing everything in her power to work against him and against the vampires. His life depended on it. If he believed she was still true to him, then all was lost.

She had to make him believe the lie—it was the only way to keep him safe. Mimi realized there was no other way out of this equation, this predicament Lucifer had designed for them. Maybe Jack had found a different way, but she did not know anymore. Something inside him had changed, she knew that now. Somehow, Jack had given up the fight.

She called out to him. *Jack? Jack, are you there?*

But there was nothing. Perhaps she was too late; perhaps he had already found Schuyler and was doing whatever it was he had decided to do.

Kingsley began to speak. "As you all know, we have long been engaged in a battle for control of the seven gates that guard the Paths of the Dead and keep the demons and their brethren in Hell. The Silver Bloods have been on a mission to destroy them all so that Lucifer may return from the underworld. So far, due to the courage, loyalty, and ferocity of our remaining Venator teams, the Gates of Hell remain standing, even as we have weathered heavy losses in the struggle against the Nephilim."

He took a deep breath. "But that is not why I have called you all here today. We have since learned that the attacks on Hell's gates are merely a distraction. For our enemy has focused his arsenal on something much more important. The Gate of Promise, Gabrielle's gate, guards a bisected path. One path leads to the underworld, and the other path is a way back into Paradise."

There was a collective gasp from the room.

Kingsley waited until they had settled down. "We have also learned that Lucifer has discovered a means of harnessing the godsfire, and he means to use this weapon to wage war upon Heaven itself."

The room buzzed with fear and anticipation.

"We have to stop him," Kingsley said. "We cannot allow the Dark Prince to reclaim what is not rightfully his."

"How are we supposed to do that?" someone finally yelled out.

Kingsley smiled. "I'm glad you asked," he said. Always the charmer, even as he was rallying the troops for battle. "We have two advantages in this fight. One: Lucifer will not be able to take Paradise without the key to the gate. I have dispatched a team of Venators to protect the gatekeeper and take her to a secure location. There is little chance of the Silver Bloods finding her; and without her, they will not be able to take the gate. The other is . . ."

"Stop!" Deming cried. "We can't discuss our plans now. Not in front of her." She pointed to Mimi, almost daring her to take out her sword. "This is not my sister! This is a traitor! *Aperio Oris!*" the Venator cried. *Reveal yourself!*

The mask slipped away and Mimi stood in the middle of the room. Her long lustrous platinum hair falling on her shoulders. A smirk on her face.

"She's working for the Silver Bloods! She is no longer our Regent!" Deming yelled.

Mimi was trapped. The Venators had surrounded her before she could unsheathe her sword. She looked around—at the faces that stared at her with abject hatred and fear. They would kill her. Slowly. And they would enjoy it.

Now was the moment of truth. She looked at Kingsley and waited—waited to see whether he understood, whether he'd seen their "battle" for what it was. A charade, a ruse, a desperate deception to save her love and her Coven.

But the blue of his eyes turned icy, and she knew she had lost him, finally. That he had given up hoping. Her plan had worked.

He believed she was false.

He believed in the lie.

She didn't know whether to rejoice or despair.

"Seize her," he said.

FORTY-ONE

Tomasia (Florence, 1452)

She was a princess, trapped in a castle. Andreas had ordered her to bed for the remainder of her pregnancy. She was alone, with only the Venators assigned to her protection—loyal Bellarmine, stoic Valentina. When Andreas visited, which was rare, Tomasia tried to talk to him, to determine whether he presented a threat to her unborn offspring, but he would not discuss it. Instead he insisted that she rest, undisturbed, in her chambers. She had asked for clay so that she might work on her art; perhaps then she would not be so lonely. He had relented, and she spent the days consumed with her work while Andreas went hunting with his new partner, Ludivivo Arosto.

Ludivivo, one of the conclave, had always been like a father to Tomasia in the past. In this cycle she had only met him once or twice before Andreas had essentially forced her into solitude. She recalled only a slim, fair-haired boy, who seemed better suited to life as a scholar than to that of a slayer of Silver Bloods. But when Andreas came to visit, he related tales of his and Ludivivo's many successes. It almost made Tomasia envy them, until she imagined trying to chase after Silver Bloods with her present girth.

"You are making tremendous progress on your sculptures," Andreas said, examining the tableau she'd laid out. It was the most elaborate piece she had ever attempted. Three figures surrounded a gate: one, a woman, was lying on the ground. The other two, both male, stood above her, facing one another. She had not yet begun work on any of the faces; she was sculpting from memory, and the memories were becoming harder and harder to bear.

Does Andreas not remember? she wondered. Does he not see what I have created, where my mind has gone? Or is he so fixated on keeping me from knowing his plans for my child that he chooses to ignore it? She was certain he was making plans. He had no reason to believe that her child would be any different from the one Simonetta had carried.

"What do you do with the others? The other demon-born children?" she asked one afternoon. "You must not kill the Nephilim. They deserve only our pity."

Andreas told her not to worry, that he had trained the Petruvian priests to care for them.

"My child is innocent," she told him. "She must not be harmed."

"What is yours is mine," Andreas had promised. "But

perhaps you should get more rest; put away your work for now and return to it when you have recovered from the pain of childbirth," he said, inspecting the sculpture more closely.

Tomi looked at her unfinished sculpture and thought of the many sacrifices that Andreas had made to ensure that they were reborn to this life, here in Florence. Perhaps he was right. Perhaps she needed to clear her mind.

Andreas left the room, and she heard him speaking in low tones with Ludivivo, who had been waiting outside her door.

"It is coming soon. She must never know," Andreas was saying. "She cannot ever remember that Gio was Lucifer, in human form."

Did they think she was not aware of what she had done? Did they think she could not hear?

"We will erase her memory," Ludivivo said. "She will not know that there ever was a child, let alone that one has been taken from her."

"The child must die," Andreas said. "Quickly, before Lucifer becomes aware it ever existed."

"You need not worry," Ludivivo said. "I will take care of everything. Patrizio will see to it."

Tomi had been right—they planned to kill her child. She felt a furious hysteria rise in her soul— She would not permit it! She struggled to sit up in the bed, but she was too weak. She could not even move. What was this? She was bespelled, she realized: trapped, confined to the bed.

Andreas returned to the room and planted a kiss on her forehead.

"Sleep well, my love. Soon this will all be over."

The only other visitor to her prison was her friend the warlock, the guardian of the timekeepers. "You must help me," she said. "I fear for my baby. Andreas will not allow it to live." The warlock did not argue. The Norsemen were supposed to be neutral in the skirmishes of the lost children of the Almighty, but this one was fond of Tomi. He was a great admirer of her art. "I will see to it. I will help you. I will steal you away tonight. I must prepare, but I will see to it."

"Promise me," she said, gripping his arm.

"I will not fail you, my friend."

But that night was too late. It was not long after the warlock left that the labor pains started. At first they were subtle, almost possible for Tomi to ignore. When they grew sharper, stronger, more frequent, she called for the midwife. "Help me," she said. "Call my friend back."

But instead, the midwife brought Duc Patrizio de Medici, along with Tiberius Gemellus, the Silver Blood Enmortal, who was now in Andreas's loyal circle.

"Iacopo would not come, nor Margherita, so it is just us," Tiberius was saying. "They refuse to be a part of this. They suspect what is happening."

Tomi stirred—the names were familiar—her friend

Iacopo and his bondmate Margherita. What was Andreas planning that was so terrible even the Angels of the Apocalypse refused to participate? Where was her friend the timekeeper, who had promised to help her?

"We must move her quickly," Patrizio said.

"Where are you taking me?" she cried. Where were her loyal Venators? Why was she alone?

"Somewhere safe."

By then she was too tired, too weak, and in too much pain to protest. They brought her underground, into a dark basement smelling of mold and dust and decay. Tomi hoped that the birth would be quick, but it was not to be so. The pains stretched out for hours and into the next day. She grew weak and feverish. It became difficult to separate reality from dreams, for she had not slept; though occasionally she closed her eyes and disappeared for a few blissful seconds.

By the time the midwife insisted that she begin to push, she was delirious. Andreas entered, with Ludivivo. Why was she surrounded by so many men? What was happening?

"Dre—please, what is going on?" she begged.

They were waiting.

"Do not kill her," she begged. "Do not kill my baby."

"We will not harm her," Andreas said. "Ludivivo has found a family. This is why Patrizio is here," he said soothingly.

"We will take care of the baby." Patrizio nodded. "Do not fear, our dear Gabrielle."

Tomi was too weak to protest, but she took some comfort in the knowledge that her baby would not die. She was not strong enough to keep them from taking it, but if it was alive, surely she would have a chance to find the child again.

She began to scream. The pain was unbearable.

"Shhh . . ." the midwife said. "Andreas, she needs something to drink. A cool jug of water, perhaps."

"I will fetch it," Andreas said. "No harm will come to your child, my love, I promise."

And with that, Tomasia finally was able to push.

inn's dorm was all but abandoned when Schuyler arrived; everyone must have gone to the party, or to some other party. Or the library, she supposed—there must be some people in college who actually spend time studying. Wherever they were, she was happy they were gone; the front door was miraculously open, and she was alone.

Which gave her time to study the paintings. There were four of them, one on each wall. They were beautiful. If Schuyler had ever wondered whether Ben and Allegra were really in love, she didn't wonder now. Only someone who completely adored the woman he was painting could have infused such emotion onto the canvas. Surely her mother had had a chance to see them, before she fell into a coma.

The tricky part now was figuring out a way to extract the blood from the paint. Assuming, of course, that it was Ben's. Schuyler had only had time to sense the faintest aroma of blood when she'd looked at the paintings. If the blood didn't belong to her father, there was no point in destroying them.

How to be sure? Schuyler walked up to one of the paintings and stood as close to it as she could, breathing in deeply. Yes, she'd been correct the first time: there was definitely blood mixed in with the paint. But something about it smelled strange. Was it because her father's blood was somehow special? She couldn't be sure. She inhaled again. There was something familiar about its scent. Well, it would be totally awkward if someone walked in right now, but . . . she stretched out her tongue and licked.

And in that brief second, her hopes were dashed. She knew as soon as she tasted it. The blood wasn't Ben's.

It was Allegra's.

Vampire blood was supposed to disappear when it hit the air, but Schuyler's mother must have found a way to preserve hers. She must have given it to him, to help him with his work. It was a sweet, if strange, gesture, but either way, it was of no use to Schuyler.

Schuyler consoled herself that at least she wouldn't have to damage the paintings, and with them her future relationship with Finn. She would have to come up with another plan. Nothing left to do but go back to the hotel and sleep.

Oliver arrived at the airport just in time, wearing the same clothes he'd had on the night before and looking pleasingly rumpled. "Oliver Hazard-Perry, I never thought I would see *you* doing the walk of shame," Schuyler teased. "Good night, then?"

"The best. Who knew I could enjoy a kegger?"

"I don't think it was the party that was so much fun."

"Perhaps not," he allowed.

"How did you leave things?"

He sighed. "Well, that's complicated. We'll be in touch, of course, but I can't imagine anything will come of it until after . . . everything."

The sojourn back to the States had been a monumental one for Schuyler personally, but the problem at hand still remained. The Venators were meeting tonight, and while she had faith in Kingsley's leadership, Schuyler knew she was the one destined to bring the vampires salvation. But all she felt was useless.

Remember who your father was, her mother had told her. *Remember him when time stands still, when you stand at the crossroads, when the path opens before you.*

What did it mean?

The flight to London was smooth and uneventful, made easier by the comforts of first class. They disembarked to find a driver holding a sign with Schuyler's name on it. Kingsley had arranged for a limo to pick them up at Heathrow, Oliver explained. "How thoughtful," Schuyler said. "And how unlike him."

"People can change," Oliver said pointedly.

"Noted," she said.

They sank into the plush leather seats while the driver put their luggage in the trunk. With a low purr, the car exited the airport. Schuyler looked out the window as they moved onto the highway. It was always so hard getting used to the whole driving-on-the-other-side-of-the-road thing—she was glad she never had to do the driving herself.

"I don't know my way around London all that well," Oliver said, "but I feel like we're going in the wrong direction. Kingsley said the safe house was in Islington, which is that way."

Schuyler tapped on the glass window that separated them from the driver. "Excuse me? Are we going the right way? I don't know if Kingsley gave you the proper address. . . ."

The driver didn't appear to hear her, and he didn't lower the glass.

"What's going on here?" Oliver asked.

Schuyler started banging on the window. "Hello? Can you hear me? Hello?"

Still nothing.

"I'm starting to get a very bad feeling about this," Oliver said.

"Is there any chance Kingsley didn't send this car?"

"Come to think of it, he did mention he was sending a Venator team. Not just a driver. Damn it! What should we do? Should we try to jump out?" Oliver tested the door. "Locked."

"We can force it," Schuyler said. "I could take the door right off the hinges if I wanted to."

"While the car is moving? I'm not sure that's a good idea."

Just then, the car stopped. They'd pulled off the highway and were in a clearing. Schuyler heard a click and tested the door. Unlocked.

"As soon as I open it, we run," she said.

But no sooner had she said the words than someone else opened the door for her.

Schuyler froze. The feeling she'd had all along—she'd been right after all—someone had been watching and waiting . . . and now the watching and the waiting had ended, and whoever it was had come for her. She knew, she felt it, and she hadn't done anything, hadn't told anybody—and now they were both in danger. She wanted to kick herself for being so stupid. She would never see Jack again, never get to know her newfound family. She'd failed in her task, and this was her punishment.

"This isn't good," Oliver said.

"Get out of the car," a cold voice said. "Now."

"Where are you taking us?" Schuyler screamed as her assailant pulled her out of the car.

"Not *us*," he said. "You."

Then Schuyler blacked out.

In a flash, she and her captor seemed to be somewhere else, somewhere familiar: falling, falling deep into the glom, and away from the light, though Schuyler felt like they were still moving.

They stopped. Schuyler tried to keep herself from throwing up; all that motion had made her nauseous. It was dark, but as her vision started to clear, she realized where she was. Hell.

The Venators grabbed Mimi and brought her to a room on the second floor of the house, then left her alone. *Really? Would it be that easy?* She tried the handle. Locked. Enchanted-locked, too, not just regular-locked, which would be easy enough to pulverize. She looked around. They'd taken her to a library, the walls filled with books from floor to ceiling, ladders on wheels propped against every shelf so browsers could slide back and forth between the higher rows. Too bad she wasn't much of a reader.

The Venators left her in the room for so long she actually started looking at some of the titles. She picked a book with a familiar-sounding title and settled into an enormous leather chair to read. She barely had time to process a word before she fell asleep.

She awoke to the sound of low male laughter. "Such

a threatening figure, all curled up in a chair like a puppy."

Kingsley.

Mimi yawned and stretched her arms over her head, well aware that he was watching.

"A kitten, then. A very, very sexy kitten."

Mimi started to stand up, but Kingsley blocked her. "No, you stay where you are for now. I want to have a conversation with you, and I don't want you pulling out that little needle of a sword, like you did the last time we saw each other."

Mimi held up her hands and sat back down. "You're the one with guards at the door," she said. "You're in charge now."

"I've spent a lot of time thinking about you," Kingsley said. "A lot more than I wanted to, given how you've been behaving. But I really wanted to figure out what was going on. One minute you travel to Hell for me; the next you never want to see me again; then you throw a fight with me to get me to steal the grail. You let me win, I know. Don't even try to tell me differently. I know you."

Mimi started to interrupt, but Kingsley held up a finger. "I'm not done. I want some answers, and if at the end of this conversation you still want to do a little sparring, that can be arranged. But be warned, my darling, that if I'm not satisfied with what I hear from you, this will be the last fight we ever have. One way or another."

"Fair enough," she said. So this would end how it was supposed to.

"Here's what I'm thinking: given your sudden shift in attentiveness toward me after we got out of Hell, I'm guessing that you were forced into making some sort of deal with Lucifer. I know you entered the underworld thinking you'd happily sacrifice Oliver for a chance to save me, but he turned out to be too good a friend. See, the thing I've known about you from the beginning is that no matter what you want people to think, you're not a bad person. Even on your worst day," he said gently. "Unless, of course, you're missing something vital. Like your soul."

She stared at him.

"I think you traded your soul for mine, and that's how you freed me from Hell. You couldn't sacrifice Oliver, so you sacrificed yourself. That's why you were so cold, as if you didn't care about me at all. Because you didn't."

Mimi shook her head. "What a lovely story you've told yourself. I'll tell Lucifer you're not just a weakling these days, you're delusional as well."

Kingsley sighed. "You can insult me all you want. I know it's a charade. But what I can't figure out is what happened after that. Because, as much as you'd like me to think that you're working for the devil himself, I know you. I can look into your eyes and see that you're there and that you still love me."

"You couldn't be more wrong," Mimi spat. "I'm just a much better actress than you think I am."

"You aren't, though," Kingsley said. "I know you think

you are, but you're not. And somehow I get the feeling that this whole thing you've orchestrated is simply a way to set us up for some sort of fight to the finish that I'd rather not engage in."

"As if you have a choice."

"Maybe I don't," he agreed. "But you had your chance to kill me back at Rosslyn Chapel, and you didn't take it. Not only that, but you set up that meeting. I think you *wanted* me to take the chalice from you, to save you from having to bring Lucifer something he so desperately needed."

So he'd understood everything, after all. She so desperately wished she could tell him that he was right, that she'd loved him all along. But the necklace she wore was burning, as if on fire.

"I knew that was you from the beginning. Of course I did. I know where Dehua is. I sent her and Sam to look after Schuyler. I wanted to have this conversation in private, but of course Deming is a bit impulsive, and now everyone knows. I had to let them take you."

Mimi shrugged.

"Why are you here, Mimi? Does it mean what I hope it means? That you've returned to us—to me?"

"Never," she said. "Why would I ever settle for you when Jack is waiting for me?" She wanted to make him angry, angry enough to fight. She could goad him into it, use that male vanity against him.

"Jack isn't waiting for you, and we both know it,"

Kingsley said. "So what's your game? Why are you here?"

"I'm here for you." She leaned back in the chair and thrust her leg forward, kicking Kingsley's knee as hard as she could. He buckled, and she was able to get past him and unsheathe her sword. "A fight to the finish, isn't that what you said?" She swung hard, with the goal of inflicting some sort of flesh wound, enough to get Kingsley riled up.

He was quick, though, and he darted out of the way before her sword could reach him. His weapon was in his hand before she saw him retrieve it, but she was quick too—she parried his thrust, and the metal swords made a clanging sound that echoed in the room.

"It doesn't have to be like this," he said as they sparred.

"This is the only way it can end," she said. "And it needs to end. You should have killed me when you had the chance."

"I could say the same for you," he said.

They fought like the equals they had always been, blocking each other's jabs, ducking each other's blows. As always, Mimi was amazed at how well matched they were. She didn't have to think about whether she wanted to win this fight; it was all she could do to maintain her ground.

And then, all of a sudden, she couldn't maintain it anymore. Kingsley had forced her up against the bookshelves, and though she'd scaled one of the ladders to get away from him, he'd used his sword to slice through the stair on which she stood, which sent her tumbling to the ground.

Kingsley stood over her, his sword pointed at her throat. "I'm going to give you one last chance," he said. "I don't want to have to kill you. But I can't have you jeopardizing everything we stand for. Lucifer cannot return to Heaven. I won't permit it. Say something, anything, so I don't have to do this. Please."

But Mimi remained silent.

FORTY-FOUR

Tomasia (Florence, 1452)

omi woke up exhausted in her own bedroom. From the window, she could see the red roofs of the city, the sunlight dappling on the terra-cotta. Why did her body ache so? Last she remembered, she had been up late into the night, working on her sculpture. But when she looked at it, it seemed unfamiliar. Who were these people—the woman on the ground and the two men standing above her?

She was cold and trembling, and her body ached with sorrow. What had happened? Why couldn't she remember? Where was Andreas?

The last thing she remembered was chasing a Silver Blood on those same roofs, jumping from house to house until they had caught up with him on the top of Brunelleschi's unfinished dome. The hooded stranger who had carried Lucifer's mark.

"Did I fall? Is that why everything hurts so much?" she asked.

"Yes." Andreas nodded. "The Croatan hit you with a blood spell. Ludivivo and I have worked long and hard to keep you here with us in this cycle."

"A blood spell! How long have I been asleep?"

He told her, and she could not believe it. So many months. But there was no reason for Andreas to lie to her. He came to sit by her bed and rested his head on her shoulder.

She pulled him to her. "They are growing in strength, our enemies."

"Yes," he murmured.

"Do not be troubled, my love. I am whole." She looked down at his dark head, expecting to feel the usual surge of affection that came over her every time she saw him. But something felt different. She felt . . . empty. Numb. She pushed the sculpture away from the bed.

"Displeased with your work?" He stood up from her embrace. "Why don't you lie down, and I'll fetch you a cool jug of water. You aren't well. You're still healing."

A cool jug of water . . . why did that sound so familiar?

"Yes, I suppose that would be a good idea." She had survived a blood spell; she was lucky to be alive. So that was why. There was no other reason she would feel so odd.

Was there?

She looked down at her belly, at her pale white legs, and in a flash saw a river of blood, saw a baby's head crown, but the memory went as quickly as it came—and she did not understand, did not know what it meant. What baby? What was all that blood?

But something in her soul grieved, something in her soul died that day. . . .

Tomasia would live the rest of that cycle with Andreas in Florence, never knowing that she'd had a child, or that the child had been stolen from her. And Andreas and Ludivivo would never know that Patrizio had betrayed them, that instead of destroying the babe, Patrizio had raised the girl as his own; had killed his own daughter so that Lucifer's spirit could remain on earth. The girl was known as Giulia de Medici, child of Duc Patrizio de Medici. When she was sixteen, she tried to kill herself, as she would attempt to do in every cycle of her immortal life.

In the White Darkness, Allegra and Charles sat together at the piano in the Cotton Club. 1923.

"So that is how you hid her from me," Allegra said. "And that is how I betrayed you. I knew. I always knew. The guilt and the shame at my betrayal has haunted me for centuries. As has my anger toward you for what you did to my daughter."

"I failed you, Allegra."

"No, Charles, we failed each other. Because Florence was merely a consequence of a decision you made long ago. This is not where it began, our estrangement. Not here."

"Yes," Charles said. "You were never able to forgive me for it. Look at that sculpture you made."

Allegra stared at the sculpture on the table in Florence so long ago. A sculpture that harkened back even farther in their history. A woman on the ground. Two men above her. One with a sword to the other's throat.

"This all started in Rome."

ow fitting that Caligula had hidden the path in a theater—his entire life had been a charade. Perhaps that was the idea—that Lucifer was laughing at them as he worked toward their destruction. Bliss forged ahead, not quite sure what she would find, or what they would do when they did find the blockage.

"Bliss?" Malcolm said. "I feel kinda weird."

"Weird how? Like, it's-dark-and-you're-freaked-out weird, or like, the-passages-are-closer weird?"

"Passages weird," he whispered.

"Well, at least we know we're in the right place," she said. "What do we do now?"

"It gets worse the closer I get to the passages," he said. "We need to keep going."

They walked toward the center of the courtyard. In the faint light of her phone, Bliss could see Malcolm's face turning green. "Looks like we're on the right track," she said. "I'm sorry you have to go through this." Malcom's stomach was sensitive to the slightest evil. In the past, his sickness warned the pack of an imminent attack by Hellhounds.

He waved her off. "It's what I signed up for. I'm fine."

He didn't look fine, though. She hoped they found something quickly. At least they had time to explore—it had only taken them minutes to get to the center, where Malcolm quietly turned and threw up. "This is it," he said. "It's right here."

"What's here?"

"An open passage, which is why I feel so terrible."

"Lawson's the only one who can open a portal," said Bliss. But as they walked closer, she saw that Malcom was right. The air before them shimmered, and finally a light began to shine, brighter and brighter, until a tunnel stood before them.

"I'm going in," Bliss said.

"Not by yourself you're not," Malcolm said.

"I have to. You have to let them know we're here."

"Stop arguing. We're right here," came the voice of Ahramin. Edon and Rafe were right behind her. "Hurry. I think the hotel's getting suspicious about us."

"All right—Mac and I will go first, then the rest of you will follow."

Together they walked into the light. Bliss felt the now-familiar disorientation of being in the passages, having no idea where she was. But unlike in times past, they didn't stop; instead, the swirling sensation slowed down, and she found that they could move around in the light.

"Where are we?" she asked.

"I'm not sure," Malcolm said. "I think we're near the place where something bad happened. Let's just keep going and see what happens."

But before they could take another step, there was a rumbling sound, and Bliss felt the ground beneath them disappear.

She was falling, falling, into the abyss, into the void, into the nothingness of time and space.

It felt as if she were falling forever. She couldn't tell if it had been minutes or hours before she finally passed out. She came to and realized she was being held. She could feel strong arms around her, and she opened her eyes. She could see the light of the passages above her, faintly, but all was dark. "What—? Where am I? Who—?"

"Don't worry, I've got you," a voice said.

Lawson.

"How did you get here?" she asked, even though she had already guessed.

"From the other direction. I was able to open a portal. This is it. This is the break in the passages, the rift in the timeline. See how the tunnel stops right there?" he asked.

"Mac, are you okay?" Bliss said.

"Here," Malcolm said, taking off his glasses and wiping them with the bottom of his shirt.

"Where's everyone else?" Bliss asked.

"I think they're still in the passages; I can hear them," Lawson said. "They'll be all right; they went the other way. We'll catch up with them later."

"How did you find us?"

"I was just ahead of you in the passages, from the other direction, and I saw both of you fall, and I jumped."

"Where are we?"

"The abyss. Limbo. We need to get back up there," he said, pointing to the light far above them.

"How do we do that?"

"Together"—Lawson held each of their hands—"we'll jump."

They were back in the tunnel. Back where they had started. Bliss could see the rift now. There were two passages meeting in the middle; two mirrored tunnels meeting in a point. The fissure was broken. They had attempted to cross it, and that was why they had been thrown into Limbo.

"What is it?"

"Time stopped here," Lawson said. "The fissure means it was manipulated by someone. It stopped and then the passages forked in two directions, whereas time should only go in one way."

Bliss stared at the rift, and she remembered something she had learned during the Committee meetings, when she had first been inducted into the secret world of the Blue Bloods.

Only one vampire in the history of the world has had the ability to stop time.

"Now is the hard part," Lawson said. "You need to concentrate. Try to put yourself in Allegra's mind, or in—" He couldn't say it; Bliss could hear it in his voice: *In your father's.* "Either one of your parents might be able to show us what happened, if they were here. Focus, and I'll go into the glom and try to see what you see."

Bliss closed her eyes. *Show me,* she thought. *One of you, please, show me. Now.*

Then she saw.

A woman running through the passages. She was frightened, and Bliss felt her fear. It was vibrating all around her.

Bliss stared at her.

The woman stared back.

It was Allegra, and not Allegra.

She looked different. This was her mother in a different cycle.

But it was her immortal spirit that Bliss recognized.

Gabrielle.

"Run!" Gabrielle said. "Run!" She ran toward the fissure, toward the darkness.

Bliss gasped and stumbled, and Lawson caught her.

"What's wrong?"

"We have to help her!" Bliss said.

"There's nothing we can do from here," Lawson said. "All

we can do is watch and try to understand what happened."

"I don't want to understand! I want to make it stop before whoever that is gets her."

"Why, what's wrong?"

"I know who's chasing her. I know why she's running away, and he's coming closer now. It's . . . it's my father."

FORTY-SIX

Schuyler

hat was more surprising than finding herself suddenly in Hell was who had taken her there. How had she not recognized his voice? How had she not recognized him from the very beginning? He had disguised himself—an illusion, she saw now—and she hadn't even noticed; hadn't given a second glance to the black-suited chauffeur holding the sign.

The illusion was gone, and now she could see him clearly. His shining blond hair and glass-green eyes. She could feel his body against hers, and his breath on her cheek. He was alive— her heart leapt at that—Jack was alive! She had tried so hard to suppress her feelings, to stop herself from worrying—but to see him in front of her made her realize how truly she had believed he was dead. But her happiness was hers alone. He did not share it and she did not understand why. She stared at his face: why was he scrowling like that? And why was he so cold? His skin was like ice to the touch—as if he were made of marble. He was like a statue.

This was not the joyful reunion Schuyler had been dreaming about. There was something wrong with Jack. He was not himself. What had happened to her love?

"Jack—what's going on?" she breathed, turning to him even as he held her like a prisoner.

His gaze was cool and distant. There was no spark in his eyes, no warmth there. He was Jack, but somehow not her Jack. Schuyler began to feel very afraid for the two of them.

"I don't understand," she said. "Why are we here? What's going on? Jack—what's happened to you?"

He did not answer, and Schuyler realized what she had been loath to admit to herself. That the presence she'd felt—those eyes on her—it had been him all along. She had sensed it, and had tried to reach out to him, but there had been no response, and so she'd tried to forget about it, had tried to convince herself that she felt nothing. That she was seeing phantoms; that she was kidding herself.

But of course she knew. She knew he was in London; she knew he had been watching her. She had been waiting for him to come to her, to show himself, and now he had. Had he seen everything that had happened to her? Was he there when she met her grandmother? When she visited her father's grave?

She looked deep into his eyes, and found him staring back at her blankly. It was as if the Jack she knew had been completely erased. She felt her stomach clench, and tears come to her eyes. Even if she could not put her arms around him, since he held them at her sides, they were so close that she could turn her face and press her cheek against his cold one.

"Where are you taking me?" she asked, even though she suspected she already knew. "You're working for Lucifer again, aren't you?"

He did not deny it.

"But why? Why now? What happened to Mimi? Did you kill her?" Schuyler sucked in her breath. Was that what happened? Was that why he was so changed? Because he had killed her?

"Azrael lives."

"As do you. So, how?" She struggled against his hold and pressed her body against his. She had hoped that his body would remember hers at least—that somehow, in some way, he would acknowledge their deep bond. Whenever they were together, there was always so much heat between them, but still, Jack remained ice-cold and indifferent. Was there any way to bring him back to her? To make him remember? "I don't care," she said. "You don't have to explain anything. I just want you back, Jack. Please, don't do this. I know this isn't you."

"You don't know anything about me, Schuyler, you never have. You've never understood what it means to be one of the Fallen."

"How can you say that? After all we've been through?" She thought of everything they had done together—remembered the first time they had spoken, outside of that nightclub in New York—all those secret nights in the Perry Street apartment—their bonding in Florence—and the last night in Cairo. . . . He would always be hers, and she his. He was her great love, and seeing him, even like this, brought a joy to her senses, regardless of her fear and confusion.

Jack was alive.

And yet Jack was dead.

Where was the boy she had pledged her life and love to? Where was the boy who'd held her so close she couldn't breathe sometimes? Where was the boy with the serious smile and the poetry and the books? The boy who had taken her to Vienna on a whim? The boy who knew her even better than he knew himself? Who knew everything about her, every inch of her body, every flutter of her heart. Jack was hers—he owned her, she loved him deeply, and even like this, she loved him still. Where was Jack? What had he done to himself?

"Jack, it's me," she said softly. "Let me help you."

"You don't know anything," he said again. "And I saw you with him."

"What? With who?"

"With *him*," he spat, and she realized he was talking about Oliver.

Schuyler wanted to laugh, it was so absurd. "You know

there's nothing between me and Oliver. Not anymore. Not since I left New York to be with you. Remember? He's just my friend." She loved Oliver, but she had never loved him the way she loved Jack. Jack knew that. He'd known it from the beginning. It had almost broken her best friend—and herself to admit it—but it was true. There had always ever been one boy in her heart. Only Jack Force.

"I know what he wants . . . and what you want. What you've always wanted."

He'd seen her kiss Oliver, she realized. His grip around her tightened, but there was no warmth in it, only anger, only violence. He could break her in half, she realized; snap her like a twig; kill her without a second thought.

"That wasn't what it looked like; you of all people should know that," she said. "I was kissing him good-bye."

"Like you did me?" he asked with a smirk in his voice, and now his hold on her became so painful, it was all she could do not to cry out.

"How can you say that to me?" she asked. How could he sully the memory of their last night? It was all she had of him. She knew he wasn't himself, but it still hurt.

"Because there's nothing you can say that I want to hear," he said with a cruel smile. "Our bond is broken. It was never forged. There is nothing between us now, and there never has been."

"You don't believe that, I know you don't. Not truly. Why are you doing this?" she whispered.

"Because this is who I am," Jack said.

Schuyler understood what he was telling her now—that evil was always part of his nature. He was a Dark Angel. He had been fighting for the Light, but he had given up at last. Whatever had happened between him and Mimi, it had changed him, just as Schuyler had feared.

She was going to die. She understood why he had come for her. She was going to die at his hands. This was how it was going to end. Lawrence had warned her; Mimi had warned her. Yet she and Jack had ignored all the signs, all the warnings. They had fought to be together, and this was how it would end. Their love had been futile, damaged, cursed from the beginning.

Jack continued to hold her so close, and Schuyler whispered in his ear. "I know you. I know this isn't you. And even if it is, I still love you. As much as I always have. You will always be mine. Take me—I am yours. Take whatever you need from me, I will give it gladly. I will always love you, I promised you that when you left, and it's true now." She looked at him, and no matter what happened, she knew that it was true. She would always love Jack. Even like this. Even if he no longer loved her.

But Jack did not answer. He was transforming before her, into the fearful vision she'd seen before. The terrifying horned angel with the magnificent wings, clad in golden armor. Abbadon, the Angel of Destruction. The Dark Angel of the Apocalypse.

"What does Lucifer want with me?" she asked softly.

"I think you know."

"The Gate of Promise."

"You are the key," Abbadon said. "You will bring us into Paradise. And Heaven will crumble under our domain."

PART THE THIRD

THE SINS
OF THE FATHER

While everyone's lost the battle is won.
—The Killers, "All These Things That I've Done"

I *remember everything now.*

I had decided to walk after the performance. The music moved me, it was so beautiful and sad. But I was happy. We were happy then. You and I. We had learned to love this world, and we had not yet known despair. I had discovered something that could change our world forever, and I'd meant to tell you but I wanted to be sure. It was a wonderful secret, and I'd planned to tell you that we would soon be home in Eden.

I went past the courtyard and down the steps, and decided I would take the passages to visit our friends in Lutetia. But as I walked down, I heard something—a noise, something different. And I followed the noise to its source. The tunnels were different, and I realized I was no longer in this world, but in another. I was not even in the passages anymore.

I was on a different path.

I heard his voice, booming in the darkness. The voice of our friend and emperor. Gaius. The one they called Caligula. Addressing his people.

I turned the corner and I saw.

Their eyes glittered crimson and silver; their fangs outstretched. I saw their hunger and greed, and I knew all was lost. That Gaius was Lucifer, hidden among us, and that he had discovered the Paths of the Dead, and he would lead an army of the Fallen and demons to take this world.

So I ran.

I ran away, to tell you, to warn you, to warn us all about the betrayal that was in the Coven, that we had nursed and nurtured among us.

I ran.

And Lucifer followed me.

FORTY-EIGHT

Mimi

ingsley's sword was at her throat. "Why is this happening again?" he asked. "Why do we always seem to find ourselves here?"

"Destiny, I suppose," Mimi said, finally breaking her silence; though she knew it probably wasn't the time for joking around.

"You know I love you," he said.

"Do you? You're so in love with me you've been running around with half the girls in London?" she said with a raised eyebrow.

"They meant nothing—and I did nothing with them. I tried to forget you. God knows. I was mad. I tried to find something—anything—that would make me forget you. But no one could. I've been faithful, I swear. Appearances can be deceiving. You of all people should know that."

Mimi continued to glare at him even as she felt a tremendous sense of relief.

Kingsley brushed his sword on her skin like a caress. "And I know you love me. You told me that you'd love me no matter what, and I should remember that. So why are you trying to get me to forget that now?"

"Because this is how it has to end," she said.

"You know that's not what I want," he said, but Mimi could see doubt in his eyes. He didn't understand why she was doing this, and that was good. She needed to confuse him, to convince him that she was hateful.

He was better off without her. He'd have a chance at happiness, at a better life. He could find someone else, someone who wasn't so complicated, so difficult. Someone *nice*. That was a word no one would ever use to describe her.

Kingsley's sword hovered at her neck, then slashed at the collar of her blouse.

"Hey!" she cried. "Careful! It's Chanel!"

But his eyes were locked on the emerald stone sitting at the base of her throat.

"Is that what I think it is?" he said, horrified.

Lucifer's Bane. The Star of Heaven. A treasure more precious than the stars themselves. Given by the Morningstar to his dearest love.

"I told you, I am with him now," Mimi said. "He is my Dark Prince and master."

FORTY-NINE

Schuyler

On the shore of the river of gold, the victor's city shall once again rise on the threshold of the Gate of Promise.

He had taken her to the gate, hidden deep underneath the oldest standing church in the city: St. John's Chapel in the Tower of London. Down beneath the church, in the tunnel that led to the Paths of the Dead, and toward the stone altar in the middle of the passage.

The Gate of Promise was a slab with a circle cut out of the center, and paths had been carved into the stone surrounding it. Almost like one of those puzzles with a miniature pinball in it.

Jack laid her on the stone, and it felt cold upon her back. For the first time, she was truly afraid. She understood now what the grooves in the slab were for, and how the gate would be opened. A pathway of blood. Once again, the gate's destruction would demand a sacrifice.

"Jack," she cried as he leaned down toward her neck, his fangs outstretched, until she could feel their sharpness on her skin and a trickle of blood. His body lay heavily on hers, and she could feel their hearts beating in tandem. She had told him the truth—that he could take what he wanted from her—and when he sank his fangs into her neck, she felt the same shudder of ecstasy and pleasure that it had always brought her. Her blood mingling with his. She felt his spirit overwhelm her, and she opened herself to him. He was drinking from her so deeply, and she surrendered—if this was death, then she would welcome it. She wanted to be one with him, for all eternity. She could feel a change within him, a quickening, an excitement. He was cold no longer, but warm, so warm again. But he had never taken her like this before, and she felt dizzy and weak. He was taking too much from her, too much blood—and it fell upon the stone, and the etchings on its slab came alive, awakened, opened. . . .

And still he drank as he held her down, keeping her hands at her sides. His grip was like ice, shackles around her wrist. Pleasure and pain, life and death, blood and sacrifice.

Finally he stopped and released his fangs, but now she could feel his warm breath on her cheek. He whispered in her ear, and for a moment, Schuyler thought she was safe. That he had returned to her at last.

Jack shook his head. "I'm not going to kill you," he said softly.

"Because I am," said an unfamiliar voice.

Schuyler looked up to the sound and saw that Lucifer and his armies were massed behind Jack. The Fallen angels, their demons and trolls; Hellhounds and every creature of Hell were ready and waiting.

For the sacrifice.

For her blood to open the gate.

FIFTY

Gabrielle

I could feel him. He was calling for me. His voice, so beautiful even then. He was saying:

Gabrielle. Do not fear. Do not fear me. I love you. I will not harm you.

Stop.

Stop and listen to me.

Gabrielle, my light. Stop for me.

But I knew if I stopped I was lost. I knew that he had planned this all along, from the very beginning.

As I ran away from him. I saw someone in the passages.

A girl.

She had beautiful red hair and green eyes.

My daughter. My daughter with him. I could see it in her sadness. The scar through her shirt. I knew what had put it there. I could see the remnants of your sword shattered in her soul; knew that its power had healed her.

I understood then, that this was not the end.

This was only the beginning.

But maybe there was hope.

There was a boy with her. A wolf. And I knew. I knew how to get help.

I could see the past, the present, and the future.

I brought her close to me.

I whispered in her ear.

FIFTY-ONE

Bliss

"Mother."

"Lupus Theilel. My wolfsbane."

"What is happening to you? We can help."

"You cannot stop this from happening. He will come for me. And it will be done."

"No!"

"There is nothing you can do now."

"No," Bliss sobbed. "He will destroy you."

"Listen—the wolves—the Praetorian Guard—they will rise here—they will help Michael defeat the demons and their king for now. . . . And when Lucifer returns, you must have them by your side." Gabrielle looked at Lawson. "Fenrir, it is up to you to restore what has been broken."

"We cannot free them. The passages are blocked. We have been unable to return to the underworld," Lawson explained.

"This is our only chance, then," Gabrielle said. "He will take me, and he will be distracted. When it happens, the path will be open." She turned to Lawson. "Open the portal and it will take you where you need to go."

"We can't leave you here!" cried Bliss.

"It is too late for me."

"Mother . . ."

"It has already happened," Gabrielle said. "Nothing can change that."

She turned away from them and kept running.

And they saw him.

Lucifer.

He appeared in the tunnel as his true immortal form. He was beautiful and golden, his wings stretched to their full span. He stopped Gabrielle from running, appeared right in front of her.

Took her in his arms.

"Gabrielle."

Now!

"Lawson! The portal!" Bliss whispered.

He did not hesitate. He took her hand and Malcolm's in his.

The passage opened before them, and they jumped through.

The Prince of Darkness, the King of Hell, the Morningstar, the Lightbringer, Lucifer the Archangel of the Dawn, stood before her. He was so beautiful, just as he had been on that mountaintop in Rio, when Schuyler had first seen him. His beauty was painful to behold. His light was stronger than the sun's. He was Heaven's son personified.

Schuyler could not move. Jack no longer had his arms around her, but she was held by a dark enchantment, bound to the stone altar. She was so weak, she had lost too much blood, she could hardly move even without her bonds.

Lucifer smiled and caressed her hair. "As beautiful as your mother, perhaps even more so."

"Don't talk about my mother. You don't know anything about my mother," Schuyler said, finding it difficult even to speak.

"On the contrary, my dear. Your mother and I . . . well, let's just say we are very, very old friends. I know Gabrielle perhaps too intimately. I finally understood this was what she was hiding from me. It was so easy to find after all. So this is what she had been planning. Salvation. Redemption. There will be no redemption today. Only revenge and triumph."

Lucifer bent down by her neck, and Schuyler cringed away from him and closed her eyes tightly, preparing for his fangs to pierce her skin.

But he suddenly recoiled. "Abbadon! You drank from her!"

"My apologies, my lord, the temptation was too great." Jack bowed.

"Yes, I see," Lucifer growled. "No matter." The Dark Prince took his sword and cut her throat, opening her jugular, and her lifesblood poured out of her, onto the stone tablet, opening the gate. A river of blood . . .

So this was death. Schuyler had wondered if she had inherited the immortality of her mother's kin, and now she knew. She had not. She was mortal. She could die, and she would die now. Today.

She could no longer speak, no longer think. But she held on to the one thing that she knew was true. Her love.

Jack . . . Jack . . . my love . . . help me . . . she sent. Even if he would not answer, she still held on to him. He was all she had at the last.

Only Jack.

She stared at him, at his blank eyes, and she prepared for death, prepared for the end of her life.

I have nothing to regret. I regret nothing. She had tried and failed everyone—her mother, Lawrence, the Coven. She had failed Jack as well. By falling in love with him she had doomed him. But even so, she could not regret their love. She had tried her best and she had lost.

She closed her eyes as her life drained from her.

Then, at all once, through the fog, as if from very very far away, Schuyler heard him. Heard his voice in her head.

Jack's voice.

Reaching out to her like a lifeline, a light in the dark. Just as she'd hoped. Perhaps the Sacred Kiss had returned him to her somehow.

But when he spoke, his voice was cold and cruel.

Only your father can help you now, Jack sent, as he stood at Lucifer's side, watching her die.

FIFTY-THREE

Mimi

"**I** don't believe it," Kingsley said, staring at the emerald stone that yoked her to Lucifer. "I don't believe it for a second."

But Mimi was tired of waiting and tired of playing this game. He was so close to her and so dear, and if she did not do it now, she would never have the courage again, and so she pulled on his sword and brought it against her throat, wanting to end it all, to save him even if she could not save herself.

She waited for death.

But death did not come.

Kingsley was faster, stronger, and instead of letting his blade cleave her in two, he directed it toward the heart of the emerald.

"No!" she screamed.

The emerald burst into White Flame and disappeared.

Mimi blinked her eyes open. She was alive and Kingsley was alive. The terrible dark burden had fallen from her shoulders.

She threw herself into his arms and sobbed.

Kingsley clasped her to him and they fell backward to the floor, and he was kissing her, and she was kissing him with a passion that surprised even her.

He was smiling. He was so handsome and brave, and he held her as if he would never let her go.

"How did you do that?" she asked.

"The godsfire. We have equipped all of our swords with the power of the Holy Spirit. It destroyed Lucifer's Bane. So what's going on? Are you going to tell me?"

She told him everything, just as the door opened with a bang.

Oliver stood there, babbling and hysterical. He had used the Venator's code that Kingsley had given him in secret to track them to the safe house. "Schuyler! They took Schuyler—they're bringing her to the gate!"

FIFTY-FOUR

Lupus Theilel

They had returned to the underworld, collected the rest of the pack in the passages, and returned to their former home. Bliss could see the smoke, smell the fire, and breathe the ash of the barren lands, the forgotten world, where nothing grew and everything was dead. The eternally gray skies hung above them.

"I hope you remember your way around here," Bliss whispered.

"Like it was yesterday," Lawson replied. "Come on, the wolves are in their dens."

"What about the trolls? And the masters?" Malcolm asked.

"What about them?" Lawson smiled.

"You are not afraid," Bliss said.

He shook his head. "Your mother. The Angel of the Lord. Gabrielle. She called me Fenrir."

Bliss realized he had never believed it before. Even after he had destroyed Romulus—even after everything he had been able to accomplish. Lawson hadn't believed in himself. Could not accept that he was the one who would lead the wolves out of enslavement.

With a great roar, Lawson transformed into the great wolf, and Fenrir stood before Bliss. He was larger than Romulus; larger than any beast of Hell.

His strength will break our chains.

In his spirit we shall be reborn.

Bliss looked at the pack: they had transformed as well. The wolves stood in a circle around her. Their eyes were shining with the blue crescent sigils that marked them as Fenrir's own.

She was alone.

She was no longer a vampire.

But as she discovered, she was no longer human either.

She looked down at herself. Her claws. Felt the sharpness of her fangs. Different from the vampire fangs. She felt the strength in her body, in her animal nature.

She was one of them.

Whatever her mother had done, she had done this. Given her the wolf gift. Given her the strength to belong.

Lawson nuzzled her. *You are truly one of the pack now. Run with me.*

The wolves howled, a battle cry, a warning:

We are coming. We are coming, my brothers and sisters.

Fenrir has returned.

We shall break your chains. We shall lead you into freedom.

We shall bring war upon our enemies.

Arise, arise! It is our time. The War of Heaven is upon us. Arise, wolves of the den, wolves of the guard. Arise and defeat the enemy we slew once before.

FIFTY-FIVE

Schuyler

My father? Schuyler wondered, even as she felt her consciousness beginning to fade; as her life-blood seeped out and death approached.

My father?

Why would Jack tell her that her father could help her? How could he be so merciless to say such a thing?

My father is dead. My father is buried in the ground. He is no help to anyone.

Then she realized . . .

Her father.

Her immortal father.

Charles Force. Michael. Her father. This was Allegra's secret. This was the key of the twins, the *sangreal*. Schuyler had had a human father to create a new life, but somehow, she was also Michael and Gabrielle's daughter.

Schuyler remembered those days at the hospital, at

Allegra's bedside, and her intuition, the thought that had popped into her head when she'd seen the gray-haired man kneeling in her mother's room, asking for her forgiveness. What had she called him then? *Father.*

They had the same dark hair, though his had gone gray. They shared a bond that neither of them had acknowledged. For Allegra's secret had been hidden so deeply when she'd broken the bond, when she'd married her human familiar. The truth of Schuyler's heritage had to remain a secret, even from her own father.

Father.

Help me.

Help me.

Father.

From the White Darkness, a sword appeared in her hand.

Michael's sword.

The Blade of Paradise. The Golden Sword of Heaven.

Her father's sword.

She gripped its hilt and slashed at the invisible bindings that held her, and she could feel the strength returning to her body, could feel the wound on her neck begin to heal. She leapt from the stone table, holding her sword aloft.

Lucifer roared and urged his dark armies to her destruction, and Schuyler cowered as the Dark Prince lunged toward her with hatred in his eyes, his own sword blazing white with the fire of Heaven.

But the blow never landed, as Jack threw himself upon her to shield her from the attack.

"Jack!" she screamed.

He looked at her tenderly, and she knew that he had never been false. That there had been a reason for his actions. He had drunk from her, she realized now, to keep Lucifer from doing the same.

"Hey you." She smiled and traced a finger on his cheek. "Where have you been?"

"Right here, always," Jack murmured, kissing her all over her face, her neck. But there was little time for tenderness.

Lucifer reared up with ferocious strength, and the Dark Prince loomed over them. His fangs bared, he was no longer beautiful, no longer bright as the sun, but revealed as Hell's eternal king, as the horrific monster he was, dark and twisted and evil. Schuyler held on to Jack and prepared for Lucifer to do his worst.

But out of the shadows, out of the darkness, powerful beasts emerged, ready for blood. The wolves of the guard.

FIFTY-SIX

Bliss

*T*he wolves crashed into the battle, meeting their former masters with tooth and claw. With froth on their lips and blood in their mouths. For revenge. For victory. For freedom.

They had followed Fenrir as he raced back through the passages, toward the Gate of Promise, which Gabrielle had shown him, and appeared at the stone tablet just as Schuyler held Michael's sword aloft.

"Destroy our enemies!" Fenrir roared. "Make them feel our wrath, our revenge!"

Bliss saw Schuyler through the chaos and wanted to run to her, but there was no time. The battle was upon them. They would fight or they would die. The wolves had thrown off their chains; they were savage and ferocious. Demon-fighters. Demon-killers.

Silver against flesh, the White Fire of Heaven against the

beasts of Hell. The wolves fought bravely and courageously, but their numbers were no match for the godsfire, for the flame that seared their very souls.

They ran howling to the edges, howling in retreat.

Until a blaze of light shone from the darkness.

A light that was just as bright as the godsfire—even brighter—this was the light from the Holy Grail, blessed by the spirit of the Son of God. The true light of Heaven.

The Venators had come.

The Angels Araquiel and Azrael had come to fight for the Light, to defend Heaven's Gate against its enemies. They flew into battle with a team of angels, arrayed in their golden armor, while everywhere, horns, horns, horns rang in triumph, just as when Michael had led the angels so long ago.

Their swords were aflame with the godsfire, and their hearts were pure and joyous as they fell upon the demons and their Silver Blood brethren.

They said there was no more beautiful sight that day than Araquiel cleaving the demon Leviathan in two, and bringing death to the death mongers. Azrael was a mighty valkyrie, her talons aflame with the light, and the demons cowered and fell upon their swords and scattered.

With the wolves at their side, the angels fought valiantly, and the stone tablet ran red with the blood of their enemies.

Azrael knelt down, taking a breath.

"Victory is ours," Araquiel said.

"Yes," Azrael whispered. But she stumbled, clutching her stomach, where she'd been wounded. The Black Fire had worked its way into her blood. It would consume her— she could feel its poison eating into her soul.

"You are Azrael. You are stronger than this," Araquiel said in despair. "You cannot leave me now."

"I don't want to leave you," Azrael whispered, but her lips were cold on his cheek, and he knew she did not have much time left.

His tears fell upon her face, bathing her with his sorrow.

FIFTY-EIGHT

Schuyler

She couldn't find him. She couldn't see where he had gone. They had been separated in the chaos of the fight. *Jack—where are you?* But all was smoke and flame, all was anarchy and war and ruin. The wolves were all around, and the Venators were fighting with every ounce of their souls. The vampires had transformed—they were angels now—just like at the battle that had cursed them to darkness. Now they were in the final battle for redemption, struggling to return to the paradise from which they had been banished.

But where was Jack?

Where was her love?

Schuyler fought bravely and steadily, wielding her father's blade, finding her way toward the forefront, until she found the two angels fighting against each other, the Dark against the Light, their golden swords clashing over the tablet. Then one slipped . . . and . . .

Schuyler held her sword against his heart.

Lucifer lay on the stone tablet.

Michael's sword holding him there.

Schuyler could taste the victory of her people. This was it. Her chance to destroy him once and for all. To destroy the Dark Prince with the archangel's sword.

"You don't want to do that," Lucifer said calmly.

"Believe me, there is nothing I want more," she said.

"You can't see behind you," he said. "But I can. Abbadon, would you like to describe what's happening right now?" Lucifer asked. "Tell her what's going on."

Jack? What's happening?

Do what you have to do. Take your chance. Do not think about me, Jack sent.

"Oh, how sweet," Lucifer said. "He's going to sacrifice himself."

Schuyler knew. She could see it in the glom, in her mind's eye, even without turning. Victory would be hollow.

Danel held a blade under Jack's throat. Schuyler could kill Lucifer, but Danel would kill Jack. She would win but lose her love.

And then she saw that it was not the first time someone had faced this choice. That once upon a time in Rome, her father had stood at the same crossroads.

FIFTY-NINE

Gabrielle

I could feel his arms around me. His wings surrounded me, their softness on my skin. I could feel his breath on my cheek, and his lips were on mine.

Gabrielle.

Then he stopped.

You were there. You had found us.

Michael.

You held your sword against his throat.

Victory at your grasp.

Kill me, *Lucifer whispered,* and you kill Gabrielle.

The demon held me in his arms, held the sword at my belly. He began to plunge the knife into me.

But time froze.

In that split second when the world stood still.

And you dropped the blade.

Pulled the devil's sword away from me.

329

I fell to the ground.

Lucifer saw his chance and he slipped from your grasp.

I lived.

But you could have had your victory, Michael. We would have been rid of the demon that plagued our people, the demon that brought shame to the angels and cursed us into darkness. The demon who wanted Heaven for himself.

You should have let me die.

See what you did?

We believed you had vanquished the Dark Prince.

That you had sent him down to Hell.

But you did not.

You saved me instead.

We thought you had rid the world of evil, but instead evil was allowed to return to the world, allowed to fester. Allowed to return in the form of my lover so the two of us would become further estranged. Allowed to hunt our kind over the centuries. You knew why the Blue Bloods were dying. You knew the Silver brethren were responsible. You kept it from me. You let them take us. You allowed the vampires to be taken, to be sacrificed, to hide your failure. You trained the Petruvians to kill innocents, and so the war continued between our kind. As your weakness grew, the Gates of Hell weakened as well. The borders between the worlds disintegrated.

You were corrupted by your love.

By giving in to your love, you let evil flourish in our world.

And so I kept my secret. About the path that I had found. Kept the secret of our salvation from you because I trusted you no longer. Especially when I saw them. The young ones. Drained. Full Consumption. That's when I ran into the arms of my human familiar. That was when I finally stopped loving you.

This was your father's great failure, Gabrielle whispered into Schuyler's ear. *Will it be yours? Will you choose love over all?*

So this was the choice, Schuyler saw. This was her destiny. This was what her mother had prepared her for.

Schuyler struggled against it. This was different. It was not the same. She had Michael's power and his sword. The wolves at her command. The Venators armed with the power of the Holy Spirit. She could *save* her love. She could save Jack, she knew she could, just as her father had saved Gabrielle. It was different this time. She would withdraw the sword. She could not sacrifice Jack. Not after everything they had been through; not after everything they had fought for. They had fought so hard to be together and she could still have both, victory and her love. She could still win, she knew it. There would be another chance. The battle was not over. She would not kill Lucifer right then. She could not sacrifice her love. Never. She could never lose Jack. She loved him too much. She would let the devil go.

My father's failure.

My failure.

"Schuyler!" It was Oliver. Her friend. He was covered in ashes and blood, and he, too, was holding a sword. What was he doing in the middle of this battle? Oliver was going to get killed. He was the only human. And seeing him made her remember her mother's words:

Remember that when you arrive at the crossroads. When time stands still. When the path is open to you. Remember who your father was. . . .

Schuyler had two fathers.

Her human father.

Stephen Bendix Chase. Who had none of Michael's glory; who was a simple human man. Whose only strength was in his ability to do the right thing. A good man. One who'd told Gabrielle to do her duty and return to Michael. Because love was not the answer to every question. Because real love meant sacrifice.

Sometimes love means letting go.

Schuyler knew what she had to do now. What she had been preparing for all her life. Every moment with Jack had always come down to this. Always. There was no escape. No happy ending for the two of them.

It was time to say good-bye.

I love you.

Always, Jack sent. *Always and forever.* He had always been true, and she was glad that she'd never doubted him, not for a moment. Their time was up. No time for even one last look, one last kiss, one last . . .

In the glom, she felt his spirit reach out to her. He was so very beautiful, an angel of the Light. They were together;

he was with her even as the angel Danel brought down his sword and plunged it into Abbadon's dark heart.

Schuyler cried in anguish, but there was nothing she could do.

"JACK!" she sobbed. "JACK!"

But she had made her choice.

Jack crumpled to the ground, but he was dead before he hit the stone.

Abbadon was no more.

For the first time, Schuyler saw the fear in the eyes of the Dark Prince.

Lucifer gazed at her in wonder. "You loved him," he rasped. "And you let him die."

Schuyler looked at him pitilessly, and with a mighty thrust, she plunged Michael's sword into the heart of the demon.

There was a great explosion, as the very universe trembled under the force of his death. The demons screeched, the Dark Angels screamed. Their grief was unbearable, and even Heaven itself trembled under the destruction of its greatest son. It was as if the very substance of time had been rent in two, and for a moment, everything was still and silent as the passages healed and fused into one.

Schuyler collapsed under the weight of her sword and her grief.

* * *

The Silver Bloods cowered at the death of their prince, their king. But the vampires and wolves took heart from the victory. They fought with renewed vigor, as the madness of triumph brought them strength and ferocity.

Lucifer was dead.

The Dark Prince has been vanquished.

The Light of the Morningstar extinguished.

The wolves howled their triumph.

The battle was over.

SIXTY

Azrael

She saw Abbadon at the crossroads and tried to call to him, but he was already gone. She floated for a moment, above the battle, and then realized she could return now that his death had healed her wound. The bond between them, that had ever yoked them to each other, had been broken. Finally broken.

Abbadon was dead.

She was free.

Azrael opened her eyes.

Saw that Araquiel had tears in his, and she wiped them away.

His face was joyous and filled with sunshine, but for a moment they dimmed. "Abbadon is no more. I am sorry. I know you loved him," he said, his voice hoarse and broken.

She nodded. "I will miss him till the end of my days. But he was right to do what he did."

She realized that Abbadon had been playing a game. He knew Lucifer had discovered their deception and so he had crafted one of his own. Had pretended to be Abbadon of the Dark, when always he had been working for the Light.

They got up and surveyed the remnants of the scene. Many had fallen. Of the Venators, both Sam and Deming had lost their twin. Many wolves had lost their lives. There was grief and there was sorrow, but there was also hope. They had fought and won. Heaven was secure. Lucifer vanquished.

"Why do I feel so alone?" Azrael said. The bond was broken. She was empty. Her twin, her star, her brother, her enemy, her love, gone. She wept for Abbadon.

"Never," Araquiel said. "You will never be alone again. Not if I have anything to say about it."

There was someone helping her up, and at first she thought it was Jack. But when she opened her eyes, she saw that it was not.

Michael stood before her. The immortal angel had returned from the prison of the White Darkness, from the Hell that he had created for himself, from the darkness of his failure. Her father was white and pure. The pure light of Heaven shone from his eyes.

He smiled at her gently.

"My daughter," he said. "I am so very proud of you."

There was someone with him.

Gabrielle. Eternal angel. Her mother. She was so much more beautiful than she had ever been. She had returned to her full glory, to her full magnificence. So this was the Uncorrupted. Schuyler now understood what that meant.

Free of sin.

Full of joy.

Beauty and light.

There was someone with them. Schuyler's father. Bendix Chase. He looked strangely inconsequential next to the two golden angels, but Schuyler saw his kind blue eyes and she was glad. The three of them smiled at her.

But there were so many more. Lawrence was there as well, and Cordelia; Kingsley and Mimi, Bliss and Lawson. Oliver. Dylan. Jane. So many of them looking at her, watching, waiting.

"What now?" she asked.

Then she saw that the gate had opened, that the way before them was filled with light.

"Lead us," Gabrielle said, pointing to the path. "We will follow."

It is said among our people that Gabrielle's daughter will bring us the salvation we seek.

The Redemption of the Fallen had begun.

AFTER

ABSOLUTE
BEGINNERS

As long as we're together,
The rest can go to hell.
—David Bowie, "Absolute Beginners"

chuyler had chosen to go to college about as far away from New York City as she could while still remaining in the contiguous United States. The campus was beautiful, dotted with palm trees and reddish-tinted buildings made of stucco. She had joked with Oliver that it felt more like going to a country club than a university, as there was even a man-made lake for sailing lessons.

Three years had passed since the final battle. It was the first week of May, and Schuyler's friends were making plans for the summer—traveling scholarships, working internships; everyone ready to leave, ready to go. Schuyler was sitting on the grass with them, watching their animated faces, laughing at their jokes, but when they asked about her plans she shrugged.

She thought she could stay right here for as long as possible—watch the days get longer and the nights shorter, enjoy being young for as long as she could, even as she had celebrated her twenty-first birthday that September.

A breeze blew, and she gathered her things and hopped onto her bike, thinking she would stop by the library to pick up a few books for research on her thesis. She had finally decided on a major—had been tempted to follow her sister's path, but decided it was ultimately not for her, to Finn's disappointment. While she was drawn to art, she wasn't passionate enough to study it seriously.

Finn had moved to New York for work, and it was her cherished dream that the two of them could share an apartment in the city one day. But as much as Schuyler missed her sister and the city, she was enjoying being far away from so many memories. It was too soon. Schuyler enjoyed her anonymity in California. No one knew who she was, no one asked her questions about her past.

Lawrence had always advocated finding and fulfilling a passionate interest: *Do not waste your life on drudgery*, he had told her during those endless lessons.

So she had chosen a subject that fascinated her: History. Because it was said that those who did not study it were doomed to repeat it, and after what she had been through, that seemed reason enough to choose it.

She parked her bicycle and walked into the library, to her usual carrel, but discovered the librarian had given away her reservation to someone else by mistake. Schuyler sighed and settled at one of the big long tables in the middle of the library, where several students worked side by side.

She'd barely spread out her books when she noticed someone reading across from her. A boy. He looked so familiar.

He was reading about Roanoke.

SIXTY-THREE

Mimi

*I*n all her lifetimes, Mimi Force had always had the *perfect* bonding. The perfect dress, the perfect venue, the perfect party.

This was unlike any bonding she had ever attended.

For one thing, it was in the underworld.

But somehow, Mimi liked the idea. There was something unseemly about it, and she liked the edginess of it. It felt just a little bit wicked in a time when there was little room for wickedness.

She had stood in the gardens of Elysium, she had tasted the water from the fountains, and when she was given a choice, she had chosen to come here.

With him.

They didn't belong up there. Eden wasn't home anymore. Not for the likes of them. She was made here. She was the Angel of Death. The one who would bring the

Horsemen to the Apocalypse. What did she need the light of Elysium for? She was made of fire and brimstone, smoke and shadow.

They chose to come home.

"Are you sure?" he had asked.

"I'm sure."

Mimi liked having her own kingdom, her own domain. And the Duke of Hell needed a bride.

Besides, what more could she ask for when everything was perfect? There was a lot to do in the underworld, and they were going to make it beautiful. Things were going to change around here, now that the wolves were free. Hell was about to freeze over.

"We're going to transform this place," Kingsley said. "No one will be here who doesn't want to be here, and those who stay will help us rebuild."

Their bonding ceremony was going to take place somewhere that would have been inconceivable a few short years ago: a rose garden, one that Kingsley had tended with his own hands.

He stood in the middle of the flowers. He was still Kingsley, his hair rakish, his clothes just a little askew. And what was Mimi wearing? She didn't care. She could have been wearing rags; perhaps she was. It didn't matter.

Kingsley handed her a bouquet.

"Still sure you don't want a big party? With your friends, or whoever?"

She shook her head. "Jack is gone, and Bliss is one of the wolves now. Schuyler and I were never close. Oliver, maybe, but he's so busy. It doesn't matter. Everyone else . . . they're not important. Only you."

"Shall we, then?" Kingsley asked.

She nodded.

Mimi said the words she had been waiting to say her whole immortal lifetime, words that would matter to the person hearing them.

A new bond. To replace the old one. One of their own making, of their own choice.

"I give myself to you," Kingsley said, hands in hers. "And I accept you for who you are. You are the world to me."

Mimi smiled at him, a blazing, terrifyingly happy smile, and she felt as if she would burst from joy. Kingsley swept her off her feet and into his arms, and she knew she had made the right decision.

But then again, Mimi Force was rarely ever wrong.

SIXTY-FOUR

Bliss

One of the things that was so wonderful about living out of time was that you could live in any moment and any place in history. Last week they were in Vienna, in the 1920s. Then they'd spent the summer in Newport in 1870, and bounced around to the early '90s Seattle. They followed the rules of timekeeping, making sure never to leave a mark or cause a ripple.

They were only there to observe and to guard, to make sure that history unfolded the way it was supposed to. So far, there were no other rifts, no mirrored passages.

Bliss had been a Texas cheerleader and a New York socialite, but she decided she liked this new incarnation best. She was a member of the Praetorian Guard, one of a pack of wolves, and mate to its leader, Fenrir, who would always be Lawson to her.

It had happened naturally—there were no words exchanged, no pretty vows, but Bliss understood they were past language, past needing a ceremony. They were mated and it was done.

The pack was scattered over the timeline with the rest of the wolves. Edon and Ahramin were broken; some things were beyond repair. As for the boys, Mac and Rafe, they had delighted in their newfound freedom, strutting in the armor of the Praetorians once again.

Once in a while Bliss and Lawson would visit Oliver in New York and Schuyler in California. Bliss missed her Aunt Jane, but she understood the Watcher's choice to return; to follow Gabrielle and Michael back into Paradise. Like many of the Fallen, Jane had tired of earth and its sorrows.

But Bliss was tired of grieving. Now was the time for joy and contentment.

In the past few years, she and Lawson had lived all over the world, in every place and time, and yet they always returned to the marvelous forest encampment with the fanciful tree houses that the wolves had built. It wasn't far from Arthur's cavern, and it felt most like home. Lawson liked living in the open air, liked living in the trees. His wolf soul needed the forest, needed the refuge of wood and leaf.

"We're finally home," Bliss said, coming up behind him and putting her arms around his strong torso. She held him tight and leaned against his arms.

He turned around and smiled. "You are home to me," he said, and nuzzled her cheek.

She sighed. She had been looking for a real home all her life, and finally discovered that home was in Lawson's arms.

chuyler couldn't stop staring at the boy in the library. It couldn't be, could it? It couldn't be him. He looked different somehow, even if the physical attributes were the same: the golden hair, the sloe-eyed green eyes. But it was impossible. He was dead. It had been three years already, but it was as if it had happened yesterday.

The boy looked up from his book and caught her eye.

She put down her books. "I'm sorry to bother you, but . . ." she started.

"Yes?" he asked.

"It's just . . . you look like someone I used to know."

"Do I?" His lips were pressed together, almost as if he were trying to keep from laughing.

It was impossible, and yet . . . "It's you, isn't it?" she asked.

Jack Force smiled. For it was him, and Schuyler wondered why she had not seen it from the beginning. But it was as if a veil had been lifted, and she could see him clearly now.

She wanted to throw her arms around him, to embrace him right there in the middle of the library, in front of everyone. But she was too afraid that it wasn't real, that maybe she was hallucinating. It was just too good to be true, and she could not bring herself to believe it.

"Where have you been?" she asked.

"Right here, always," he said.

And now her heart was bursting in her chest, and she felt as if she could not breathe. Jack. Alive. She felt as if she could not breathe from so much joy.

"Come on," he said, and led her outside to a park bench, their books forgotten.

"Hey," he said, taking her hand.

He pulled her toward him and held her close. Schuyler was trembling all over. She wanted to cry, but she was too happy. She kept her hand on his, gripping it tightly, unable to believe what was right in front of her.

"How?" she asked. "I don't understand. But really, where have you been all this time?"

"Looking for you," he said. "I was gone, and when I woke up I was on the side of a road. Someone stopped and picked me up and took me to a hospital. I had no idea who I was. But it came back to me, slowly."

"I saw you die."

"I did," he said. "But like all the vampires, I was given a

choice, and I chose to return. I've been looking for you ever since."

"I was right here, all this time, waiting," she said.

She had led the Fallen back to Paradise, and in the Garden of Eden, the vampires had been forgiven. The curse was lifted, and the lost children of the Almighty were given a choice. They could ascend into Heaven, or return to mid-world and continue their immortal life. But the path back home would always be open to them when they tired of their life aboveground. Paradise would welcome the just and the good among them, as it was for the Red Bloods. Redemption was in their hands now. Salvation an individual choice.

Most of the Fallen had chosen to go back home to the Garden they had lost so long ago. But Schuyler had decided to return.

She was half human. She still had family and friends, and she couldn't imagine that Paradise would bring anything but sorrow without her love.

She brought Jack's warm hand to her cheek and saw that he was still wearing his bonding ring on his left finger. Just as she wore hers. Their matching rings glinted in the sunlight.

"What happens now?" Schuyler asked. But somehow, she knew. They were together. They would have children one day. She was half mortal; she was blessed with the gift of procreation. Children. Hope. Blessings. There was so much to look forward to.

In truth, this was just the beginning of their story.

Then finally, they were kissing, and his mouth was on hers, and she felt his arms encircle her waist and she was sitting on his lap, and he was holding her and kissing her and she was kissing him back, and his head was against his chest and she ran her fingers against his soft hair.

Jack had returned to her. Jack was *alive*.

"I didn't know," she said. "I missed you so much. I didn't know you would come back to me. I thought you were lost forever."

"You made a sacrifice," Jack said. "And Heaven rewarded you."

SIXTY-SIX

Regent and Conduit

Oliver Hazard-Perry watched as the Conduits made the final adjustments—wiping a surface here, adjusting a picture frame there. It had taken three long years to rebuild the Repository, but it was finally done. The gleaming shelves were once again stocked with the books and documents of the real history of the world, and the Conduits were busy updating files, keeping track of every remaining member of the Coven.

Oliver understood the choice that Schuyler and Jack had made to keep away. They craved a normal life. After Schuyler graduated, they had told him of their plans to settle in California, near her grandmother. They sounded happy and content, and Oliver was happy for them. He was happy for all of them—Mimi and Kingsley, Bliss and Lawson, his friends and equals.

But there was business to attend to, Committee meetings

to discuss, regulations to be enforced; new Venators needed to be trained to fill the ranks. The Coven had to be rebuilt for those who chose to stay.

Oliver was glad that his studies at Columbia did not interfere with his work. He needed to be here, in New York, near headquarters. There was so much work to do—so much to clean up. There were still Nephilim around, and the Gates of Hell, while secure, would need to be guarded once more. The Praetorian Guard would keep the Passages of Time safe from harm, and Kingsley and Mimi would keep an eye on the underworld.

Oliver still could not believe his luck. He had knelt at the foot of the Almighty. What reward did Oliver seek? He had asked for the dearest wish he'd nurtured since he was a child, and it was done.

"How's it going?" a voice asked.

He looked up and smiled.

Finn Chase stood with a hand on a cocked hip. She was so beautiful, and her blue eyes sparkled with life and merriment. She had moved to New York for work, since Oliver had offered her a job.

He nodded. "We'll almost there. We'll reopen on schedule."

"Good," she said, sitting on his desk. "Do we have time?" she asked. "Before?"

He smiled. "We have all the time in the world."

Then he took her in his arms and inhaled her sweet

scent, and she swooned against his body.

He bared his fangs—those needlepoint incisors—and sank them into her neck, and drank deeply of her blood.

She was his, body and soul. Her blood sustained him, and together they would forge a new path.

They were together.

Vampire and familiar.

Regent and Conduit.

Until . . .

THE END

Acknowledgments

The Blue Bloods series changed my life—and words cannot express how grateful I am to the people who brought it to life and to the people who welcomed my characters to their lives.

But I'll try.

The folks at Disney•Hyperion have believed in the book since the beginning, when the *Mayflower* sailed off with vampires on board. Thank you to everyone who had a hand in its long gestation.

The superstar Blue Bloods Team at Hyperion: Suzanne Murphy, Stephanie Lurie, Jeanne Mosure, Nellie Kurtzman, Jennifer Corcoran, Andrew Sansone, Ann Dye, Dave Epstein, Simon Tasker, Elena Blanco, Kim Kneuppel, Tanya Stone, Laura Schreiber, Drew Richardson, and Mark Amundsen. Thanks to the fabulous home office team: Kady Weatherford and Michelle Falkoff.

Special thanks to my lovely and wise editors over the years: Brenda Bowen, Helen Perelman, Jennifer Besser, and Christian Trimmer. Much love to my current editor: Emily Meehan. Lifesaver and editrix extraordinaire. Thanks for your patience and brilliance, Em!

Thanks to my agent: Richard Abate. Friend, confidant, partner-in-crime. More than a decade's worth of madness!

Thank you to all my foreign publishers, especially Samantha Smith in the UK, Shane Cassim in France, and France Desroches in Montreal.

Thank you to my foreign agents: Melissa Chinchillo and Mink Choi.

Thanks to my family: All the DLCs and Johnstons. Especially the immediates: Mom, Aina, Steve, Nicholas, Josey, Chit, and Christina. We miss you, Pop.

Big kisses and hugs to my dear friends in life and letters: Ally Carter, Rachel Cohn, Deborah Harkness, Alyson Noel, and Carrie Ryan for their support, encouragement, sympathy, and good humor.

Very special thanks to my fellow hard-living chocolate-eating, wine-water-drinking denizens of the writer's cave (LindaVista and DeadlineKona): Pseudonymous Bosch and Margie Stohl, who fixed the snags in this manuscript and brought in the rescue boat when I got stuck.

Most of all, thanks to my husband, Michael Johnston. Co-creator, ally, and soul mate. And my daughter, Mattie Mat: Everything is for you.

My dearest readers: Thank you for your love of the story and the characters. I hope I did well by you. You guys were an inspiration and a motivation. Thank you for everything.

Melissa de la Cruz
The Blue Bloods Series
December 22, 2004–July 23, 2012